The Ber

Producer & International Distributor
eBookPro Publishing
www.ebook-pro.com

The Berlin Girl's Diary
Tzvia Golan

Translation: Zoe Jordan

Contact: tzviag7@gmail.com
ISBN 9798820702259

The Berlin Girl's Diary

TZVIA GOLAN

~

CHAPTER ONE

"Petting Zoo" — some mischievous teenagers had spray-painted the words on the outer wall of Kibbutz Mishmar HaAliya's cemetery, but the wall did not make a fuss. Miraculously, the cursive graffiti letters in black paint had not come off, even when it got wet in the rain. The words were sprayed very close to the spot where Nisim puts his chair and sits on the days when he is on guard duty.

Sometimes, the smells of the cow shed and the chicken coop met his nostrils, strong and pungent, but Nisim liked the natural smells as they are. Nor did Nisim try to wipe away the graffiti.

"Why erase it?" he said to Avner Bock. "Why not laugh a little? You could laugh too, Avner. We work hard, anyway, with you as director of ceremonies and me guarding the dead, and as the person who protects the landscape around here, and sometimes builds coffins, too, it can't hurt to have a little fun." The way he said the "l" in "little" was melodious, and he rolled the "r" in "Avner" with a prolonged, almost endless smile, in his characteristically festive mood.

Every morning, Avner wakes up at exactly six thirty, as if he had an actual clock inside him. He never arrived anywhere early nor late. It had been a long time since he had said the morning blessing upon waking, not to mention performing the ritual hand-washing. He had abandoned those customs and no longer believed in divine providence. He had been raised on tradition, but since the disaster, he had his doubts and, angry at God, he abandoned all of it.

Until the disaster, he had grown up with his father and mother in a modest, pleasant apartment in Ashkelon, not far from the kibbutz. His father, Nahum, had come to be known as a special man, and members of the kibbutz occasionally invited him to perform religious ceremonies. The people who lived on the kibbutz marveled at the mild-mannered man's extensive knowledge of all things pertaining to the occasional functions for which he was summoned.

Once he was asked to lead the Passover Seder, another time to run a Bar Mitzvah ceremony, and as the years passed, they came to ask him to lead the burials at the cemetery, especially for locals who wanted a touch of religion for their deceased loved ones.

Nahum was always available and always willing to be of service. Not one of the people on the kibbutz knew that his work in the cemetery actually gave this gentle man the greatest satisfaction. None of them knew that the memory of a pogrom at the cemetery of his hometown was etched in Nahum's heart and that he would never forget the terrible destruction of the tombstones. It seemed that this work was almost a kind of corrective, and Nahum saw it as a kind of sacred work. He had often taken Avner with him, for him to learn the trade, and felt sure that he was setting his son up for a professional future and livelihood.

After the disaster, nothing returned to the way it was before. For years, Avner tried to root himself in the work to which he was accustomed, and only occasionally did he regret that he worked with the dead his whole life.

In time, his wife Chaya joined him, and she would joke that they would never go out of business. "Avner, people will always die, sooner or later."

She meant well, of course, but every time she joked about the subject, Avner would cringe a little inside.

Sometimes, he shared his deliberations with his wife. "If there was some divine providence, wouldn't he see all the human suffering down here?"

Chaya observed him sadly and replied, "God doesn't work for any one of us, Avner. He doesn't owe anyone anything." Sometimes, they would argue furiously, until she softened and gave in. She couldn't bear his painful argument that if there was a God in heaven, his mother would not have suffered so much, poor thing.

After every one of Avner's visits to his mother, his faith would weaken ever more, until he stopped behaving like a religious man entirely. At first, he still maintained the outward appearance, but with time, as doubts overwhelmed him and kept him from sleeping, he eventually abandoned everything and came to terms with reality. He focused on his work, regardless of the beliefs and origins of those who came to the cemetery.

With exemplary punctuality he would get up, shower, dress carefully, and sometimes not even eat or drink a thing. He knew that Nisim would have already prepared their morning coffee.

Nisim also gets up with the sunrise, leaps from his bed with characteristic lightness, to perform the ritual hand-washing and recite the morning blessing, "I give thanks." He would tuck his wayward side locks behind his ears, dress hastily, and go to work for the day. If it had not been for Bracha, his wife and mother of his six children, he would go to work in sandals, even in the winter, even though his skinny body could hardly keep warm. What luck that she was so attentive, she even made sure that his shirt matched his pants and that he didn't forget his sweater.

On days when there was work to do at the cemetery, Avner would call Nisim the evening before. "Tomorrow there's a funeral, we need to do some weeding, water the plants a little, freshen up the place."

On such days, Nisim would be in a great hurry and even leave the house without so much as a sip of anything or a taste of the bagels that Bracha made him.

For more than twenty years Nisim repeated the same ritual with precision; like his morning had been etched by an artist, never to be altered. Bracha wakes up with him, smiling, her mood as pleasant and at ease as his.

Bracha is sensitive to Nisim and can see it on him when someone has died. To this day, he feels deep grief at every death. Bracha sends him off with a container of fresh vegetables: green kohlrabi sliced thin, peppers in every color, little cherry tomatoes that she called bite-size tomatoes, and a big thermos filled with his favorite coffee.

Nisim always looks at her lovingly, which makes everyone who knows them wonder: *what's their secret?* How do you maintain the spark like that, they asked, and Nisim would smile and say that he doesn't know, she is simply wonderful, he has no better explanation than that.

When there is no funeral, there is less rush and Bracha tries to delay him another moment, to persuade him to have a sip of something, and he reminds her that punctuality is already a part of him, he can no longer go anywhere late after so many years with Avner. Indeed, tardiness is not acceptable where Avner's family comes from.

Nisim recalls with a smile how Avner Bock once told him, "Yemenites are the *yekkes* of the Sephardic Jews."

By now, Nisim liked to be punctual like Avner and hates to be late. Maybe he should buy a big clock and put it in Avner's office, just like that, as a gift, he thought one day. Yes, soon he would go to a shop and buy one. A moment later he smiled to himself. What a paradox: what would Avner need a big clock in his office for? After all, he's never late or early, but always precisely on time.

On mornings when there is a funeral, Nisim arrives to the cemetery early and waits for Avner Bock to arrive, dressed festively as befits a day when the cemetery is bustling with people.

Avner usually sits with Nisim and the two exchange a few words about the weather.

"Today is awfully hot," said Avner. "But tomorrow they said it will get chilly again."

"Summer isn't here yet." Nisim smiled because that's the way he is, even when he says serious things he always looks like he's about to smile. "It's not yet summer, which awaits us in Tammuz, may god have mercy..."

Avner knows that Nisim actually loves summer, and that he suffers from the cold, but he also knows that Nisim won't really complain when Tammuz comes, because Nisim is one of those people who is always happy with his lot, and almost never complains.

Then Nisim poured cafe for Avner, who asked, "What is this coffee, why is it not brown?"

Nisim looked at him as if he fell from the moon and said, "Come on, are you joking? You've drank this coffee a million times and now you think to ask?"

Avner takes a sip, an inadvertent smile spreading across his lips. Nisim doesn't ask what's funny. After so many years of working together, he reads Avner like an open book, and he knows that if Avner is smiling, it is probably some funny story that he will tell momentarily.

"You won't believe this," Avner said with his usual opening.

Nisim responded with a wink. "Why won't I believe you? Do you usually lie to me?"

"No, I don't." Avner suddenly looked pensive. He does not lie, but he is never sure that others aren't lying. Either way, he resumed his story.

"So, Chaya joined a diet group."

(Every time Nisim heard that name, he thought to himself how fate works, offering us gems better than we could have imagined. How ironic is it that the name of the wife of Avner, who worked with death all his life, was 'Chaya,' meaning "alive" in Hebrew.)

"Your wife? To a diet group? But she's stick-thin!"

"Yes, she's nuts like that, she's afraid of putting on one pound, but that's not what I wanted to tell you. Are you listening?"

"Always," said Nisim.

"So the leader of the group said that the difference between a thin woman and a fat woman is that the thin one looks at the ingredients of something and how many calories are in it and then decides if she will eat it or not, but the fat woman eats it first and looks at the packaging afterward to see how much weight she will gain."

"That's you, Avner." Nisim laughed. "You've been drinking white coffee for years and only now did you think to ask!"

As he was speaking, Nisim poured himself some more, and the sweet smell spread through the little office. "There's no coffee better than Marty's coffee," he declared with pride.

By now, Avner knew that 'Marty' meant "my wife" in Yemenite Arabic, just like Nisim knew 'danke schon' and 'bitte schon' and when he said those words, a big smile spread across Avner's face.

***

The two sit and wait for the relatives of the deceased, as they usually do on days like this, and then Avner will conduct the burial in a dignified way, even playing a recording of the 'kaddish' when there was no one to say the prayer.

Sometimes, when there was a funeral of the kind that Nisim doesn't like, Avner calmed him with gentle words, and Nisim gave in humbly, but asked that it not happen in the future. But Avner did not promise a thing, he was careful with his words, because he knew that promises must be kept, and this promise, here, at Mishmar HaAliya, was a promise that he would have to break from time to time.

But that does not interfere with the relationship between the two, and they will go on sitting together until the ceremony begins, and they will talk about shared memories, the living and the dead, love and hate, peace and evil, and anyone who looked at the two from the side cannot help but wonder at this deep friendship they have forged, the kind that allowed for pleasant conversation and total openness, the kind in which it is possible to sit comfortably in silence, as if they were longtime spouses who had found serenity in the strength to go on living.

***

The next morning Nisim parked his little car in the entrance, and got out quickly. A full day of work awaited them. Nisim had some gardening to do, he wanted to tidy the grounds and also build a coffin for the following day. He thought about what Avner had told him on the phone.

"Listen…" Avner said. "A messenger arrived at my house with a strange package."

"Strange?" Nisim repeated. "Why? What was in it?"

"It was a letter from a woman named Eva Reich, and a diary too!"

"A diary? Do you mean like a planner? Because I also got one of those in the mail, from my insurance company."

"No, not a planner!" said Avner. "A diary, a journal! Of some woman that I don't even know."

"Sounds interesting," replied Nisim.

"Yes," said Avner. "I told you. It's weird. Anyway, I will talk to you tomorrow. Come early, we'll be up to our ears in work."

Now, as Nisim got out of his car, he heard Avner call him through the little window of the office, "Come in, I have to show you this."

Nisim entered the office, and Avner pulled a letter and a little package wrapped in brown paper out of his bag.

"I flipped through the pages a little," he said, and pulled the package out of its wrapping.

Nisim put his kippah on his head, crossed his arms as he felt the chill in the room, and looked at Avner inquisitively. "Anything interesting?"

"It's still not clear to me. It's a bit of a strange letter." Avner set it down on the table. "She requests that I write and deliver her eulogy."

"Interesting indeed," said Nisim. "Maybe she doesn't have any family to do that for her?"

"She actually does have family, whom I still know nothing about. But it seems she wants me to be the one to tell her family who she really is!"

Nisim looked thoughtful for a moment. He wound one of his sidelocks around his finger and tucked it behind his ear.

"Tell her family who she is? What, they don't know? I don't think I understand."

"I told you it's weird," said Avner.

"Maybe it's some kind of prank?" Nisim asked. "After all, there's no shortage of crazies in the world, as you know."

"You think this could be a prank?" Avner asked.

Nisim, to whom the idea that it was a prank suddenly seemed so logical, developed the theory further. "It sounds like an episode from the "Mission Impossible" series. You remember that show?"

"Of course," replied Avner.

As two people who had grown up in Israel during the 1960s, they had a lot of similar memories.

"So, you remember those instructions that they had at the beginning of each episode? They would play instructions on a tape, and afterward it would self-destruct. So, maybe it really is a prank, who knows, it's true there's no shortage of crazy people."

"There's cash, a lot of cash actually, inside the envelope," Avner stated and sat down. "If someone decided to prank me, he wouldn't pay so much money for it. This isn't a prank. This is real."

Nisim burst out laughing. "Believe me, Avner, any moment some guys will burst out of someplace with their cameras. You came off totally decent, you didn't even take the money!"

"I don't think it's funny," said Avner. "And anyway, we have a ton of work to do today." In an uncharacteristically authoritative tone, he gave Nisim his tasks for the day. In addition to the gardening work, he also had to build a coffin, clean the grounds and the bench out in the middle of the cemetery, maybe someone would want to sit there tomorrow at the funeral.

Nisim had never had a problem with hard work. He was willing to do whatever was needed, but still he felt pretty sure that it would turn out that someone was making a joke.

"Look," he said. "You have to be thorough. If you received a package with a diary, you should read the whole thing before deciding, and I am pretty sure that by the end it will become clear that it was a joke. Don't you think?"

"I don't know," said Avner, looking troubled.

"Fine," said Nisim. "I will get to work and meanwhile, you read. If it turns out that it's all a prank, then we'll be done with that, and if not… it shouldn't be too much trouble to say a few kind words about someone, right?"

"It's not really such a big problem, just I'm not sure how much I can say about this person just from reading the diary, after all I don't actually know the deceased."

Nisim knew that if there was one thing Avner couldn't stand, it was a job not well done.

"Say," he asked. "Do you ever listen to those radio shows where all kinds of people call in to talk to experts about their problems?"

"I don't really have the patience for that kind of nonsense, but let's say I did, so what?"

"I can't stand it either," Nisim felt compelled to apologize, and removed the kippah from his head in embarrassment. "Just that it happens some-times that the radio is on, so I wind up hearing these people who call in to specialists and get their opinions based on cards, or handwriting or God knows what."

"It's really just a lot of nonsense, those programs," said Avner, but Nisim wasn't finished.

"Nonsense or not, all of the "experts" tell people these general things that could apply to anyone, and that nobody would object to. So you can do something similar. Just say a few words along those lines and be done with it."

"I'll manage it somehow," Avner replied. "But my main problem is the late woman's request that I tell her family who she is. It really is one of the strangest things I've heard in my life."

"Really strange," Nisim agreed. "But roll with it, as they say."

"Fine." Avner smiled. "I'll roll with it."

"Great," said Nisim. "Okay off to work."

"But tell me, Nisim, what if the deceased was some kind of criminal?"

"Mission impossible for real, huh?" Nisim declared and smirked.

"Wait. Just think for a second, maybe she was some kind of undercover assassin?"

"God help us, where are you going with this?" asked Nisim.

"I'm kidding," said Avner. "Really, just joking."

"Fine. Listen," said Nisim. "First, read the diary, and then you will know if she was some kind of crook. I imagine you will discover that she was not, and even if she was, it will be an interesting story."

Avner nodded. Of course he had to read the diary first, and maybe the answer to the question who Eva Reich was would not be so bad. He held back a laugh when he said what he said, but in any case, deep in his heart, he felt a kind of distress signal and a feeling in his belly that there would not be a simple, straightforward solution to this, that it would be more complicated.

Nisim knew him well enough to know that he was still troubled.

"You know what," he said. "Saying a few kind words is easy, so you can just perform that part of the request. You will eulogize her and that's it. Where is it written that you have to do everything she asked?"

"In all honesty, I would love to just ignore that part completely," Avner replied. "But I can't."

There were more than a few bills in the envelope. He couldn't refuse, unless he returned the money, and he didn't have so much as the slightest idea to whom he would return it.

"You know," he said. "She wrote that she knows that it's to take money for burial services, but that here in Mishmar HaAliya, because it's a kibbutz, the rules are different. She looked into it."

"Interesting!" said Nisim. "She sounds like a smart lady, eh?"

"Yes," said Avner thoughtfully. "So, what was it you said? To just carry out part of her request?"

"To tell half the truth…" Nisim smiled, and now Avner smiled too. They often spoke about movies they had seen in the theater or on television. It was a shared interest. Many times they saw courthouse dramas, where people swore to tell the truth, the whole truth, and nothing but the truth. "Nobody in the world knows that much, it's a false oath," Nisim had said once.

"Yes," said Avner. "To tell only half the truth, because nobody knows the whole truth anyway."

"Exactly," said Nisim.

"So, now I have to read the diary until the end, properly, not just to flip through it. That's a lot of work, and not a lot of time."

"Yes, you must and you will. Read it and figure out who this woman was, and then say a few things about her. Simple, no?"

~

CHAPTER TWO

I was born in Berlin, Germany, in January 1930, to my father, Yosef Berliner and my mother Elsa. I was a light-haired baby with freckles. I don't remember much from my early childhood, apart from the things that Maria told me years later. Maybe my memory is deceiving me by now, but not long ago, during a visit to my hometown, I saw two little girls playing with a rope right in front of my parents' home in Alexanderplatz and my heart ached with the intensity of feeling. I don't know if I myself remember playing with my sister or if I'm remembering Maria's stories, but I can really feel the jump rope wrapped around my wrists, and can almost hear my older sister Anna trying to teach me.

"Here, take this end, and jump, high…" said my sister. "Not like that, you're just falling, here, watch me do it." She jumped lightly and tried to show me how to do the same. "Wrap the end of the rope around your hand, okay?"

I remember that I tried, and my wrists hurt, but my sister didn't let it go.

"Swing the rope high, now skip, when it's right at the top, here, like this."

More than anything I remember observing my sister with a puzzled look, wanting to understand her instructions and not managing. Now when I think of it, it seems to me as though my big sister was hurrying to help me grow up, as if she knew deep inside that there was no time, that we had to squeeze a lot into the short time we had, because soon it would all be over. On the other hand, as I already mentioned, my childhood is fragments of memories intertwined with Maria's stories and my reflections at the end of my life.

My early childhood years were very pleasant. In the mornings I walked happily to the Jewish nursery school and in the afternoon I played in my mom and dad's fine fabrics shop. My parents, my sister Anna and I, were a happy family. We didn't want for anything. Our fabric shop was flourishing. My parents worked there from morning to night, we had a good life and plenty. We were considered wealthy, maybe even very wealthy.

We had good relations with our neighbors and all of the tenants in our building, even all the residents on our street. Next door to our shop there was a store selling wool and buttons, owned by a couple. They were husband and wife, Ludwig and Maria. They had a wonderful relationship, as I understood from my parents, but they never had any children.

The secret of their relationship, I heard my father tell my mother, was the quiet. They were quiet for whole days at a time, sitting, him on the stool at the entrance and her on a little chair in the shop, quiet. He would have a newspaper spread across his knees and she — with a little thimble on her finger, would patch holes in her husband's clothes, sew buttons back on, and not speak. Maybe they felt that quiet would invite better luck.

Sometimes I heard Dad say jokingly that Ludwig and Maria were born old and tired, that God help them when they actually got old. And Mom would say thoughtfully that Ludwig and Maria were dear people and it was terrible that God had not blessed them with children, even though they were good, kind people.

I remember that when Mom would talk about our good neighbors, Dad would quiet her. "You know, Elsa, the walls have ears!"

***

Avner stretched out in his chair. The diary was interesting, he thought to himself, intriguing, even. He felt great sadness in light of what was written, how she said that soon it would all be over. He knew that that was life's way, even in his own life. Nothing lasts forever, and certainly not happiness. He supposed that the people she mentioned were very important to her, but did not know the nature of the journey on which he was embarking.

***

My father was a gentle man in appearance and temperament who pampered us. Although I was a young child, I remember well how he would come into our room. My sister and I would be in our bed, and Dad in the middle of the room, on the carpet decorated with diamond shapes, telling us exciting, fanciful stories in German mixed with Yiddish. For her part, my mother would listen from the room next to ours and from time to time offer commentary, mainly if it seemed to her that Dad was speaking Yiddish instead of German.

But Dad would smile in the dark and keep on telling us stories, with an emphasis on faith in God. I even remember how he once said that since monotheism had become popular in the world, people had not stopped producing new idols for themselves to smash to smithereens. It's interesting how sometimes full phrases are etched in my memory, even those that I didn't understand.

Dad told bible stories with a hint of a smile, stories of global explorers with a hint of myth, telling fables with descriptions of animals from unconventional perspectives. That was how the eagle "Hanipopo" came to be king of the birds and an answer to the lion, king of the beasts, who boasted a long tail and mane of hair.

We spent the weekends and sometimes the holidays, too, at the home of Uncle Karl von Bock and his wife Alice. They lived in a big house, and I remember that the walls were covered with pictures, including drawings of angels and geometrical shapes whose names I did not know.

Uncle Karl was a serious man who did not let us run wild. I remember him, tall and strong, with a thick moustache, light hair and big, blue eyes. When we were wild he would look at us and usually that was enough to make us stop and behave ourselves. I don't know if I remember that because they told me about it afterward or it really is burnished in my memory, but there was a time when we played in their living room, and Anna accidentally knocked over a vase which stood in the corner of the room. The vase broke into shards, which Aunt Alice gathered up quickly before Uncle Karl could see. She must have done it so fast that she wasn't careful and cut her finger on one of the shards. Perhaps that is why I remember that scene, because my aunt's finger was bleeding and there was a bloodstain on the carpet, a stain that she scrubbed for a full hour to remove.

When we would stay over there, he would wake us up early in the morning and insist that we go out for physical exercise. I don't think that any of us liked getting up so early and going out into the cold in order to exercise, but on the other hand, it is very possible that I owe Uncle Karl my good health and the fact that I survived in spite of everything. Maria told me this years later, too, but she had such a compelling way of telling stories, to the point that it seemed that I remembered them for myself.

In addition to the exercise that Uncle Karl required of us and demanded that we do, he had another custom, and after the exercises he would insist that we take a cold shower. Mom would say that Uncle Karl only wanted what was best for us, that he knew about health because he was a doctor, and anyway, dad's sister Alice already had enough difficulties with him, there was no need to add further arguments into the mix.

Aunt Alice was pleasant, friendly, and smiley like Mom. She and Karl had two children, who exercised with us too. As a little girl, it seemed to me that all of us, Anna and I, Mom and Dad, Aunt Alice, Uncle Karl, and their two boys, were a big, happy family.

***

Avner wondered about the family's names, as Anna and Eva were not common Jewish names, nor was their mother's name — Elsa. He quickly checked Google to learn more and found that 'Eva' was the same as 'Chava' or Eve from the bible, 'Anna' came from 'Hannah,' and Yosef clearly came from the biblical, righteous Yosef. But Avner couldn't find any biblical sources for the name 'Elsa.' Apart from the fact that the word itself meant "noble," there was no hint of an additional source. Avner understood that the names they were given had to sound German, and the sense of impending disaster grew stronger.

***

Aunt Alice died before her time. Mom wept bitterly. She was so young, she hardly had the chance to live, and Dad tried to comfort her. "At least she married Karl, the love of her life, at least she was granted some love, but Mom refused to be comforted. Now I suspect that Mom knew that Uncle Karl was not exactly as Dad described, but she did not say a thing, and continued to grieve her sister for a long time, lamenting Alice, who had caught a terrible disease and died weighing scarcely sixty-six pounds.

The truth is that I can't really remember my aunt, nor her death, nor the events that happened at a dizzying pace at that time. I was only three years old when my aunt died. There are memories we invent for ourselves, mostly about significant events and stories that we heard later on, and Mom talked about Alice again and again. In time I heard how kind-hearted she had been, and how her righteous spirit would go to heaven, and Dad told her that it was weird how all of the faiths believed that the righteous were granted an eternity in heaven while the wicked got a ticket to hell. I remember that Mom responded to him, "sinners" and not "wicked" and Dad dismissed the difference with a gesture of his hand.

I did not go to Aunt Alice's funeral. I was too little. But I asked questions, "What do you do with her now? Is she gone?" And Anna, who was six years older than me, told me about a golden coffin, decorated with pictures of angels, and I, a little girl, believed that whoever got to have a golden coffin with angels, must be happy in the next life, the essence of which I did not understand.

***

Avner stopped reading. For a moment he was a little worried but dismissed it. Burial in a coffin was common there. It was not unusual for anyone, and the angels on the coffin, he would check up on that later, look up if that was in fashion there. He also wondered why was there so much emphasis on this detail of burial in a coffin? And then the picture grew clear: after all, the deceased had also requested a coffin, she had even paid good money for it.

Maybe the reason for her request was this memory of her aunt, who had evidently been a beloved figure from her childhood? That would make sense! He also considered the mention of the difference between "sinners" and "wicked" and could not come to a satisfactory conclusion on the matter.

He decided that he had no clear answers at the moment and resumed reading.

**

But life at home did not go back to normal after Alice died. There were questions in the air about the nature of mourning, and I didn't understand a thing apart from the fact that Mom didn't stop crying about her sister for days, maybe even until the end of her days, which were to be too few.

I did not see Uncle Karl and the two boys after Alice died. Rumor had it that he enlisted to the military, and that he had put his boys with a foster family, but Mom said that that was impossible. He would not do such a thing to children, and not to his brother and sister-in-law.

I vaguely remember that Mom wanted to look for Karl and the boys, but Dad told her that we should leave the man alone, if he chose to leave to another place, maybe that was the only way for him to get over his grief and give the two little boys a good chance at a new life. I even remember that Anna said that Uncle Karl probably had a different wife, and now he would marry her and they would have more children.

Anna wondered if the new children would be our cousins, or if since Alice was dead, the new children were no longer related to our family, but Mom got very mad at her for saying that. In time, we all came to terms with the fact that Uncle Karl and the two boys had chosen to leave.

Over the years I heard Dad plead with Mom more than once to leave everything and move to a different country. I remember him coming home one day, his face grave. From the snippets of conversation that I heard, Dad had seen a German harassing a Jew on the street and calling him derogatory names. He repeated the word "little Jew" multiple times. Mom listened to him and didn't dismiss his words as she had in previous conversations, but offered a practical solution.

"You have to change your name," I heard her tell him. "Yosef is a problem here."

But Dad was a stubborn man who stood by his principles and did not agree.

I think that Mom asked him to at least remove the kippah from his head, and he refused that too.

In that same conversation, I heard her tell him, "If you don't want to really change it, maybe at least change it a little, just one letter, to Yozef. Yozef is good, nobody will be able to tell." But dad refused.

In truth, I was glad that Mom didn't agree to leave. It was daunting to think of moving to some other place. I was already in school, and the thought of leaving my friends and the room that I shared with my sister was upsetting, So Mom flatly rejected the suggestion, and a while later, they no longer had enough money to buy immigration visas.

More than once I heard Dad talking about the kinder transport of the Jews of England, and wanted to look out for us, the girls, so that at least we would be saved, and I will return to this subject later, but Mom did not listen and I heard her tell Dad to stop worrying, thanks to her all of us were safe, all of us.

I can't remember all of those conversations. After all, I was just a little girl. But from the bits I heard, along with the things that I checked later on, I understood that my father wished for us to leave. And if Mom had listened to him, things would have looked differently.

Indeed, almost until the end of 1941, Germany's Jews still had the option of leaving. The authorities even urged them to do so, but many chose to stay until the storm passed. It's dumbfounding to think that even the Jewish organizations in Germany and outside of it were against leaving and saw emigration as an irresponsible act.

I remember I once heard Mom saying that if all of the Jews left their

German homeland, it would weaken their power.

In many sources that I read years later, even the Jews believed in the utopia of resettlement in their German homeland, and there were those who said that uncontrolled immigration to Israel was a Zionist crime. I don't know which of those things Mom heard or knew, and today I think that more than anything she really believed that it would be okay and we would all be safe thanks to her.

But we were not safe.

We stayed living in our house, but nothing remained as it was. Some time after we were sent to the concentration camp at Dachau, and ultimately, like many others, we were sent on a train to Auschwitz. But until then, we tried to stay in our home and live normally, which soon became impossible.

New, stricter rules were enacted that set us apart from everyone else. Dad was forced to add "Israel" to his name, according to the regime's strict laws. He began to call us Hannah and Chava and only Mom didn't change her name, refusing to go by "Sarah." She said that she was born Elsa and would die Elsa. Only she had no idea it would happen so soon.

∼

CHAPTER THREE

On the 9th of November, 1938, Ernst vom Rath, a German diplomat in Paris, was assassinated by a seventeen-year-old Jewish refugee. Punishment was not long in coming. That cold night, shop windows on our street were broken and shards of glass flew in every direction. There were several Jewish shops beside our house, including the bakery which produced the wonderful smell of fresh bread each day. At the end of the street was a hat shop I remember well, because Anna and I would sometimes stop in front of the display window and imagine how we would look in this hat or the other, and burst out laughing at weird hats with feathers and baskets of flowers on them.

Beside the hat shop was a photography shop. I even remember the name of the owner: Mister Greenbaum. His shop did not attract our attention when we were girls, but on that terrible night, the shop windows were broken and the store was looted. Mr. Greenbaum became a beggar overnight and would walk through the streets with the one camera that he had managed to save, film in his pocket, offering passersby to photograph them for a few pennies. Rumor had it that he had set up a darkroom in his house, where he would develop photographs for his clients.

Mr. Greenbaum even offered my mother to photograph our family all together. Mom agreed, so we stood, the four of us, beside the house, with Mom and Dad standing in the back and Anna and I in front. Mr.

Greenbaum put his head underneath the dark cloth of the camera and took the picture.

A few days later he brought us the photograph. I remember Mom's expression and that I didn't understand why she wasn't happy in the picture. She looked concerned. She called my sister and the two of them went out into the back garden.

Mom told her quietly, "Look, Annuchka, I am putting the picture here, just so you know."

I watched the two of them from the stairwell window and saw Mom put the photograph into a cloth bag, bend down, dig a hole in the earth and bury the photograph in it.

"Just so you know, Annuchka," she said again, wiping her hands on her apron, and went inside.

The incident troubled me for days afterward until I forgot about it. Now I have no doubt that many of the photographs that Mr. Greenbaum captured became the single remaining souvenir for entire families who were wiped out, just like that one picture that I have to this day, which I will mention again later.

In any case, on that same terrible night, which came to be known as Kristallnacht, Mom and Dad locked the door and sat with us, holding hands, trembling with fear. Dad wanted to help the neighbor couple who must have been frightened and alone. What if they needed help? But Mom quieted him and did not let him leave. Outside we could hear the sounds of glass shattering and blood-curdling screams. As an eight-year-old girl, I still could not understand that the end was near. Rumors from outside said that all of the Jews who worked in important jobs had been murdered. Even our bank manager, the Jewish lawyer, and the rabbi from the synagogue.

The Western world was shocked. Jewish refugees escaped to the United States, and many orphaned children were sent to England. But Mom didn't want to leave. I don't know if she was naive, if she truly believed that nothing bad would happen, or if she was just deadly afraid of change, of emigrating. She was so connected to her hometown, she loved the culture and the customs, the precision and the order, to the point that she did not realize what was about to happen. I heard her talking to Dad on multiple occasions, the terrible things that she said etched in my mind to this day.

"Did you hear about the Brauchtzigans?" she asked.

"The ones who live at the end of the street?"

"Yes, the ones who *lived* at the end of the street." Mom emphasized the word "lived" in the past tense. "They don't live there anymore."

"Did they move? Where?" Dad asked.

"They moved on… to the world to come," said Mom, with terrible anger in her voice. "They were listening to the Brandenburg concerto on the gramophone and hung themselves in the living room."

"Oy, no," said Dad. "Elsa, we have to get out of here, this country is eating its people."

"We won't just up and leave!" Mom raged. "The Brauchtzigans were stupid! Rumor has it that they were found completely blue, with Brandenburg still playing in the background!"

Were it not for what I went through afterward, the image of the couple, blue and hanging there with classical music playing in the background, would likely have remained the hardest thing I could have ever imagined.

In that conversation, one of many similar conversations, I heard Dad mention a faraway country, the name of which I had not heard until then. "We will immigrate to the land of Israel," said Dad.

Mom replied, "That's it, Yosef, you've lost it completely."

But Dad did not give up easily and I heard him talk about the wonderful country many times after, a country of sunshine and summer, year-round. "It's the only country where we can really be free," he tried to say.

Mom would not stand for it. "Germany is our homeland, there is no other country."

If it is true that words can be imprinted on a person, Dad's echoed in my ears for years after, like an unwritten will, and I have yet to tell of my leaving and my immigration to Israel.

Many others also committed suicide, while listening to Bach or Beethoven, or while reading Goethe and Schiller. Dad felt certain that Maria and Ludwig, the neighbors, were in big trouble, but there was no evidence of it. We had not yet received a deportation order. The Nazis let us repair the ruined shop and try to revive it. They did not build ghettos in Germany, preferring to deport the remaining Jews to Eastern Europe, where they received similar treatment to the Jewish people of Poland and Czechoslovakia and their neighbors.

∗

Avner removed his glasses for a moment, stretched, and set down the diary. It was hard for him to read, and the heavy feeling of impending catastrophe did not let up for a moment. He could not help comparing what Eva was describing in her diary to what had happened to him in his own life, as a child of Holocaust survivors. He never talked about it with a soul, not with Chaya, and not with Nisim.

His relatives only knew very few details: that his mother was a Holocaust survivor, alone in the world, and that there had been a disaster and his father died at a young age of a heart attack. They knew that Avner was an only child, and the rest was locked away behind the facade of a handsome man in his fifties.

Avner was tall like his father Nahum but his appearance was gentler and less muscular. He had had grey hair since an early age, but his wife reminded him that greying hair was better than going bald.

But behind the manly appearance, Avner was a sensitive man who had taught himself not to let his emotions out. The people closest to him in the world did not ask him hard questions, as if they understood that there were certain things he would prefer to not discuss. But now Eva was talking about it, and for a moment he felt that she was holding up a mirror to him, demanding of him to deal with the things he repressed.

He got up, poured himself a glass of wine, sat down and continued reading.

∗

Life at home became harder and harder as the days passed. Our shop did not return to what it had been before that terrible night, and Dad tried to support us taking odd jobs wherever he could. The bank manager's son, a short and bespectacled man named Elgar, whose father had been murdered that night, tried to help as much as he could. He tried to give us a loan because he remembered that Dad had been a desirable client in the past, but the bank didn't have money either, and offered an inflated interest rate, and there was a big fight.

Now, I never thought that I would ever tell or write what I am writing now, because I am very ashamed of what I did, but the page endures all. I also worry that soon memory problems will get the better of me and then I won't remember anything from back then. There is a little comfort in this; I can almost say that I am waiting eagerly for this forgetfulness to come and relieve my pain. But now, as I am still lucid, I will write everything and purge my troubled soul.

It was a Friday evening. Mom made a real effort for each Shabbat dinner, that it at least include hot soup and a slice of bread. The soup consisted of hot water and a few vegetables or the remains of whatever greens we had left. I went over to Mom with two empty bowls, the red one for Anna, and the blue one for me. Mom ladled the soup into the bowls, unintentionally pouring a little more into the red one. I took the red one for myself and gave Anna the blue.

Anna, who didn't know why I had switched the usual bowls, demanded that we switch back. The red one was hers! I burst into tears, complaining that it wasn't fair that Anna always got the prettier color, and Dad insisted that Anna let her little sister have her way. I ate more soup than her. For years, this story tormented me.

In bed at night, after Anna was dead, I had unbearable dreams. More than once I dreamed of a very fat woman standing over me, a cook's hat on her head, waving a soup ladle at me.

"Your sister, she died," she would scream, slurring her words. "But you eat soup and you survive." I could not shake the rhyme from my head. For a long time I was tormented by the thought that the fat cook was right.

In January 1942, we received a deportation order and were loaded on to the freight trains, first to the concentration camp and from there to the extermination camps. Anna did not hold out. She suffered stomach pains and Mom was too weak to help her. I couldn't find Dad. He had been put on a different train car, alone. I saw him one more time, through the fence. I shouted at him, but he placed a finger over his lips and signaled to me to be quiet.

I remember myself, a little girl, running between human skeletons, pleading for help. In my memory is etched an image of one woman who produced a bottle of milk, as if by magic, wet several strips of fabric that she found and placed them on my sister's forehead. She gave her milk to drink and Anna guzzled it thirstily, then threw it all up. Eventually, she stopped responding.

***

Avner sighed loudly. He was gripped by deep sorrow, and he struggled to breathe. He went a little pale as he read what Eva wrote; it was that same suffocating feeling that she described.

***

Just for the sake of comparison, and in order to catch my breath, I must take a short break from the memories and mention Meir, my husband, who died of a serious illness, but managed to live a good, full life. It so happens that Meir was also born in Berlin, but by age four he was already in Israel. His father recognized the disaster that was about to happen, and like my father, asked his wife to flee for their lives. Except my father was met with refusal, while Meir's immigrated to Israel with his wife and sons, minutes before the gates closed behind them. They settled on a kibbutz at first, and a year later moved to Tel Aviv. With their business skills, they opened an ice cream parlor in Tel Aviv and my Meir got to grow up in our real homeland.

***

In addition to the deep sorrow, Avner felt the poison of truth that he had preferred to ignore all of these years seeping into him. He was filled with admiration for Eva Reich, the survivor. "Like my mother." He was taken aback to hear himself say it out loud.

Eva was saved by an extraordinary survival instinct. His mother had survived too, despite everything, but it was not the same thing. He tried to guess how old Eva had been on the day she died, but couldn't, really. He just figured that she was not young. His curiosity grew. He wanted to know more about the family members to whom he was meant to deliver her eulogy. Had she been a mother?

Avner hoped that the diary would supply answers to his questions. All he knew now was that she had experienced horrific things in her childhood, which she mentioned here, in this diary, maybe to unburden herself of the pain, to share it with others. If his mother had done the same, maybe she wouldn't have to be in that terrible place now.

Avner forcibly suppressed the memory of the envelope he once found at home, which he'd ripped into pieces, along with whatever was inside, without reading what was written on the pages that it contained.

A slight tremor gripped him as the thought passed through him that like his mother, he also did not talk about pain or cleanse himself of all that evil. But his mother, unlike Eva, had not managed to get over her past. The fact was that Eva, whose firstborn sister had died right before her eyes, had managed to survive.

Suddenly, the question flashed through him: why did she choose him of all people to read her diary? Why him?

Avner was troubled. He looked out through the small office window. Headstones were scattered between flower beds and grass, and Nisim was out there hoeing and pruning, preparing the grounds for the following day. Avner went out of the office and gestured for Nisim to come and sit with him on the bench, the one bearing black letters of dedication to someone's beloved. They sat on the bench and Avner let out a sigh.

"What's up?" Nisim smiled at him.

"I don't understand why she chose *me*, how is that out of everybody the deceased knew, she chose me of all people, a total stranger! It doesn't make sense to me."

"Maybe she just wanted someone who worked with burial?" said Nisim. "Maybe it was entirely by chance that she found you specifically?"

"Does it seem like a coincidence to you?" Avner asked.

"I don't know, I mean, your family name starts with "B" so it's probably close to the top of the phone book."

"That's true, but if someone is looking for a cemetery, they'll find us under "Heavenly Rest," which is under "H," obviously, or if someone was looking for the name of the kibbutz, then it would be under "M.""

"Okay," said Nisim, who realized that his explanation was insufficient. "But you know, we don't have a lot of competition. With the latest photos you put on our website, anyone with a head on his neck would choose us."

Avner smiled. First of all, there was something very comforting about Nisim's simple logic, and he knew that Nisim was a voice of reason. But apart from that, there were these little turns of phrase, which Avner never knew if Nisim was altering them on purpose or not, always brought a big smile to his face.

"A head on his neck, ah? Good one, really."

"More importantly, you're smiling, Avneriko, the main thing is that you're smiling."

Avner looked at Nisim, skinny as a teenager, his strong arms like those of a working man and his eyes with a constant glint of pleasure, and for a quick moment he felt a twinge of jealousy creep between his ribs, grip his bones, try to burrow into his heart.

"You're a special man," he said, unsmiling.

"You're a fine man yourself," Nisim replied. "But tell me, are we playing "who gives better compliments" right now or what?"

Avner smiled. For a moment he even managed to forget what made him go outside in the first place. He got up and returned to his office. It was late, he had not yet finished reading the diary, and what would he do about the request to deliver the eulogy? No, he could not allow himself to get lost in thought. He had work ahead of him, and he was dedicated to do it well.

~

CHAPTER FOUR

Avner picked up the diary and stretched out in his chair. He wanted to keep reading, but the phone on his desk rang, breaking the silence in the room. He was momentarily alarmed by the sudden noise, then answered the call. From the other end of the line he heard what sounded to Avner like the voice of a young man.

"Hello," said the voice. "Who am I speaking with?" Avner never liked when people called and asked who they were speaking to. He usually replied, "Who were you hoping to reach?" But something in the voice on the other end sounded desperate, and Avner replied, "You've reached Heavenly Rest, on Kibbutz Mishmar HaAliya. My name is Avner Bock. Who am I speaking to?"

There was a brief pause from the other end, then a reply, "My name is Yossi Reich. I believe you received a package from my mother yesterday evening."

"O-ho, nice to meet you," said Avner, happy to hear from a member of the deceased's family. He immediately realized how stupid it was to say "nice to meet you" under these circumstances so he quickly added, "Are you the son of Mrs. Reich? I am sorry that we are speaking under these sad circumstances. Yes, I received a package from your mother yesterday. The messenger brought it to my home."

"I apologize," said the voice. "My sister got the message about the package and the letter from the manager of the nursing home where our mother lived. She didn't manage to get herself together and pick it up herself, you understand?"

"Certainly, but there is no need to apologize, it's really okay." Avner felt the need to reassure the sad voice on the other end of the line. "So, did they inform you over the phone?"

"Yes, by phone. The nursing home manager called my sister."

"Sounds terrible," noted Avner. There was another pause on the other end and then he heard conversation, and Avner was not sure if they were speaking to him or to one another.

"I visited her just yesterday," he heard a female voice say. "I asked her how she was, and she told me, but afterward she said some strange things."

Avner heard Yossi's voice ask, "Strange things?"

Avner felt a little uncomfortable, as if he was listening in on a private conversation, so he cleared his throat audibly.

"I apologize," Yossi said quickly. "I only got here now from Haifa, we haven't spoken yet."

"I understand," said Avner. "Should I call again later?" Mrs. Reich's daughter, who hadn't heard Avner say anything, went on speaking to her brother, ignoring the receiver of the telephone in his hand. "For a long time she just stared at me, and then started telling me stories she used to tell us when we were kids, about a knight and a princess."

Again, there was quiet on the other end, and Avner assumed that Yossi was gesturing to his sister that someone else was there, but she seemed to be preoccupied by her recent memories of the previous day's visit and carried on, "Are you listening, Yossi? She said that the princess was dead and that their love didn't triumph. Do you have any idea what she was talking about?"

Yossi was quiet for a moment, then said, "There's someone on the phone, Hani, he can hear us."

Hani ignored him as if she hadn't heard him at all, and he suddenly interrupted her, saying, "I also have some tough memories from my last visit to her. She didn't recognize me. She called me Meir and other names that I didn't even recognize. But listen, Hani, we need to figure out a few things first, then we can talk."

He returned to Avner. "Frau Shapira, as Mom called her, that is, the manager, knew that there was no chance we would come for a visit last night. My sister was there yesterday morning, and I live in Haifa. I was there two days ago myself, as you probably gathered."

"Yes," said Avner, feeling guilty about his own mother. "I understand, of course. But what a terrible way to receive such news."

"Yes," Yossi agreed with him. "But what exactly was in the package that Mom sent you?" He got the conversation back on track.

"She sent me her diary," replied Avner. "Along with a letter. She asked that I read the diary."

"I don't really understand. My mother kept a diary and we didn't know about it?"

"It really isn't so unusual these days for people to write diaries," replied Avner. He wanted to add that what was really unusual was that she had chosen a strange man to read her personal diary, but Mrs. Reich's son beat him to it.

"You should know, my mother would call me every time she wrote something new and read it to me. So, it's very strange to me that she wrote a whole diary that I didn't know about, and then chose to send it to someone she never even met."

Avner did not reply. He knew full well that there were many things that people don't know about others, not even those who are closest to them. He also knew that there are things that people choose to not know, usually to protect themselves, along the lines of "what you don't know won't hurt you." He himself knew very little about his closest relatives, how much could he really know about his mother, and how much did he really want to know?

But here, on the other end of the line, was a man who not only wanted to know everything about his mother, he was shocked by something that he didn't know. As he listened to the great sorrow in the son's voice, a small, private grief of his own crept in. He snapped back to the conversation and the things that had yet to be arranged, before sinking into himself and his personal pain.

"Your mother also requested that I give her eulogy. I hope that that is acceptable to you. Obviously if you want, you can do it, and if I understood correctly, you also have a sister. Perhaps she would also like to say something."

"Ahh… we haven't thought about that yet, it all just happened so fast. That is, you know, it doesn't matter how sick someone is, you still never really get used to the idea, and it is always a surprise." Yossi was quiet for a moment and Avner heard his sister speaking.

"We still have to do the obituary. Ask him for an exact address." Without waiting, Avner gave the information.

Yossi said, "We haven't even figured out the obituary yet, we just haven't had a moment."

"That's easy enough with our newspapers," Avner tried to reassure him. "And there are templates, where you can just add the personal details, if you want." He tried to recall the obituary for his father, but couldn't. What had they written there? "The crown has fallen from our heads?" Or maybe, "Shocked and grieving?" He couldn't remember. Maybe it was "With great sorrow and deep grief?"

"We'll write something easily enough," Yossi said. "Like I said, you can never be fully prepared for death."

"Yes," said Avner. "That is very true. Was your mother unwell?"

"My mother stood on her own two legs almost until her final day," said Yossi, sounding mournful. "It's just that damned Alzheimer's that wiped out her memory."

"Was she sick with it a long time?"

"Not really," said Yossi. "She had some memory issues, but nothing more. But in the past three months it really deteriorated."

"I can say that from what I've read up until now, she remembered lots of details from her life," said Avner, wanting to say something comforting.

"I assume that she didn't write that diary in the last few months," Yossi noted. "It's terrible what became of her, she really was a brilliant woman."

Avner felt compassion and great sorrow for the woman that he had never met. He heard the sound of someone blowing their nose on the other end of the line, and knew that her children were crying.

"I'm so sorry for your loss," he said. "And as for the eulogy, take your time and decide. Whatever you say is fine by me, of course."

"You said that she asked you to eulogize her?" Yossi asked, as it suddenly sank in that the task that had been handed over to a stranger.

"Yes, that's what she asked, and I will do the best I can to honor her request."

"But you don't know her. How can you possibly deliver her eulogy?"

"That's right," Avner agreed. "I really didn't know her personally, but I am learning about her through the diary."

"I understand that this was her request. But I have to say, I am pretty stunned by it," said Yossi Reich. He grew quiet for a moment. "On the other hand, it's sacred to me, her final request."

"Certainly," Avner replied. "Like I said, I will do my best."

Again, there was quiet and Avner thought that the conversation had ended. He almost put down the receiver, when he suddenly heard a woman's voice on the line.

"Are you Mr. Bock?" the woman asked.

"You may call me Avner," he replied.

"I'm Hani, Eva's daughter."

"I'm so sorry for your loss, my heart goes out to you," said Avner. "And as I just told your brother, I will do whatever I can to make it a respectful ceremony to honor your mother."

"Thank you," she said quietly. "But we don't have money to pay for her plot on the kibbutz. While you were talking to my brother, I looked at your website. It costs a fortune."

"Ah, don't worry about that," Avner replied. "You don't owe me a shekel. Your mother already paid good money for her plot here." He paused for a moment. "Ahh... and she wanted a coffin, she paid for that too, you may as well know. She even paid more than necessary. I will return the difference to you."

From the other side of the line he heard Yossi's voice again. "I don't think I like the idea of burial in a coffin. It's against my principles now, just as it was when my father died."

"Where is your father buried?" Avner asked.

"In Holon," Yossi replied. "And for that matter, Mom has a plot there too."

"That really is strange, but the letter I received is kind of her will, I assume, that is, nobody wrote it for her, right?"

"If you are asking if she wrote it with a clear mind, the answer is yes. Like I said, she's only stopped being herself lately." Yossi's voice broke.

"I fully understand," said Avner. "Nor am I hinting, God forbid, that someone else wrote it! On the contrary, this will is written in fine language and beautiful handwriting! There's no doubt that the person who wrote it was in full command of her faculties!"

Avner heard Yossi tell his sister, "He noticed her fine language, what a special woman she was." Avner didn't hear what the sister replied and a moment later Yossi said, "About the coffin that you mentioned, did she really explicitly ask for that?"

"Yes," said Avner, and tried to reassure him. "It's not against Jewish law. Maybe there is a preference for burial without a coffin, but it's not against the 'halacha.'"

"Coffins also cost a lot of money," Yossi whispered. "Did she pay for that already too?"

"Certainly. Like I said, she even overpaid."

"It's just like her to take care of everything, down to the last detail," her son said quietly.

"Was she a perfectionist?" Avner asked, and was pleased to have found another good thing to say about the deceased.

"Like you wouldn't believe," said Yossi, without so much as a trace of a smile in his words. "Punctual as a Swiss clock."

"The truth is," said Avner, hoping to cheer up Yossi a little. "The coffin is nearly ready. The carpenter who is working with "Heavenly Rest" is a real artist; he does amazing work, and he's also fast."

He added, "By the way, you can choose the style of ceremony and the details of the program. For instance, there are people who ask for a sound system, and they play a song that the deceased especially loved, and want to give the eulogy with a mic so everyone can hear."

"No," said Yossi. "We'll pass on the sound system, and there's no song like that."

"As you like," Avner replied.

"Lots of people will be there," said Yossi. "She was highly regarded in many places and had a ton of acquaintances, including from the time when she worked at the university. Did she mention that in her diary?"

"Actually I've only started reading," Avner said apologetically. "But I promise to read it all. In the meantime, goodbye for now, and I wish you an end to your sorrow."

He sat down in his chair, feeling exhausted and mournful. What nonsense to wish someone an end to sorrow. An illogical notion. But now, he thought to himself, one must keep one's promises. "I must keep reading."

~

CHAPTER FIVE

It was May 1944. I was fourteen and a half, and the cold blue eyes which lacked any sign of humanity looked directly into mine; he swung his stick to the right. My mother, who looked thirty years older than her age on account of hunger, fear, and how skeletal she was, faltered, a few steps ahead of me before that same pair of eyes, which, without blinking an eye, swung the stick to the left.

Mom tried to say something in German, 'fehler,' "mistake, mistake," she whispered, but the stick had moved on. I was a young girl. I did not understand that to the right there was a slim chance of survival and to the left — there wasn't. Nor did I understand what mistake it was that Mom was talking about.

From a distance, smoke rose from chimneys and the smell of charred flesh rose to my nostrils. I had not eaten meat for a few years by then and the hunger was paralyzing, unbearable. I was furious with myself that in moments like these I thought about food, but evidently the will to live was stronger than anything else. A few minutes earlier, when I saw Mom being sent to the left, and realized that anyone who looked a bit unwell was sent to the left, too, I thought that since my stomach hurt terribly, maybe it would be good if I made it obvious that I didn't feel well either, and would be sent along with Mom.

Maybe there, on the left side, they would bring us a doctor who would care for anyone who wasn't feeling well, like me. I held my belly and scrunched up my face, to show that I was sick, but an SS officer who stood beside me gave me a light smack and whispered in German, '*astrein*,' "stand up straight" and the stick before my eyes pointed to the right.

For years I never wanted to visit Germany. Meir tried to convince me that we should go on more than one occasion, thinking he might find someone from among his extended family. After all, it was his homeland too, but I vehemently refused any connection to that place. I did, in fact, return there after the war, and I'll talk about that shortly. But beyond that, I refused to travel to Germany for many long years.

After Meir died, I felt that it was his wish that I visit Germany. About four years ago I complied with that unwritten will and visited the land of my birth. I made my way to Alexanderplatz. Today, it is a lively place, appealing to tourists from all over the world, but for me it was the vague and painful memory of my childhood. I wandered a little around the nearby streets. There was no trace of the hat store or the photography shop, but I could still smell the aroma of fresh bread being baked. I proceeded on foot, my head held high, feeling a sense of victory mixed with pain. I glanced down at the sidewalk, and saw gold plaques embedded in it. I bent down and managed to identify names. Here lived the Hirsch Zorn family, there lived Mrs. Feldman, born in 1924, and perished in 1943, there lived Mr. Kaiserman, born in 1928, and perished in 1944, and so on, names etched into neat, orderly golden plaques.

I found my parents' home. The house was still there. It had been renovated but was still recognizable. I looked at the yard, where I dug in the dirt many years ago, in the place where I found the photograph which I will say more about later. A tall, strong tree with its roots in the earth now grew in the spot where it had been buried, and I thought of all those people who did not manage to put down roots anywhere, remaining refugees, without a home. I looked around. People walked down the street, hurrying about their business. I think that they live with a lot of feelings of guilt to this day. It seems that Germany really is trying to atone for the atrocities.

I stood there almost hypnotized, watching two little girls playing in the street, jumping rope and giggling, when suddenly an older woman, at least eighty years old, approached me and asked in German if I needed assistance. I looked at her. She had kind eyes and I told her who I was. Her expression grew shocked and she whispered in German that she had not yet been born at the time those atrocities took place. Funny, but I felt sorry for her. It was obvious that she knew that I knew that she was lying, but I didn't mention it.

I went on walking around the street. A large shopping center had been built where the bakery had been, and there were new stores over the ruins of the photography shop. A little farther on, where the hat shop had been, the same place that gave Anna and I many hours of entertainment, a multi-story building had been built. Our fine fabric store, too, no longer existed.

At the end of the road was the same old school, and I could see Anna and myself, dressed in our matching uniforms, giggling in the yard. If I had listened closely, I might have heard voices praying in the synagogue, 'Beit Israel,' which had been located just there, rising from the earth. Across from where I stood was the world clock and the famous television tower. I kept walking toward the Brandenburg Gate. Not far from it there was a special monument in memory of the Holocaust, hundreds of concrete blocks of different heights, that feel like a maze to the visitor walking among them. Beneath the monument is an underground museum in memory of the Jews of Europe.

I apologize, dear diary, for putting the cart before the horse, but I could not stop my pen. Mr. Bock, now, as you read this, I hope you find it close to your heart in one way or another, and since I've already put the cart before the horse, I suggest that you flip through the diary to the end, where I put a photograph that I found a few years ago. No, it is not the photograph that I mentioned earlier. That photo is in my album to this day. This is a different photograph, the one I found in Yad Vashem, the Holocaust history museum, and they let me make a copy for myself. In the photo you can see people from my street, including several members of my family. It is a rare document, which reminds me that these were really living and breathing people once.

Now, Mr. Bock, have a seat on the bench in the middle of the yard, take a moment or two and look at the photo. Does anyone from among those photographed look familiar to you?

＊

Avner quickly flipped to the end of the diary. There, between the two last pages, was a black and white photograph. There were some twenty people in it, some of them standing, some sitting. In the center sat a young woman holding a baby in her arms. Beside her was a boy about five years old and behind her a tall, sturdy man with a moustache. Beside the sitting woman stood another woman, in her arms a baby girl in a dress and beside her another little girl with a ribbon in her hair. Behind them another man, with an impressive beard and a hat on his head. A few others stood behind them, somewhat hidden.

At first glance it looked like a class photo from school, except that the subjects included babies and older people together. The faces of the adults in the photograph struck Avner as looking sad. The girl with the ribbon smiled brightly. The five-year-old boy looked like he was crying. Avner held the photograph in shaking hands. Who was he meant to recognize here?

The hot rays of pre-summer sun flickered through the hunched fig tree at the entrance to the cemetery. The tree, as old as some of the inhabitants of the place, had never borne any fruit, but stood bent as if bearing a heavy load. It appeared to challenge the world around it. Its branches drooped, the sorrow of the whole world peering through them.

Avner went outside for some fresh air and found Nisim sitting on the bench, a container of fresh vegetables in his hand. He held out a juicy piece of red pepper to Avner, who sat absent-mindedly and took the pepper but did not put it to his mouth. Tomorrow, late afternoon, the funeral would take place, and he did not know what to think.

"Have you finished reading?" Nisim asked, and took a noisy bite out of a red pepper.

"No," replied Avner. "I put down the diary when Mrs. Reich told me to check the picture that she placed between the last pages."

"Sounds interesting," said Nisim and pulled a long slice of cucumber from the box. "Here," he said, handing it to Avner. "Tastes like heaven, I swear."

Avner took the piece of cucumber, the red pepper still in his other hand, and he looked like a lost child who couldn't choose between two toys in the store.

"Well," Nisim urged him. "Eat it, I told you, it's the taste of heaven." He wiped the juice of a ripe tomato he had bitten into from his chin with a napkin. "What? What was the picture there?"

"I think that it was a picture of her relatives and people from her street," said Avner quietly, without thinking to return the vegetables to the box which sat between them. "I don't understand why she thinks that one of them would look familiar to me."

"So you don't recognize any of them?"

"No."

"Did you look really closely? Because you know, sometimes at first glance we miss things." He pulled a slice of fresh kohlrabi from the container. "Heaven, I swear," he repeated, and handed Avner a round slice of aromatic fennel.

"I looked at it for a long time. I don't know any of them, and why would I?"

"I don't know, but that is interesting," Nisim replied.

Avner bit into the fennel and said, "She even asked me if I was sitting down right now on the bench outside, you understand?"

"She did her research, huh? She knew what this place looks like."

"Kind of strange, no?"

"Strange? I wouldn't say so." Nisim smiled. "That's hardly a problem these days. With Facebook and Google there's no privacy left anymore, she probably looked online... what, did you forget that we have a website with pictures?"

"Right," said Avner. There was something so reassuring in the way Nisim approached life. If only a small part of that would stick to him maybe he would have had an easier time of it.

He pulled out a slice of sweet carrot and put it into his mouth with a sudden appetite. A moment later, as always, doubts returned and Nisim's calming words ceased to work. Why had she come to him of all people? Why did she think he would recognize someone from the photo? What the hell was all this about? His gaze wandered from the fig tree to the gravestones around him and he was quiet.

"I know you like the back of my hand," Nisim said in a soft tone. "I know exactly what's disturbing you."

Somewhat encouraged, Avner looked at his friend, who explained, "You struggle with doubt, that's your problem here."

Avner seemed to stare, and Nisim thought that he had not fully understood.

"Look," he went on explaining. "You need to write a eulogy for an unknown woman, which I appreciate is strange enough as it is, and on top of that her diary is evidently getting to you somehow."

"You read me like an open book," said Avner. "Everything you said was spot-on."

"What can I say… after so many years working together, I really do know when you're sad, when you're happy, when you're disturbed, when you're dying to let out a fart."

Avner burst out laughing. Somehow, Nisim could always make him laugh. More than once he had described something to him, that made him laugh to the point of tears, like the story about the elegant-looking woman, bustling along on her heels at breakneck speed toward her office, where, behind the door, she bent over and let out a loud, liberating fart, right in front of the astonished client, who had entered the room without her knowledge just a moment earlier.

"Good to hear you laugh," said Nisim.

"Yes." Avner sighed. "It's good to laugh," he said. His story was hovering on the tip of his tongue, about to erupt. Dozens of times he had wanted to tell Nisim what troubled him more than anything, and every time he stopped himself at the last moment. Now, too, seeing Nisim's smiling face, he wanted to free himself from the shackles of his silence, but couldn't do it.

Instead, he said, "You know, I am not a "maybe" person. I can live with "yes," can come to terms with "no" but I have a hard time with "maybe.""

Nisim held out another piece of carrot to Avner and said, "Yes, I understand. You don't know what to write and that's driving you nuts, that maybe you will write this or maybe you will write that, and you, how to say it, you are not someone who is able to handle things that are unclear."

"Exactly," said Avner, looking at Nisim with great affection. "That's quite right."

"Hey," said Nisim. "Snap out of it. What's up with you, what's with the long face?"

Avner did not respond, and Nisim added, "Listen, so she thought you might recognize someone, so what?"

Nisim was quiet for a moment, looking thoughtful. "Tell me," he began. "Did she write in her diary where she was born?"

"Yes," Avner replied. "She was born in Berlin."

A broad smile spread across Nisim's face.

"What's so funny?" Avner asked.

"Come on..." said Nisim, "I presume she looked into you a little, and knew that your family is from there too."

"So, what?" said Avner, looking for yellow pepper in Nisim's container.

"So, it's pretty clear," said Nisim. "After all, it's always like that with Jews, you meet by chance and then immediately check who knows who, and in the end someone always knows someone, no?"

"Yes, there is something to that," said Avner and Nisim, encouraged by the fact that he had once again managed to calm his friend, pulled the last piece of yellow pepper from the bottom of the container. "See, from your family name it's not hard to guess where you came from, it's a 'yekke'[1] name, no?"

"Yes," Avner replied. "What you're saying makes sense."

"So..." Nisim smiled. "There is sense to this nonsense, is there not?"

Nisim got up, went into the office and came back with two cups. He poured a little of his hot, white coffee into each, straight from the thermos, then sat down again.

"You know," he said to Avner. "Sometimes I imagine the dead, resurrect them, invent conversations between everyone, dress them in costumes, put words in their mouths, make them dance and even sing."

"Yes, I know that you are a bit of a fool," Avner said affectionately. "That's part of your charm."

"Fine," said Nisim. "I will take that as a compliment, but listen, you remember that guy who came here for a memorial service for his grandmother, and someone asked him where Block 7, Plot 5 was?"

"The one with the funny hat?"

---

1   'Yekke' refers to a Jew of German-speaking origin.

"Exactly! So you remember what that guy answered him?"

"No…"

"Okay, well that's the hilarious part," said Nisim. "He said that he's sorry, he doesn't know, he isn't from around here."

"Yes," said Avner. "That was really funny."

"So, why aren't you laughing?" said Nisim as he did a near-perfect impression of Polly from 'HaGashash HaHiver,' the famous comic trio. "I have no idea! The world is funny, so laugh!"

"You're something else," said Avner with sincere appreciation, putting his own story away once more. "I have no idea what I would do without you."

"And I don't know what I would do without me," Nisim said and laughed, placing a warm hand on his friend's shoulder, poured a little more coffee with a skilled hand. "You remember that time we said that the laughter of the two of us here could wake the dead?"

"They would probably enjoy some entertainment, no?"

"Sure," said Nisim.

"Do you think she came here?" Avner asked suddenly.

"Maybe, who knows? It seems like it, since she knows what the place looks like, no?"

Avner looked at Nisim. He was five feet, four inches or so of a skinny, jumpy man with kind eyes and a somewhat unkempt knit Kippah on his head, who lived simply and accepted life with such serenity. He remembered a deep conversation he once tried to have with Nisim. "How much would you be willing to invest in your own self-actualization?" he asked him.

Nisim had replied that he was a simple man without great demands of life, he felt that God had been good to him and given him good health, a wonderful woman, six talented children, a livelihood, and bread to eat and water to drink. No, he could not think of anything that he was missing.

Avner stared at his friend with wonder mixed with envy; here before him was a man who actually lived the proverbs that he so often recited. This was how it was for someone who had lived all of his life in praise and gratitude to the creator of the world for everything he had been given, who knew how to rejoice in everything and who never kept goodness for himself. Enviable, no doubt.

What a shame for Avner, that he was unable to approach life with that same lightheartedness, that he was tied down to his past and couldn't seem to break free.

Now Nisim tried to interpret Avner's pensive expression and said, "You know what? If this whole thing is hard on you for your own reasons, maybe we can come up with a creative solution?"

"Like what, for example?"

"She has relatives, right? So what do you say that you ask her family to deliver the eulogy? Tell them that you didn't know the deceased at all, which is true. They could definitely see it as coming from the right place, no?"

"They called me earlier," Avner replied. "I suggested that they give a eulogy too, but not instead of me."

"Who said instead of you?" asked Nisim. "Tell them to do it along with you, but let them do most of the work."

"If they talk that's how it'll go anyway, after all they are the ones who actually knew her," Avner replied and rose from the bench. "I completely forgot that there is a memorial service here today."

Relatives of the deceased gathered at the cemetery gate, and Nisim got up to open it, let them in, and perhaps sell them a bouquet of flowers.

Then he returned to Avner and said, "They bought three bouquets, those ones, and now we're out of Gerbera daisies. I'll make sure to get more for tomorrow."

"I'm counting on you," replied Avner.

~

CHAPTER SIX

I already mentioned my Aunt Alice's death, and that I wasn't at the funeral. But I want to go back to a few years earlier and say a bit more about my family. On the day that Alice died, there was heavy snow falling, and it was unbearably cold. It was November, the end of 1933, and I was three years old. My aunt was buried in a big cemetery in Berlin. I remember that I tried to listen to what my parents and sister were talking about when they returned from the funeral but I didn't understand much. Anna told me that there were few people there and that everyone cried, apart from a group of soldiers, friends of Uncle Karl, who didn't. Mom never got over the loss until the day she died in the gas chambers, as her whispers of '*fehler*,' "mistake, mistake," did nothing to save her.

Uncle Karl was a doctor who specialized in ear, nose, and throat afflictions and worked full-time at the hospital in Berlin. As I wrote previously, after the death of his wife and Hitler's rise to power, he left the house with his two sons and disappeared. There were rumors that he had enlisted in the army, but nothing was certain, they were just rumors. Today, I think that Mom knew things that the rest of us didn't, and I will return to that later.

***

Avner stopped reading for a moment. Mrs. Reich wrote that there were rumors that her uncle had joined the army. Why, then, were those rumors not investigated? Avner was troubled. If the rumors were true, what did that mean about the family? And what part of all this did she want him to tell her children? Then again, these were rumors, and Avner was familiar with the nature of bad rumors. He tried not to think about what people used to say behind his back, clicking their tongues: poor child with his crazy mother. He remembered her sitting on a bench, wearing a thin, floral dress, her legs covered in a plaid blanket, staring at some point in the distance. From time to time she would raise her hands and examine the fingers on her right hand, of which two were crooked as if someone had broken their bones. Then she would grimace, looking disgusted, and place them back down on her lap.

Unanswered questions from his childhood stirred in him, piercing his heart, rising up in his body like a tangle of threads. He got up and poured himself a glass of water. He tried to focus on the last passage and the fact that Eva Reich had been just a little girl on a freight train, on the way to a living hell, whose father disappeared and whose mother had been steered to the left, which meant death. But together with pity, he also felt a nagging doubt, that perhaps later on in the diary, there would be difficult insights to come.

He reread the last section, because sometimes you need to read between the lines, maybe he would find something to make sense of the great distress that he felt. He reread the bit about "the rumors" and tried to reassure himself: if they were only rumors, how could she know that they were true? He tried to think logically. He could tell her family members part of the truth and not all of it. That would not be a lie, and he could live with that.

He sank into his chair and closed his eyes for a moment, but opened them again quickly, because when they were closed he heard his mother, clearly, telling him, "Don't ask questions, my child, because if you ask, it will summon the devil."

He picked up the diary once more and went on reading, and it was as though Eva Reich had read his thoughts:

***

Often it is better, perhaps, not to know the details. There is a certain comfort in not knowing, and it allows a person to live with himself and his environment more fully. On the other hand, as I see it, a comfortable life is like living in a paradise of fools, and that is a place I hope to not find myself.

***

Avner was perturbed, overwhelmed by challenging, almost mystical thoughts. Maybe Mrs. Eva Reich was a mirror held up to him which reflected the pathetic life of someone who had never investigated the truth just because his mother forbid it? He suppressed these thoughts and recited the facts out loud to himself. Eva Reich was a little girl, unusually in touch with her past, who had visited her hometown and looked into archives and databases in search of her relatives, and that's it.

It suddenly sounded so logical to him, but a second later he felt concerned again. If it was so simple, why the hell had she chosen him of all people? Why not simply give the diary to her children?

Avner felt trapped so he went outside. He could hear the sound of hammering from the little carpentry workshop, and he headed there.

Nisim looked up at him. "Well, what's new?" he asked with a smile.

Avner hesitated. He couldn't bring himself to tell Nisim of his great pain. He looked at his friend, full of life and joy and said, "Nothing new. I just came to see how you're getting along, nothing special."

Nisim smiled at him, showing a row of white teeth and said, "Well if all's well, then all's well." Avner nodded and smiled.

He went back to the office and resumed reading.

***

There were many heroic stories from that time. Today, I know that many of them are meticulously documented in the Yad Vashem Holocaust museum, and that there is a whole archive which shows that we didn't simply go as sheep to the slaughter, as I heard said more than once in the street. And if I think of Ludwig and Maria again. For instance, I remember that there were also those who endangered their own lives to save Jews.

There is something touching about those non-Jews who did whatever they could to prevent the atrocities, and I will tell of one of them, a particularly unusual, special one. I just feel the need, and a kind of Israeli pride, to say that there were also strong Jews, the kind that didn't lower their heads before the tyrant, and it's enough to examine stories of uprising in the ghettos to understand how many heroes there were among us.

***

He set down the diary and mused: which unusual and special hero was she referring to? When he said the word "hero" out loud, it struck a familiar chord in him, something woke up, but now, after so many years, he was no longer sure if that was the word his mother had used. He had been a little boy, and she had been institutionalized when he was an adolescent. Since the hospitalization, it became impossible to take anything she said seriously.

He felt shame as he remembered that it had been nearly two months since he last visited her. Most times when he went to see her she didn't remember who he was anyway, so he found himself visiting less and less.

∾

CHAPTER SEVEN

They unloaded us from the freight car. I looked for Dad among the hundreds of people but didn't find him.

They led us to the entrance, where a sign promised that work would set us free. After being steered to the right, before I realized that I was all alone in the world, they led me and many more women and girls into a small chamber with old beds, ripped blankets — and cold. I think I remember the cold more than anything. Freezing cold, bones shaking, teeth chattering, and me with just a torn dress and a pair of shoes — a valuable commodity in this place — which I later sold and not even for so much as lentil stew but for a piece of bread, real bread, not wet or thrown to some animal.

Throughout the day they sent us to work. We dug trenches in the snow without knowing that the blood of our people would flow through them. They ordered us to dig with our hands. Those who were lucky were given a shovel. Soldiers stood over the trenches as we worked, ready to shoot anyone who stopped digging at any moment. It's hard to describe the kind of human relations that form between people who are persecuted, starving, and freezing from cold. A range of behaviors, from disturbing thoughts of eating the flesh of whoever did not survive, to squabbling, rage, and blood-curdling screams. But there was another side, too, which was merciful and compassionate, the side that made people in crisis actually come together and work together with the hope that the sun will rise again. There was a terrifying officer who we referred to as "the Eye." Among the barracks, huddled together, trying to stay warm, we would giggle and tell each other stories about the Eye, the man with the single blue Cyclops eye, who thought that he was omnipotent, and how he would stumble and fall into the trench we had dug. In reality he was not a cyclops, nor did he fall, unfortunately. He had both his eyes, but to us he looked like a monster with a penetrating gaze, and the blue color of his eyes looked inhuman.

The Eye would make the rounds outside in his shiny boots, and his cruelty knew no end. More than once he caught some miserable girl who appeared to be working too slowly, and performed terrible deeds on her in front of everyone, then threw her back into the trench when he was finished. We shook with fear of him, and invented a secret code: the first girl who saw him from a distance would whisper into the ear of the girl beside her, "the Eye," and so on, in a kind of unending chain, like in a game of "broken telephone." The message would pass through all of us, and anyone who had grown tired would suddenly display renewed energy, shoveling vigorously, until he passed.

I survived. My fingers froze and remained crooked, my ankles grew red and swollen, and my shoes, as I said, I sold for a piece of bread. We drank snow, we laughed and cried, and every day I was sure that I would see my mother at any moment. We willfully ignored the rumors, the smell, the smoke. Not everyone survived. There were those who died of cold, of hunger, of disease. But there were also those who made it, and even looked healthy.

I remember Davusha, an intelligent teenage girl from Poland, who spoke fluent German. One evening she disappeared from the barracks. We worried for her, we were afraid that she had done something stupid and tried to escape through the electric fence. We were also afraid to look for her, because rumors said that girls who wandered around outside were caught by young officers, who did as they pleased with them.

I remember that I didn't understand what that meant, and once I asked the older girls in my barracks. They giggled and blushed and one of them said, "they use them for sex." I didn't understand what she meant, and another said, "Are you stupid or what? Don't you understand? They undress them and force things inside them there, down there." That scared me to death.

That same night, when Davusha disappeared, I imagined her screaming as the officers pushed things into her body, and the fear rose to new levels that I didn't know existed. I slept huddled in the corner of my bunk and cried with fear. But in the morning Davusha was back, wearing a new dress, and even a sweater, a precious commodity.

I watched her come in and I listened to her speak with the other girls. They whispered together and I heard her say, "I will survive, and that's what matters. Beyond that, don't ask."

If I could have, I would have asked Mom to explain what that meant, because the warm sweater that Davusha had looked like something someone had plucked from the heavens for her. But I never saw Mom again, and her voice as she cried 'fehler,' "mistake, mistake," echoed in my ears for a long time afterward.

***

Avner stopped reading. The terrible things he had just read shocked him deeply. Eva had been so naive, so innocent, so alone, and had learned the facts of life, what happens between a man and a woman, in the most twisted way possible. The thought that maybe his mother too, who by all accounts had been a pretty girl, had suffered such shocking abuse made Avner want to shout, to seek revenge. He remembered how ashamed he had been of his mother, and now felt guilt flood his body.

He got up from where he sat and paced the room, restlessly, his hands clenched in tight fists. And it was even a mistake, he said out loud to himself, since Eva had emphasized the mistake several times. It wasn't totally clear to him why Eva's mother said that it was a mistake, and he thought to himself that the Nazis had been so well-organized that there hadn't really been any mistakes. If Eva's mother had been killed, it had not been an accident. The Nazis made no mistakes. They valued order above all else.

He was somewhat disturbed when he thought how orderly he was as a person, almost compulsively so, and how hard it was for him to leave the house in the morning without all six kitchen chairs at an equal distance from one another, and a uniform distance from the table, and moreover he was a little shocked by himself when he recalled how he had told Chaya to hang the laundry with clothespins according to the order, one blue, one white, one blue, one white, etc., because she didn't pay attention to those kinds of details, and for him, such disorder disturbed his peace of mind.

Avner pushed aside these thoughts, and reassured himself that one could be an orderly person regardless of where they came from. He swore to himself that he would not mention the clothespins again, no matter what. Besides, he must keep reading, it was already getting late.

***

I didn't really understand what mistake Mom was talking about. I was a scared young girl, skin and bones, and I missed her so much! At night, huddled in the arms of my friends, some of whom survived, like me, and later moved to Israel, I would lie there, freezing from the cold. It is hard to describe how hard it was to live with that constant hunger, and sometimes I would cry just so that the hot tears would warm my cheeks a little.

I remember my friend Regina who, as far as I heard after the war, also survived, maybe thanks to her intelligence and the wise advice that she gave us. If it was hard and cold, she said, close your eyes and let your imagination take you to a good place, where it isn't cold and you aren't hungry. I did as she said, and my imagination took me to my parents' home, big and spacious, with a huge wood stove which was always lit, and a table of food in the middle of the dining room, always set with porcelain plates, filled with delicacies prepared by our cook. I would lie like that for a long time, my eyes closed, the memories flooding in.

Here it's a holiday, the new year. Dad said that these were days of repentance and a return to the way of God, and the meal included apples dipped in honey. Before Aunt Alice died, there had been another new year holiday, when the family celebrated at Alice and Karl's home around a pretty tree, and all of us were given gifts. I didn't think then about what that meant.

I was young, it was cold, and I was hungry. I didn't stop to think how we celebrated two new years' holidays, and not even on the same date.

When you are a child, you simply accept things, unless someone chooses to complicate them, even unintentionally, as it happened not long after.

***

Two New Years' holidays? Aunt Alice was Eva's mother's sister, no? So what did that mean? Avner reread the last lines, and suddenly it all seemed so clear, to the point that he didn't understand how he hadn't caught on sooner.

It was late afternoon in Kibbutz Mishmar HaAliya. Avner knew that Nisim would come in at any moment to eat the food he had brought with him from home, and he faced a problem: What would he tell Nisim? How would he explain Mrs. Reich to him? After all, he knew how opposed Nisim was to any kind of pluralism in "Heavenly Rest." What would he say? How could he justify burying a goyish woman in the earth of "Heavenly Rest" to Nisim? But he had no choice. He had to tell him, otherwise it would be a blatant lie.

Like a Swiss clock, Nisim entered a moment later, his broad smile replaced by a look of concern. "What's the matter?"

"Nothing," said Avner, and tried to think of what to say.

"You're a little pale, did something happen?"

"There's a bit of a problem."

"A problem?" Nisim asked. "Surely something we can solve, no? After all, there's no problem too complicated that it doesn't have a simple solution, as you know."

Avner hesitated. He knew that if he told Nisim the truth, Nisim simply would refuse to bury Mrs. Reich at Mishmar HaAliya. He racked his brain for times they had run into an issue like this in the past, and apart from an incident or maybe two, in which Nisim was not involved to the degree that he was this time, he couldn't recall any such incidents. It was clear to him that Nisim would object if he knew, but not saying anything and letting Nisim work all day on something that he was opposed to, would be an unacceptable deceit.

What a bind, he thought to himself. They had had a number of arguments in the past about the nature of the place. Nisim didn't want "Heavenly Rest" to lose its Jewish character, while Avner was primarily concerned with making a living. As far as he was concerned, there was no difference between one person and another, and whoever was willing to pay and buy a plot here should be welcome.

He remembered how it took him time to convince Nisim to agree to work here. "Most of the burials here are for the kibbutz members anyway," he told him then. "And they're secular, but have nothing against tradition." Nisim was uneasy about it then and Avner had added, "Burial in a coffin, with background music, is not against Jewish law."

When this failed to pacify Nisim, Avner added, "If anyone from outside of the kibbutz comes to be buried here it'll be once in a blue moon!"

Ultimately, Nisim agreed, after Avner promised to attend to each case appropriately.

"Hey, friend-o, are you with me or what?" Nisim asked.

"Yes," Avner replied, absentmindedly. "So, there's a small problem, as I said."

"I'm listening," Nisim replied.

Avner tried to avoid making eye contact with his friend. He knew perfectly well that Nisim might turn a blind eye to funerals that were inconsistent with his worldview, but he also knew that if something strayed too far from the acceptable, Nisim would get up and leave, and he really did not want that to happen. Nisim was very dear to him. He couldn't imagine his work at "Heavenly Rest" without him. No, he couldn't tell Nisim the truth right now.

He collected himself, got up, tucked his shirt into his pants and said, "It's nothing, maybe I had a bit of a drop in blood pressure, after all you know I my blood pressure fluctuates, it's nothing, everything's fine."

He sat back down with uncharacteristic heaviness, his back more hunched than usual. Nisim looked at him with great concern but Avner carried on as if nothing had happened. "Have you finished the coffin?"

"Blood pressure? Since when do you have issues with blood pressure?"

Avner paused a moment, remembering how just that morning Nisim had asked him if he ever lied, and he had said no, and now, here he was about to lie right to his face. A white lie perhaps, but a lie, nonetheless. He got back up, stood tall and said, "Not really an issue, but sometimes, you know, a little unstable, that's all."

"Are you sure everything is okay?" Nisim answered him with a question. "It doesn't seem like that's everything—"

"Don't worry, it passed already, I told you."

Nisim didn't let it go. "But a moment ago you said that there was a little problem, so now there's no little problem?"

"Come on, when did you become my Polish mother?" Avner smiled reluctantly. "My blood pressure is up and down, it's just a small thing… did you finish the coffin?" He tried to change the subject.

"Why does it seem like you're bluffing?"

Avner smiled. He hadn't heard the word "bluff" instead of "lie" for years.

Nisim didn't understand the meaning of this smile and Avner seemed somehow off to him.

"You're acting weird," he said, and Avner stood taller, to show him that everything was fine.

"Don't worry, it's passed already," he lied. "Well, what about the coffin?"

Nisim shrugged his shoulders and looked like someone who had given up on getting a straightforward response. "The coffin?" he said. "As far as I'm concerned the devil himself can die today, I worked on it since the morning. If necessary, I can make another coffin, the one I made for Mrs. Reich turned out great, really great."

"I am familiar with your talents." Avner felt compelled to compliment his friend. "You're an artist."

"Thank you," Nisim replied, and got his food from the fridge. He poured himself a little soup into a bowl, and put it in the microwave. "Shall I heat some up for you?" he asked.

"No thanks," Avner replied. "Actually, I'm not hungry, maybe a bit later."

"So, you aren't eating with me," Nisim asked-declared and went over to the sink. He rinsed his hands, said the blessing out loud, took a bite of bread and sat down to eat.

Avner looked between Nisim eating silently and the diary on the table, and suddenly thought to himself that Mrs. Reich had a son, and what about the 'Kaddish'?[2] God help him. In fact, he thought to himself, it wasn't just that. If they didn't know who their mother was, then they didn't know what they were themselves, God help them. He had no choice, he simply wouldn't say a word about it to anyone, and that's that. But as much as that decision seemed like a relief, it was also confusing and troubling. Was not saying anything the same as lying?

"The soup is great," said Nisim. "Nothing like hot soup, it's the best thing in the world." He did a blessing over the food, stood, and said, "'Ya Habibi,' time is short and work is long."

Avner smiled and Nisim winked at him. "I know, I know, plenty of work, not much time, but what does it matter?"

Nisim went out to go on working, and Avner continued to sit, thinking. Was not saying anything lying? His memories took him back. He was a small child in a soft bed, in his room in his parents' home, before the disaster, and the next day was Mother's Day at nursery school. The teacher had said that the whole family could come, Dad and Mom, brothers and sisters, grandma and grandpa. Now he remembered how his mother had answered him, without lying, but also not telling the truth.

"Mom," he said to her, a moment before she turned out the lights in his room. "The teacher said that Grandma and Grandpa and Mom and Dad can come to school."

"I'll come, of course I'll be there, and Dad too, he will take a day off of work to come."

"Dad will come, too?" he asked, and was so happy that his mother said so again. He wanted to ask if he could also invite Hilik but he hadn't told her that he had an imaginary brother. Instead, he said, "But I want Grandma and Grandpa to come, too."

Mom came back into the room, sat down on his bed but said nothing.

"Mom," he asked directly, like an arrow straight to her heart. "Why don't I have a grandmother or grandfather?"

Mom looked at him with a dreamy expression. He didn't like it when she got like that, it always frightened him because he knew that whenever

_____

2   Jewish mourning ritual

he saw that face, she said kind of scary things, but he felt guilty. It was he who asked her again why he didn't have a grandmother or grandfather, and now he would have to listen to this talk of hers, which would probably frighten him.

"You had a grandfather and grandmother on one side, but they perished. Your dad, Nahum, he is a true hero, listen my boy, a real hero. Here, look, he gave you the name of a great warrior from the bible, because he is a hero, my boy, a real hero. He saved Jews, your father, even your grandfather resisted, yes, my boy, it is a great secret. Just that your father is a hero, that's all we are allowed to say. We can't even say your grandfather's name, it's simply forbidden. Remember that, forbidden!"

"But what will I tell my friends?" he asked. "How do I explain to them why my grandparents didn't come?"

"Don't say anything, my son. If they ask you, just don't answer. That way it won't be a lie, you just won't say the truth, get it? Got it?"

Here, his mother hadn't lied to him. She simply hadn't told him the whole truth. And he didn't lie to her either. He just didn't tell her about Hilik.

***

Among the unthinkable sights that I saw at the extermination camp, there are a few that come to mind which I will never be able to forget. Like Abrashka, the cook, who made soup and found human flesh inside the pot, threw his guts up and was shot by the Nazi officer on duty, while the rest of us stood and watched it play out, and the officer laughed gleefully. "Meat? You want meat? Here you go, fresh meat!"

Or Rivka, who got pregnant by her beloved and managed to hide her pregnancy and keep the baby underneath her dress during roll call. It's inconceivable how the baby knew not to cry or that she survived off the drops of milk that her mother somehow managed to collect from generous prisoners who donated drops from the one cloudy glass that they received for the day. I don't know what became of Rivka or her daughter because she was taken to different barracks, far from mine. I just remember her marching toward the barracks that they sent her to, carrying her baby between her legs, and only God could explain the miracle.

I remember death, disease, hunger, and most of all the paralyzing silence. I don't pretend to understand much about the human psyche, but I can say that to this day I cannot stand silence when it lasts too long.

Maybe in my subconscious I was attracted to Meir precisely because of his booming voice and his easy laughter, which you could hear from a distance. More than anything else, I loved to hear my children laughing, and the louder the better, all the sweeter to my ears. I suspect that I was afraid of the quiet. Maybe I even passed on that fear, without meaning to, to my children. I remember how my Hani, when she would go to the bathroom, would talk to us from there, nonstop. I think that she was afraid to sit in silence, and maybe that came from my fear, that if everyone was quiet, maybe they were simply no longer there. There was even a time when she called us from the bathroom, and for some reason nobody answered her, so she shouted, "Speak!"

It might seem funny now, but for me, "quiet" meant secret. Maria and Ludwig kept quiet so that the secret of the cellar would not be found out. Rivka's baby was quiet so that she and her mother would not be killed.

Back to my story, we didn't know if and or how it would all end, but in the spring of 1945, we were told to hurry out. We marched for long days, without food or water, toward the unknown. Hundreds of people fell along the way, shot by the guards or died of hunger and disease. We marched like that for what felt like eternity, and when David Ben Gurion later said that the day of victory is a sad one, he was right. Dozens, if not hundreds of thousands of refugees, some ravenous with hunger, died free from Hitler, but prisoners within their own thin bodies.

The Red Army came in and now we were refugees. Together with us were many hundreds of prisoners and forced laborers and even Nazi collaborators. Rabbis from America, along with members of the Jewish Brigade, suggested establishing separate displaced persons camps for the Jewish survivors. I was there, in the Jewish camp. Now, when I write about this, I see how I really couldn't know that my origins were different. Later on, when we were already in Israel, the men were checked to see which of them were Jewish. Among the women, of course, there wasn't anything to check and the authorities made do with testimony. Besides, I was a Holocaust survivor and everything that came with that. Nobody investigated further.

The separation of the DP camps between the Jewish refugees and the others did not come from the need to protect the refugees, but the notion that the Jews were somehow different from the rest of the refugees. In Russia, for example, they refused to acknowledge this, and the Jewish displaced persons stayed with the rest of them. Maybe there was some wish to give equal treatment to all, but it is likely that these shared living quarters led to complex situations.

I can't say anything about that, certainly I cannot judge so painful a subject, but I feel that I must say how once, when I was working at the university, there was a statistics lecturer, a religious man, with strong opinions on many issues. More than once he was embroiled in intense arguments with others whose opinions differed from his. Occasionally, ethnic, political, or subjects related to religion one way or another came up. Some of the things he said I find hard to forget. "Statistically speaking," he said once. "Six million Jews were exterminated, which is certainly an astronomical number, but the real Holocaust of the Jewish people is assimilation."

***

Avner finished reading this grim section. Additional facts became clear, but more than anything, he felt excruciating pain. The characters described in the diary were clear before his eyes: the poor Jewish cook falling to the ground and puking, the miserable mother who hid her baby when it seemed pretty clear that her fate was sealed. A feeling of national pride arose in him suddenly. He felt that anything was possible. A moment later, his doubts returned and gnawed at him. He decided to be proactive and call Eva's children.

~

CHAPTER EIGHT

"Hello," said a woman's voice on the other end of the line. Avner began apologetically, he didn't want to bother her, he knew that this was a hard time for them, but still, if possible, he had a few questions about the next day's ceremony.

"Just a moment," said the woman's voice. "I'll put you on speaker phone, so my brother can hear you too."

"Great," said Avner. 'I just wanted a couple of details about your mother. Since she asked me to say a few words. Perhaps you might be so kind as to tell me a bit about her? For example, how many grandchildren does she have, and where did she live when she married your father?"

Avner hoped he might be able to extract some details that could shine a little light, based on their answers, as to what exactly her children knew or didn't, but they weren't particularly cooperative.

"But you're the one with her diary, no?" The voice of the daughter cracked and Avner could hear her deep pain.

"Yes," he replied. "But I haven't managed to get through all of it yet."

"Ahh…" she replied. "I imagine she will write about her grandchildren in her diary. In any case, I have a daughter named Alma, she's nineteen, and my brother has two boys, Evyatar is eighteen and Itamar is twelve and a half."

Avner assumed that he would get to that in the dairy, and didn't know whether or not to ask about spouses. He feared it might seem like a nosy question, and he didn't know if they were even married. There was quiet on the other end of the line and then Hani said in a quiet voice, as if to herself, "I can't believe it, Shoshi was always afraid something would ruin Itamar's Bar Mitzvah."

"Shoshi?" asked Avner.

"My sister-in-law, my brother's wife," Hani replied as if she had read Avner's thoughts. And my husband's name is Gideon, in case you want to mention any of them in the eulogy."

The son joined the conversation, "By the way, we also have a few questions."

"Go ahead," said Avner, his mind already racing with thoughts of how many new people in this story may or may not know their status in terms of 'Halacha,' or "Jewish law."

"Let's agree that tomorrow, after the ceremony, you will hand over the diary to us," said Yossi.

"Ahh… that might be a bit of a problem, since your mother requested that I destroy it, and I would hope to do as she asked, if possible."

"Absolutely not!" Yossi declared loudly. "I did not agree to that, not at all!"

"Whatever Mom asked is supposed to be sacred, you know," the sister interrupted. "You said that yourself, earlier."

Avner listened to their arguing with interest, as it could solve his problem, because here exactly was the crucial matter as far as he was concerned. What the mother had requested was sacred, so said the daughter, and the son replied that that was true, but the way he saw it, it should be enough that they were giving in and burying her at the kibbutz and not the plot that she already had, beside Dad, in Holon.

Avner tried to think quickly. It had happened more than once that he had drawn incorrect conclusions. Maybe this time he was mistaken too? If she had bought a plot at a regular cemetery, maybe he was totally wrong about her? How could he be so sure what she was? He had to read to the end to draw any conclusions. Maybe she had converted, how did he know that she hadn't? He was tempted to ask her children if they knew anything about that, when he heard them on the phone. "Mr. Bock, are you still there?"

"Ahh… yes, I am. I hope that everything works out for the best." He felt compelled to reassure them…

"How do you intend for tomorrow to go? Because from what I saw on your site, I understand that you'll conduct the ceremony according to the family's wishes, right?" Hani asked.

"Yes," Avner replied. "Do you have something in mind?" He was still worried about the 'kaddish' that was meant to be read during the ceremony, but the son replied, confirming Avner's concerns. "Mom raised us traditionally," he said. "She would light the candles on Friday nights, and we said the blessing over the wine, and she kept kosher, and lived according to Jewish tradition."

"Yes," said the daughter, her voice warmer now. "If that's not written in her diary, well, now you know."

"That's definitely important information," said Avner, and thought to himself that if she raised her children in the spirit of tradition, maybe he really had rushed to conclusions.

"Tell me," he heard Yossi say. "Do you have any idea why she chose to send her diary to you, of all people?"

"No," said Avner, in total honesty. "I really don't … but I still haven't finished reading. Maybe it will become clear later on."

"The truth is we really don't understand, but I hope that we will by tomorrow, at the funeral," said the son.

"My condolences for your grief, really, and I promise I will do the best I can," Avner replied, ending the call.

Avner sat down in his chair. He had a few more chapters left to read. He would read a bit more this evening, but he was getting tired already. Maybe he would lay his head down on the table and doze a little. Nisim had already gone home. The place was a little scary at night, but he would go home soon too. Just rest a little. He didn't want to drive when he was so tired. He put his head down on the table.

Avner dozed, and before him stood the figure of a woman. He blinked. She looked familiar to him but he could not recall from where.

"Look," she said to him. "You are someone who only hears what he wants to hear. That's how you've been your whole life: repress, repress, repress." Every time she said the word "repress," the tone went up to a scream.

"Only what you want to hear. You put words in the mouths of others so that they will say what you want to hear. Like an anorexic girl who believes that her therapist told her that she doesn't have an eating disorder, like someone with suicidal tendencies who thinks his psychologist says that he just had a dream about death."

Avner wanted to respond. He didn't understand what she wanted and who she was anyway that she was telling him what was wrong with him, but she shrieked, "Repress, repress, repress!" And disappeared.

Avner woke up in a panic, but the nightmare did not leave him. He knew that the woman was right. He was furious about what she had said, but it was accurate. He had never really dealt with things. He always chose the easy way, the noncommittal way. When something bothered him, he disappeared. When he had too strong or too painful a memory, he set it aside and didn't touch it.

He nearly smiled to himself as he recalled how Chaya had bought new shoes for herself and the girls and brought them home inside their original shoeboxes. She had put the three boxes down on the kitchen table, no more, no less. But Avner could not tolerate it. Shoeboxes, and on the table? That had been a tough one and not just because it felt messy. It was too painful, too reminiscent.

His father had bought inconceivable amounts of tranquilizers for his mother, and God knows how Dad counted the pills every day without getting mixed up and knew if Mom had taken her daily dose or not. Those pills had been kept in a shoebox, on the table in the corner. It was rare that anyone came over to visit, but if someone did happen to come by, he wouldn't find a vase with flowers on the table but that shoebox.

Throughout his entire childhood that box had been there, at eye level, bearing silent witness to the situation. Now that he was older, he didn't deal with that pain, just demanded that no shoeboxes enter his home nor, God forbid, be placed on the table. Chaya hadn't done it on purpose. She simply forgot, or maybe she didn't even know. Avner wasn't sure if he had told her that story or not. But then he'd had a fit of rage and knocked the three boxes off the table. The girls cried, Chaya had stood there stunned, and he'd shut himself in his room afterward for many hours. Now he sat and smiled with embarrassment. Repress, said the figure. It was so true. He considered calling Nisim, but decided not to. That was all he needed, for Nisim to think he was crazy.

A sliver of moon rose in the sky, and darkness covered everything. Avner felt frightened and didn't know what to do. He had never done a ceremony for someone whose identity was unclear to him before. On the one hand, he couldn't lie so brazenly and let her son say the kaddish. There was a limit. After all, it was pretty clear to him that he hadn't really been mistaken in his earlier conclusions. Though far from religious, he still felt a meaningful connection to the faith and couldn't take part in this kind of deceit.

What could he do with the fact that she wasn't Jewish? To return the money they had received and send Mrs. Reich elsewhere? Was that ethical? After all, the woman had left a kind of will, how could he violate it? But then, would he stand and tell her children that she hadn't been Jewish, just like that, to their faces? He couldn't do that! It could have crazy consequences for their lives! He simply couldn't be the one to deliver such loaded news.

And then, from one moment to the next, he had discovered further disturbing information. Her daughter had a daughter. If his concerns were justified, then Eva's daughter would also need to convert, as well as her granddaughter, God help them, what a mess. There was no choice, he had to go on reading; maybe there would be a miracle and she had converted. That would solve a lot of problems. But the darkness all around was frightening, he couldn't stay here alone. No, he would go home now, and maybe read a bit more there.

Avner left the cemetery and walked right passed the "Petting Zoo" graffiti on his way to his car. He drove home, deep in thought.

A heavy night fell on Mishmar HaAliya; the flower petals closed, burying hidden dreams, the nice ones and the nightmares among them. Here and there flew the tooth fairy, making little children's big dreams come true, and smiling at the little dreams of the big people, the adults. No, she could not make everything come true. She was just a little fairy, with extra fragile wings.

In his home in the nearby kibbutz, Nisim slept soundly. Bracha, his wife, slept beside him, at ease, the smell of the desire that had been present a few minutes earlier still hanging in the air. Tomorrow was a new day, the sun would rise, Nisim would get up, do his ritual hand washing and give thanks to God, and at the doorstep Bracha would smile at him and hand him his thermos of coffee and his container of vegetables. The blessed routine gave him strength, joy, and a near-constant smile.

In the meantime, Avner lay in bed, unable to fall asleep. The more he thought about things, the larger the questions loomed in his mind, growing larger and suspicious, as is their way, so that it was not long before there was no distinction between facts and assumptions, between truth and doubt, and the suspicion took shape, like a golem, got up on its legs, went through the wall of logic, dancing and skipping in Avner's mind.

Sweating in his bed, he drank from the glass of water that stood on the side table and tried to fall asleep. Sleep eventually took him by surprise, when the night watch was replaced by the morning shift, and Avner was granted the mercy of deep, thoughtless sleep.

~

CHAPTER NINE

Nisim woke up early, washed his hands and said the morning prayer, showered, and dressed hastily, then left the house equipped with his thermos of coffee, sandwiches, and fresh vegetables. Bracha had added sandwiches at the last minute. She sensed that he was a bit troubled, maybe he wasn't eating well. Even though it was early summer, Nisim shivered slightly.

Bracha handed him a light sweater. "Take this," she said and winked at him, smiling. "On the inside, you are a warm person, but on the outside, God help you…"

He was first to arrive to the cemetery, as usual. A dark-skinned *yekke*, he thought, smiling to himself. He parked his car and got out, then sat down on the chair under the sign "Heavenly Rest," right beside the graffiti on the wall.

A few minutes later Avner arrived. "I have an eye infection," he said, rubbing his eyes lightly. "It's this erratic weather this time of year. It gives me all kinds of trouble."

"What's going on with you, yesterday you have blood pressure issues, today an eye infection. Have you become a hypochondriac?" Nisim laughed, and Avner understood that the mispronunciation was intentional this time.

"It's always like this during the in-between seasons," said Avner. "Annoying allergies, but what can you do?"

Nisim followed him into the office and poured him some white coffee. He had finished building the coffin. He had even nearly finished the gardening, and the hole in the ground was already dug, just needed some finishing touches. Another moment of coffee, in complete silence, and Nisim would replace his white shirt with a work shirt and go out to finish digging.

Avner sat before his desk, his eyes burning from the infection and lack of sleep, and opened the diary to continue reading.

***

The mass extermination ended on November 3rd, 1944. Led by the murderer Heinrich Himmler, the Reich's Minister of the Interior, the Germans were afraid that the Red Army would enter the extermination camps before they had finished disposing of the evidence of the atrocities that had been committed there. Himmler gave instructions to destroy the buildings and the crematoria and to move the survivors to camps in Germany. He also ordered that anything that could not be transferred be burned but some prisoners, particularly the Poles, managed to save important documents, which to this day offer conclusive evidence of what happened there.

In January 1945, the Red Army entered southern Poland and senior Nazi personnel and soldiers withdrew, taking tens of thousands of refugees with them and marching them in what later came to be known as the "Death March." I was there. Those who were too sick or too weak were left behind, but by the end of January, we were liberated by the Red Army.

I no longer remember which of my friends marched with me and who was left behind. I remember that we were three girls around the same age, sick and without a drop of energy remaining, but we held one another's hands and marched. I remember that I thought of Davusha, that even the sweater she had received didn't help her, and that truth be told nobody had helped her, not even those Nazis who used her body night after night, and in the end she didn't make it.

My friends and I marched in the snow, with torn fabric for shoes, instead of those that I had sold for a slice of bread. I walked upright, standing tall. I have no idea where I drew my strength from. I was skin and bones, all alone and above all, frightened. But I had a strong will to live. I saw what the Nazis did to those who faltered along the way. Anyone who showed signs of exhaustion was shot to death at once. I don't think I heard anyone talking for a long time. The only thing I heard were the occasional shouts of the persecutors, the sighs of the persecuted, and the sounds of explosions, followed by unbearable silence. I don't know which of those left the deepest wounds, but I have no doubt that if later on I raised my children with incessant concern for their survival, I can "thank" Himmler and his friends for that.

We walked and walked for many long days, I don't even know how many. One night we arrived at a place where there were a few warehouses. They crammed us like chickens into one of them and ordered us to lie on the floor. We whispered among ourselves and figured that the Nazis had decided to let us rest for one night. In the morning we heard loud whistles outside. A murmur passed between us. In another moment there would be a formation and all of us would be forced to come out of the warehouse and stand outside, let them count us, and continue marching.

I looked at the two girls at my sides and they looked back at me with an expression that said they had come to terms with their fate. We knew that we wouldn't manage to get up, we couldn't go out into that terrible cold, and we would not be able to go on walking. I think that in all those years, that was the only moment when I really gave up. I no longer cared if I died, I could not go on marching through the snow with frozen feet and indescribable pain in my belly.

So, with that unspoken agreement, we decided to not go out, which meant that a Nazi officer would come in at any moment and shoot us to death.

My friends whispered, "'Shema Israel,'"[3] and even I muttered something.

The whistling stopped, there was silence, then we heard footsteps approaching. Terrified, we looked toward the door but nobody came in. We didn't understand what was happening but a moment later one of my

---

3   Jewish prayer recited upon waking, before sleeping, and as a Jew's last words before death.

friends pointed at a hidden opening behind us.

When we had arrived in the darkness of night we had not seen that the wall behind us was cracked open. A tall soldier now entered through the opening, dressed in the uniform of the Red Army, a big pack on his back and a rifle across his shoulders. He looked at us for a few moments without saying a word and then asked, "*Ebraika?*"

I didn't know Russian and didn't understand what he was asking, but my friend who understood replied, "Yes…"

The soldier looked at us for another long moment and then suddenly began to cry. He took the pack from his bag and pulled out '*tfillin*, a *tallit*, and a *siddur*.'[4] As he cried, he stood and prayed before us while we watched him in complete astonishment.

After he finished praying, the soldier sat down beside us and told us a little about his own background in a whisper. His wife and children had all been sent to Auschwitz and never returned. He had managed to escape and was the sole survivor from his whole family. Then he proudly told us that he personally knew a Jew named Anatoly Shapiro, a battalion commander in the Red Army. Anatoly, the man told us, had given him a uniform, and recruited him into the Red Army. A considerable group of soldiers, he said, were hiding in the area, planning to fight the Nazi enemy to the bitter end.

When he finished speaking, the soldier suggested that we stay inside the building and keep on praying that the Nazis continue on their way.

"Only come out when there is total silence outside," he said. Then he took bread and canned food from his backpack, bundled it together, handed it to us, then explained where to go and how to hide along the way. He left out through the cracked wall and disappeared.

We did as he said and hid in the warehouse until we heard the convoy continuing on its way. The Nazis must have given up counting people this time. Miraculously, we found new energy to go on walking. It is hard to explain the joy that we felt when we saw houses at a distance. I was a fifteen-year-old girl, with almost nothing in the world, apart from two refugee friends like me and the will to live.

I don't know why we parted ways when we arrived at the city. Each of us

---

4   Jewish ritual objects

went in a different direction. Today, when I think about it, I wonder how it was that we didn't stick together, but I've long since stopped trying to make sense of what happened there. In any case, I roamed for a few days without really knowing where I was. I remember that I saw houses with their doors open and dared to peer inside one of them. The house was almost entirely empty, the furniture broken, but I couldn't believe my eyes when I found a pot with milk on the stove, evidently heated not long ago, because it was still warm. I drank it eagerly. In the refrigerator, I found leftovers which helped me get back a bit of my strength and stand on my feet.

On the street I saw people walking, their heads bowed. I think that the German people were afraid of what had happened and the magnitude of the atrocities was beginning to become known. At some point I realized that I was a free person. I walked on foot for a few days, every so often entering another abandoned house, finding something warm to wear, shoes for my feet, and most of all, something to eat. In one house that I entered I found people: an old woman and a few other refugees lying on the floor. The woman asked me if I had seen her son Alfred and pulled out a photo from a drawer. The man in the picture was tall, wearing an SS officer uniform. I told her that I hadn't seen him, she sighed and let me rest a while in her house.

The next day I went out and kept on walking, entering other abandoned houses along my way. In retrospect I understood that many people simply fled their homes out of fear of the Red Army's bombs, leaving their homes wide open. I also learned that the remaining Nazis shot anyone who dared to help Jews and let them take refuge in their homes. To this day I fear for the fate of that German woman who was looking for her son Alfred and gave me temporary shelter.

I continued on my way. Here and there, a few good people threw some food my way. More than once I asked people outright. Some of them didn't even answer me. Most of them preferred to ignore the strange refugee, and there were even those who raised an eyebrow at my German. I wandered the roads for a few more days and found myself with other refugees in the same situation. Rumors suggested that we head west toward the border of Poland and Germany, so we did. There was an unusual power in that group of survivors. We arrived at a kind of camp on the border, and with the help of locals, built a small city of our own with the intention of preparing ourselves for a new life. We built a small hospital, a school, and even a farm. I was too old for the school. Only children under the age of twelve attended, and I was already nearly sixteen. But since I was a strong young woman, I worked on the farm, and afterward in the hospital. I didn't have any medical knowledge, but a big heart and a lot of common sense. I've always believed that a person can learn more from experience than from school.

Members of The Joint came to help us. Angels, we called them. They helped us with food, clothes, and of course money to build everything. In time, many of us immigrated to the United States, but a smaller group, including myself, asked for permission to immigrate to Israel. I don't know if I can explain it properly in words. After all, I was a refugee, without anything, with no family.

At the camp I met a family who had had unbelievably good luck. All of them had survived: Mom, Dad, the older daughter, and the younger son. They had found one another after the war, whole in body and even in mind. Such miracles were by no means common. All the rest of the refugees looked at them with unbridled envy. It was known around the camp that the father of the family was an expert shoemaker, and that the Nazis had needed him to make and repair their boots. Miraculously, he had managed to convince them that his young son, Leibleh, was also an expert shoemaker even though the child didn't know how to hold an awl, and so the two of them survived. Meanwhile the mother was a seamstress and her daughter would do deliveries to the houses of high-up officers' wives, so they too survived.

The daughter — her name was Dina — who was around my age, loved me from the first moment. She would call me to their barracks, night after night, where I received a hot meal and a smile from the mother of the family. Something in me made them want to protect me, to save a soul, and they suggested that I join them as a member of the family and travel to the land of endless possibilities, the United States. I deliberated over that option for many days.

I so needed the affection they gave me, and the idea of joining them and making a new life in a huge, free land where, it was said, money grew on trees and wealth and happiness flowed through the streets was tempting, but the image of my father standing in the kitchen of our house in Berlin, waiting to go to Israel was like an unwritten will for me, like my father's final request, and I couldn't think how my life would look if I did not do as he had wished. At the same time, I also had a strong desire to return once more to my parents' home, to see if there was any trace of them, or if anyone I had once known remained.

I do not know to this day how the members of that remarkable family managed to save money for themselves, and I don't know how I was so lucky, but as soon as I so much as voiced my desire to return to Berlin for a few days, the father gave me some money and even accompanied me to the train station.

The thought that maybe, just maybe, I might find some member of my family there was perhaps childish or irrational, but people in my circumstances wanted to believe that something good could be waiting for them around the corner, that they deserved some good news, that after years of suffering, there might be something else.

It was not easy to find the house, but I found someone who was willing to show me the way. I stood there a few minutes, then entered and went up the stairs to the first floor. The door was closed and the smell of cooking wafted from the apartment. For a brief moment my heart rejoiced. Another moment and my mother would open the door and welcome me with hot soup. That moment was quickly replaced with dismay. I knocked on the door, weakly at first, then stronger. The door opened a crack. Through the thin gap, an old woman peered out and asked me who I was and what I wanted. This was not my mother. This was a strange woman, who now lived in my home, cooking in the kitchen that had been ours.

For a moment I wanted to shout, but I realized it was preferable to be friendly. "'Guten Tag,'" I said, hoping that my friendliness would help me, but the woman tried to close the door in my face. I stopped it with my foot, and the woman shouted that I should get out of her house or she would… I didn't wait around to hear the rest of the threat. I went downstairs. The faint hope of finding my mother at home finally vanished.

I stood in the yard for a few minutes, praying that some relative would show up, maybe even Uncle Karl or one of his sons, but nobody came. I was about to go when I suddenly remembered. It's amazing how some things are etched in the memory and never erased. I went to the corner of the yard, bent down and dug in the earth. The hole that I dug seemed big but I didn't find anything until suddenly I felt something soft at the tips of my fingers. From out of the hole I pulled a tattered cloth bag. It contained snippets of the photo taken by Mr. Greenbaum the photographer. I shoved it into the pocket of the coat that I had found in one of the abandoned houses and got out of there.

For years I held on to that bag and didn't dare look at the pieces of the picture, until one evening, when I was sitting with Meir in the living room of our home in Givatayim, I told him things that I had never spoken of up until that point. I think that that was the first time I cried, a painful, liberating cry, weeping that comes from deep in the soul. I cried for Dad, and was glad that I had fulfilled his wish to immigrate to Israel. I cried for Mom, who shouldn't have had to die and was killed because she was married to Dad. I cried for Anna who didn't find the strength to survive. I cried for Aunt Alice who died too soon. I cried for Uncle Karl and the two boys.

Meir sat and listened to me for a long time. He didn't want me to give up. He wanted me to keep searching for relatives in case someone had survived. More on that later. But then, that same evening, I took out that bag with the torn picture pieces for the first time, and Meir fit them together like a puzzle. In the torn picture, everyone looked fragmented, incomplete, like in reality.

Meir took the pieces to an expert photographer who, in a generous artistic deed, healed the rifts and prepared a photograph for me as a keepsake. In the photograph I saw Mom smiling, standing somewhat in profile, Dad hugging her around the shoulders from one side, one hand on Anna's shoulders and me, a little girl with blond curls, smiling at the world and not yet knowing how evil it could be.

When I returned by train from Berlin to the camp, I was reunited with Dina, Leibleh, and their parents. The next day they left for the United States and I parted from them in tears.

This seems like the time to mention that Meir and I did a fair amount of traveling. We went to the United States together more than once and one time Meir decided that we should appeal to the authorities and look for our relatives. I know that it sounds crazy, like looking for a needle in a haystack, but we succeeded in finding Leibleh in Brooklyn. I remembered his family name, Lederman, because I remembered that his father was a shoemaker. Meir took care of the rest.

Leibleh is an Ultra-Orthodox Jew today, and lives peacefully with his wife and children. Meir and I met him at a cafe, on our last trip to the U.S. His parents had died by then and his sister was living in Australia. He looked well and happy. He told us that he had changed his name to Arieh.

"You know," he said. "'Leib' is "lion" in Yiddish and 'Arieh' is "lion" in Hebrew, so it's not like I'm ignoring my past."

He was a diamond-dealer, and contributed big sums of money to Israel on a monthly basis. I know that Meir wanted to ask him why he donates to Israel but does not live there, but I wordlessly thanked him for not criticizing Leibleh. When we left the cafe, he had tears in his eyes, but they were tears of happiness.

***

Avner set down the diary and wiped away a stubborn tear. This woman's unthinkable story, this woman who for some reason had chosen him to be the one to read these things, both moved him and stirred up repressed thoughts and memories of his own. Suddenly he thought of Leibleh, now Arieh, and that he really had been victorious, with the image of that haunted boy standing on his own two feet, leaving hard memories behind and giving himself such a strong name… that seemed like another mirror being held up to him.

Reluctantly, he recalled how his mother had told him that he had the name of a great warrior from the Bible. He couldn't help but smile to himself at the irony. The name of a great warrior from the Bible? Him? How was it that so great a biblical fighter suffered so many insults as a child? How was it that such a great soldier didn't ever manage to defend himself?

Avner could think of many times when he had not lived up to his name. One particular memory came back and played out before his eyes: he was a youth in early adolescence. He was not yet five feet, less because it was only at age sixteen that he suddenly began to grow tall. But then, short and unimpressive, none of the girls from class, not even the plainest of them, so much as looked at him. One time, the biggest bully in class seemed to think that Avner was looking at Nirit, a beautiful girl who seemed like a magical creature out of a fairy tale. The bully ran after him, caught him, and pinned him against the wall. While closing in on him, he screamed, "You little shit. Are you hitting on my girlfriend?"

Avner tried to respond, to explain, to apologize, but the bully went on shouting, "Say it out loud: I'm a little shit midget!"

Insulted and hurting, Avner managed to break free and ran home. He found his mother sitting on the window ledge and one look at her expression made it clear that there was no point in requesting help from her.

~

CHAPTER TEN

I soon realized that it was not so straightforward to follow through on my father's wishes and simply move to Israel. I joined a group which organized as a kind of underground movement. I wasn't among the organizers, but I felt like part of something and that feeling was wonderful.

Among them there were dozens of young men and a few brave, solo young women like myself. An unusual kinship formed between all of us along with a particular pride. We were free, we had a vision, and we were linked by a strong desire to move to and live in the land of Israel.

Our goal was clear: to transplant Jews from Eastern Europe, controlled by the Russians, to central Europe, where it would be easier to arrange for the move to the promised land.

We tried to move as many Jews as we could to Italy and France because immigration to Israel passed through the Mediterranean ports. To transport displaced persons through the Alps, among them children and the elderly, most of them survivors, via extremely challenging terrain, was an almost impossible act requiring much resourcefulness, but the spirit of freedom was blowing full force.

The organizers forged connections with locals who, in exchange for a fee, helped us determine the best routes. Border guards were also bribed and many refugees were moved through Italy and France, where they were organized into camps, and from there transported to ports where illegal immigration ships docked.

It was hard to address the refugees' needs. Sometimes, looking on from the side, I was astonished at these people who until now had nothing and suddenly, when there was someone to look out for them, they wanted more and more. It reminded me of the stories my father would tell, lying on the rug in Anna's and my room. Sometimes he would choose a biblical story, usually to teach us something important, like the story of the sons of Israel being enslaved in Egypt for four hundred years, and how the moment they got out of there they began complaining to Moses, their leader.

I could almost hear my father telling us: human memory is short. From the moment they were freed, they became slaves to their cravings and desires. That was exactly how the refugees behaved. They made demands, complained of hunger and cold, and all of that on top of the challenges of organizing the ships and managing the cunning authorities that opposed our plans.

I stayed in Paris for several months. The Parisians looked at us like aliens, wretched, but there were also those among them who wanted to help. One day a senior city official came and suggested that we sing as a choir in a central square in exchange for pay. It seemed crazy and far-fetched, but those were times in which the impossible became possible. They brought a music teacher for our group of youths and we soon learned French songs, which we sang together in the streets for a few coins. Who would have imagined that these were refugees from Eastern Europe singing the songs of Edith Piaf in the City of Lights?

One morning I woke up with a terrible headache. I felt exhausted, fatigued. and unable to eat. Throughout the day I lay in bed and coughed a dry, troubling cough. Within a few hours my body temperature went up, I had chills, terrible stomach pains, and — though I don't like to mention it — bloody diarrhea. Today, looking back, I wonder: I made it through the previous torments, the hunger, the filth, the cold. And here, of all places, when I had a place to sleep, clothes to wear, and food to eat, was when I fell ill with typhus.

Among the refugees there was one doctor, an older man with white hair and a constant smile on his face. He visited me every day and gave me medicine, which he had managed to hang on to since the days of the camps. Weak and tired, I finally rose from bed after two weeks.

Outside they were talking about the ship on which we would all soon sail. In retrospect it was clear that I wasn't fully recovered, and the typhus returned again later, if less intensely. I will tell of that soon.

I remember that the last evening in the camp was tense with anxiety and expectation. We were told that we would board the ship which would take us to Israel that night, but I, still close with the organizers, heard the argument with the owner of the ship. He demanded a sum of money that we did not have and claimed that the risk that he was taking on himself required such an amount. I don't know how my friends managed to obtain so huge a sum, but then came the Italian captain who was supposed to sail the ship and demanded still more money. His image is etched in my memory to this day. His name was Aberto. He was short and muscular and had a particularly impressive moustache. I remember hearing him say that he knew the British would prosecute him for this, and my friends tried to convince him otherwise.

He looked angry, threw his hands in the air, and then shouted at whoever stood before him: '*vada al hell*' — "go to hell" — turned and left.

But my friends did not despair, and the money that they had already paid to the ship's owner did not go to waste. We remained at the camp for another full week before a new captain, Biaggio, appeared, and we boarded the ship of illegal immigrants to Israel.

We were on the water in that little ship for twenty-one days. We didn't understand the meaning of its name then, but I assume that if we had understood '*L'Negev*' ("to the Negev desert") we would have been proud that we were going to make the deserts bloom, but also afraid, because the lack of water was our biggest fear. If I remember correctly, we were some fifty people on the '*L'Negev*.' The trip was rough, like hard labor with seasickness. Water would seep into the belly of the ship, to where our bunks were. We scooped out water every time it leaked in, using big buckets and sponges.

Meanwhile, the immigration representatives had provided us with food and drink, but a number of complications arose. One problem was that the meat that they had given us was pig meat, and another was that the water was murky and rusty, and we had to drink from old barrels. I must say, in all truth, the pork was tasty, very fatty, much juicier than chicken, and for anyone who had been hungry for years, a meal of one cut of meat and two dry crackers a day seemed like a feast fit for a king.

***

Avner thought of the refugees, the terrible hunger, the need to survive, and felt tremendous admiration for Eva, who even if she hadn't been Jewish, was hesitant about eating pork. He recalled the vacation he and Chaya had taken two years ago, to a hotel in Antalya. It had promised to be "all inclusive" and they entered the dining room both suspicious and hungry.

He didn't touch the juicy-looking pork but he didn't hold back too much and garnished his green salad with a thick layer of croutons which had been made with lard. He knew that it was lard because his friends had been to the hotel in the past and told him, but to Chaya he played it off as if they were "innocent" croutons. He enjoyed the flavor until Chaya asked to try it too, and he grew anxious. To mislead her or keep quiet? He kept quiet. And she ate it. And enjoyed it. At night, in their room, as he was holding her, he couldn't live with the lie.

"It was made with lard, that's why it tasted so good," he told her.

"Lard?! Why didn't you say so?" She sat up in bed. "Have you lost it completely?"

` Now he read Eva's writing with the unavoidable thought in his mind: she ate pork because she had been through years of hunger and because she had no choice. But him? He was just a glutton. He went back to reading, and it was as if Eva had read his mind once again.

***

I remember Edgar, the son of the bank manager, throwing his guts up when he heard that the meat he had eaten was pig. Edgar didn't recognize me when I went over to him. I introduced myself and explained to him that God would forgive anyone who ate pork right now, I had no doubt about that. But Edgar did not believe me, and for days lived off just the crackers and smelly water. In any case, the food ran out after two weeks, and before us was still a long journey of at least a week, without food.

I sat on the side of the deck, tired from pumping water, hungry and thirsty. I had terrible stomach pains and I realized that I was sick again. By then I felt I might not make it. I think that I fell asleep and dreamed a strange dream. In my dream I was a ballerina and Anna was my teacher. She showed me how to do the steps, and I tried and failed. Anna produced a rope and tried to teach me how to jump over it.

"Here, like this," she said, but I couldn't do it. Anna didn't give up. "Here," she said, winding the ends of the rope around her arms. "Swing it up high and skip." I tried and failed.

I don't know how long I slept, I cuddled up to the dream of my sister, and in the depths of my heart, maybe for the first time since everything began, I wanted to reach her, in that place in the sky which I believed existed. Imagination and reality are intertwined for me. Did I really fall asleep or had I fainted? What I remember for sure is that suddenly I felt water drops between my lips. I opened my eyes. Above me was a woman bent over me with a concerned expression, dipping a cloth into the water in the barrel, and wetting my lips.

I thought that I had died and this was heaven, but the woman stroked my head and said, "Eva, dear, I can't believe I found you here." Hot tears dripped from her eyes and I tried to understand if I really had arrived in heaven.

"Who are you?" I asked her, and she didn't answer me, just went on crying and wetting my lips.

"How do you know my name?" I whispered and she stroked my head.

"Why are you so good to me?" I tried again, but she put a hand over my mouth and whispered, "God in heaven, you survived, Eva, you made it."

I wanted to ask again, but she put a finger over her lips as if to say quiet, and whispered to me, "Don't call me by my name so that they won't know who I am and nothing bad will happen to me as it did to my beloved Ludwig."

"Maria!" A soft cry burst from my lips and she smiled at me and quieted me again.

"I will look after you," she said.

"But how did you get here?" I whispered.

She smiled again. "Connections, you know, never hurt anyone."

I will get ahead of myself and say that Maria arrived at Israel after the war in which she had harbored seventeen Jews in the cellar of her and Ludwig's shop. I kept in touch with her until the day she died, about a year ago.

Years after the run-in on the ship, in her house in Israel, she told me how Ludwig was caught while he went to stock up on food. "Someone must have reported him," she said, and I saw the angry look in her eyes.

"How evil do you have to be to do something like that?" She had waited for him at the designated hour and he didn't come home. "I still believed he would come back until the middle of the night," she said sorrowfully. "But then someone knocked on the door." The man who knocked on the door was able to tell her that he had seen Ludwig hiding food inside his clothes for the fugitives in the basement, and how he had seen the same man start shouting, "Thief, thief!" Then it was just a matter of time until the cops would catch him.

Maria cried telling me about that night as if it had been just yesterday. The anonymous man who told her about Ludwig offered to help her escape before the Gestapo came for her too.

"I had nothing to stay for," she said. "I didn't even have any belongings, apart from the apartment which I couldn't stay in anyway. Just memories, you know?" She then opened the basement door and told the Jews who were hiding there what had happened. "They cried in despair," said Maria. "But they understood that they had to get out and flee for their lives."

Maria said that she didn't want to remain on German soil, and the way she saw it, to go and live in the land of the people for whom Ludwig had given his life was the only thing to do.

I asked her how she could be sure that Ludwig was dead, after all, they saw him caught, not more than that. Maria's expression grew grim and she said, "I know he is dead, dear Eva, I just know."

But back to our meeting on the boat. "Connections never hurt anybody," she said and smiled, and at that same moment I thought that if there was a heaven, this must be exactly how it felt. I was lying there exhausted for some time with Maria at my side. I heard the people around me talking. I didn't really understand what everyone was talking about, but fragments of sentences began to come together.

"She didn't have to die," I heard them saying, "She wasn't even one of us," said someone, and I think I heard the voice of Edgar say, "Just because her husband was Jewish, just because of that those scoundrels killed her too."

Someone asked him if he knew her and Edgar said yes, he knew the poor thing. What bad luck. And someone else said she was tortured too, those villains, and someone else added that they raped her. I was mesmerized by the voices and the words: raped, beat, scoundrels, her daughters died, her husband was murdered, they took their store, there were valuable goods in there, probably silk, not just your average fabric shop. A thriving business, scoundrels, burnt it, just because of him.

I didn't know for sure if they were talking about my family. On the one hand — a fabric shop, that was our store. On the other hand they said that both of her daughters were dead, which wasn't true. If I had understood that this was their way of exaggerating, if I had understood that this was how people add incorrect information to make a better story, maybe I would have immediately grasped what they were talking about. But I was so weak then that I didn't even understand that they were talking about my mother. I couldn't even understand the part that they repeated, that she was killed because of her husband, just because of him. It was confusing and I did not grasp the full meaning of things.

For years afterward I imagined that conversation in my ears. I even checked the facts. I wanted to know if what I heard on the ship, with my eyes closed, starving, tired. And alone, was fact or fiction. But I didn't say a word of it to a soul. I only ever told Meir. I understood that pain should be kept inside and not shown outwardly. We must be strong, because only the strong survive.

∗∗∗

Avner set the diary down on the table and wiped his eyes again. He knew that it was no eye infection but hot tears streaming down his cheeks.

He thought about this woman, who had gathered the strength from God knows where, after all those horrors that she had experienced, and begun a new chapter in her life. After all, he knew that she had married, had two children, even worked at the university and toward the end, she had written down her life story. In addition to all that, she had not given up on answers. She sought the truth.

He returned for a moment to the diary, to the words. "I checked the facts…" and again felt as if she was making him look himself in the eyes, encouraging him: look, my friend, look.

More than anything it was clear that Eva Reich represented strength, she was a woman who had fought for her basic right to live and had not let herself off the hook in any way. Here was a Holocaust survivor who had overcome the worst horrors in the world, and had not found herself, like his mother, hospitalized, in a thin, floral dress, a plaid blanket over her legs, gazing at her hands with their crooked fingers, placing them back down on her knees, her eyes empty.

Now he had nowhere left to run from his memories. He got up, poured himself a glass of water, sat back down with his eyes closed, and the picture in his mind grew clear.

On the day that his mother was hospitalized, he was an adolescent, around sixteen years old. A year earlier, his father had died in his sleep. With his death, the nightmares returned to the house and his mother stopped functioning. She sat for hours, staring into the distance, until the day when he came home and once again found the people in the white robes. At first, he still wanted to say something, to explain, after all, she had already been hospitalized in the past and returned home, so why go through it again? He looked at them afraid but could not make any words come out of his mouth, as if someone had turned him mute.

He ran to the bedroom, but his mother was not there. From the bathroom he heard the sound of running water and for a few seconds he did not understand what all those people were doing there, with his mother in the shower. A moment later, the bathroom door opened and two women in white robes took his mother out, walking her toward the living room. The box, he thought to himself, I have to open the shoebox on the table, to count the pills, she probably forgot to take them today. But he didn't know how many pills had been there yesterday, because since his father had died, nobody was counting them.

"Maybe check, maybe she didn't take her pills," he mumbled, finally able to say something. He knew that if she just took a pill she would fall asleep and everything would pass.

He even checked once inside the box and saw what was written on the back of the package: tranquilizer, to be taken after meals, not recommended for use over a long period of time, addictive, liable to cause side effects, do not take if pregnant or breastfeeding, consult with your doctor before taking.

"There's no point in checking," one of the women replied in a gentle voice. "The pills won't help her anymore."

A tall woman, who wasn't wearing a white robe, turned to him and introduced herself by name, but he didn't catch what she was saying. She tried to reassure him: they would look after him, social services wouldn't abandon him, but he just stood there frozen to the spot and watched as the people in the white robes took his mother out on a stretcher.

After they left, more people came to the house and joined the tall woman. They talked to him, but he didn't remember what they said. He just remembered how, robotically, he had shown them where his clothes were and where there was a big suitcase.

The tall woman helped him pack and they took him from there. That night he found himself in a religious boarding school in northern Israel. He was there for two years, and didn't make friends with anyone. They called him "the weirdo" and he heard them tell one another that he was an odd duck, but he didn't care. Sometimes he was invited to spend a Sabbath or holiday at the home of the school's principal, but he usually avoided it and spent whole Saturdays alone in his room. The director tried to speak with him but he would go quiet and not reply.

For several weeks he did not go to his parents' home until one night he snuck out of the boarding school and hitchhiked back. The key to the apartment was still in the fuse box in the stairwell. He entered his childhood home slowly. The shoebox still sat on the table. He opened a window to let in some light. A blinded cockroach jumped from the table and skittered into the corner of the room. He let it get away. Then he went to his room, smelled the sheets, picked up a soccer ball that had lost its way and went back to the living room. On that first visit, he sat for a few minutes, got up, left, locked the door, and slipped the key into his pocket.

Since then he made it a regular habit and would escape home every now and then, sit there for an hour, with tears in his eyes, not daring to enter his parents' room. He knew that if he went in, the whole picture would return to him, and he did not feel he could handle that. It was too hard, too painful, almost impossible. He would sit in the living room and remember how he heard his mother's cries from their room, and how he got up, still half-asleep, and ran to the doorway, and how he saw his father lying there, his eyes open, not moving or responding.

He knew that if he went into his parents' room now, he would see his father again, touch his hand, feel the cold of his skin, and hear the heart-rending cries louder than ever.

One day, on one of those visits to the empty house, he summoned his courage and headed for his parents' room. He stood at the doorway and looked inside. The bed was still unmade, the windows were closed and the air smelled stale. He didn't open the window, but turned on the ceiling light with no lamp shade. The lamp light flickered for a few minutes, then went out. There was a bottle of perfume on the dresser and on the bedside table a book covered in dust. He picked it up with a shaking hand. "House of Dolls" by Ka-tzetnik. He leafed through it a little, afraid of what was inside and placed it back down on the bedside table.

Then he opened the drawer beside his mother's side of the bed. There were many items loose inside it: a few pieces of jewelry, lipstick, a powder box, and envelopes with letters. He looked at a few of them and found that they were addressed to people he didn't know. One big envelope caught his attention, and he picked it up. The envelope was addressed in unfamiliar handwriting: "Sarah Bock, documentation." It was stamped with "Holocaust and heroism documents, Yad Vashem Museum." He didn't open the envelope. He didn't have the strength. With a shaking hand he returned it to where he found it.

On the next visit he planned to take the envelope with him, but when he arrived, the tall woman emerged behind him. "Hello Avner, I'm from social services, perhaps you remember me?" He was quiet and she said, "We think that you need a little more help than what you have received until now."

Avner looked at her in surprise and asked, "But how did you know I was here?"

She smiled at him and replied, "The rabbi, the director at your school, told me that you go home sometimes."

He wanted to ask her how the rabbi knew and why she had come here, but she beat him to it and said, "Let's go inside and speak?"

They entered the house and sat down in the living room. Avner was mostly silent, and let the woman talk. "We understand that it's hard for you on weekends at the boarding school," she said. He said nothing. "The school director said that you are alone on weekends, but we know a nice family on the kibbutz where your father, bless his memory, worked, and they are happy to host you on the weekends."

He didn't reply and she went on, "They aren't religious, but they would certainly be willing to observe the Sabbath and keep kosher for you. They really loved your father." She got up and went to the kitchen, poured some water into a glass at the sink and handed it to him.

"Look, the house is neglected, you know, and it's not a matter of a day or two. We are looking for a longer-term arrangement for you."

He gave her a puzzled look. Until then he hadn't thought that he would never return to living at home with his mother. The woman must have read his mind and said, "Your mother, unfortunately, won't be back. The doctors unanimously agreed that she won't be able to return to a regular life."

Now, as he remembered this, he smiled bitterly to himself. "Regular life," as if there was such a thing. But then, when the woman from social services said that his mother wouldn't be back, suddenly tears streamed down his face.

The woman tried to encourage him. "I really do feel your pain," she said. "But we have to think ahead, you're still so young."

He didn't answer, just got up, went to his mother's room, opened the drawer and took out the brown envelope which seemed to be waiting for him there. He picked it up and ripped it to pieces. Shreds of paper drifted through the room like the crumbs of his life and the woman from social services approached him and hugged him tight, with real warmth.

After that he found himself at the kibbutz for the weekends and holidays. There was someone to look out for him and make sure that he didn't remain alone at the boarding school. His hosts on the kibbutz made sure to take him to visit his mother. She didn't recognize him.

He only returned to his parents' house once more, but stood outside and didn't go into the apartment. He wandered around for a few minutes outside the building, then turned to leave. He wanted to die. He no longer saw any reason to go on suffering. He found himself walking toward the pharmacy. There, to the pleasant face of the pharmacist, he muttered, "I need... my mother wants... she has difficulty sleeping... she is asking for the pills she always takes."

The pharmacist looked at him with pity and called to his wife to come to the counter for a minute. Avner stood there, his shirt rumpled, dark circles under his eyes which were swollen from crying, and was quiet.

"Do you have a prescription?" the pharmacist asked. She turned to her husband and said, "His mother always takes Brotizolam to help her sleep."

"But his mother is not here, didn't you hear that she was hospitalized a long time ago?" the pharmacist asked in a whisper.

She answered, "Maybe she is on a little vacation?" She turned back to Avner, with a questioning look on her face.

He was silent, and she smiled a crooked smile and repeated the question, "Where is the prescription?"

He muttered that the prescription was at home.

"Look," said the pharmacist. "Your mother always buys the pills in the blue box, but without the prescription I can't give it to you, they could close my business for something like that."

He didn't answer and the husband said, "Hey, young man, are you sure everything is okay?"

But nothing was okay. He wanted to go to sleep and not wake up again. He wanted them to help him end the pain that pierced his heart.

The pharmacist's compassion overcame her and she looked like she was reconsidering. She pulled the blue box out of a drawer and said to him in a tone usually reserved for small children, "Look, it's written here explicitly, this requires a prescription from a doctor, so run home and bring the prescription, okay?"

Now, as he sat, with the words, "I checked the facts…" before his eyes, he knew that he had deprived himself of the chance to learn anything real about his roots. He now knew for certain that it was not concern about violating his mother's privacy that prevented him from opening that envelope and reading, but the need to protect himself from the truth, from the fear, and from the things that his mother had told him. "If you ask, my child, the devil will come and take your father and me, and you too. He won't take pity on anyone."

So he had torn up the envelope and its contents, maybe because he believed that he was tearing up the hard reality and erasing it, and maybe he had also hoped that he could destroy the sorrow that was always hovering over him.

∾

CHAPTER ELEVEN

Maria, that guardian angel, who saved seventeen Jews and me, should be honored for her heroic deeds. I curse the fact that I did not make sure of that, out of concern that doing so might expose my own past. If that makes me selfish, I accept the accusation, because there was not a day in my life when I did not think that my Maria deserved a designation from the Righteous Among the Nations and I didn't do a thing. The little that I can do, if anything, is to dedicate a few words to her here.

She was born in 1918, in Berlin, to a small, modest family. In her childhood, she was a pious Christian who attended church, where she met Ludwig, whose death she never got over. Even as a child, her mercy, compassion, and concern for others were striking. Twelve years younger than her, I would watch from a distance as she fed milk to a hungry kitten, jumped into the street to take in a stray puppy, or would try desperately to not step on an ants' nest. Over the years I also saw her come to the defense of weak children, fighting off their bullies.

She grew into a tall, upright, golden-haired, beautiful woman, and married Ludwig in a humble wedding ceremony. The young couple moved in beside us and together opened a little store for wool, buttons, thread, and knitting needles.

My parents said that what preserved Ludwig and Maria's unique partnership was their silence. They were quiet together for hours, only speaking through their glances.

Dad would joke and even act out little scenes of the quiet couple. "We have to buy buttons." "How many?" "Ten." Then go quiet for an hour.

Mom would scold him. "Quiet is a good quality," she would say. "They are doing a kindness, you know."

Dad would smile sheepishly and say that he knew and would explain that the little scenes were just camouflage for the real reason for their silence, and we shouldn't talk about it out loud, the walls have ears.

Now seems like the right time for one little story that Maria told me years later, at her home here in Israel. Among the refugees that hid in the little cellar were a brother and sister. They were the only remaining members of a big family that had been entirely wiped out. On the day when Maria was forced to flee and opened the cellar door, the brother and sister left too and fled east.

With tears in her eyes, Maria told me how years later she heard the story of the sister, by chance, on a radio program on Holocaust Remembrance Day. The sister, who spoke on the broadcast, in Hebrew mixed with Yiddish, said that at the time of the deportation to the camps, she and her brother had hidden under a bed as the Germans dragged the rest of their family from the house; they never saw them again.

She and her brother then snuck out and, mercifully, were taken in by a Christian couple who owned a little wool shop. In the store there was a rug which hid an entrance to the basement. The woman told how she and her brother found refuge there, how the shop owners would bring them food and how grateful she was to find these nice people. She said that the two left the hiding place later on, out of fear that they had been found out, and fled into the snow, where her brother disappeared.

The woman went on to say how when she arrived in Israel, she met someone from their hometown who told her that he had seen her brother here in Israel, in Haifa. She collected pennies, bought herself a train ticket, then sat for many hours at the Haifa train station. There, a miracle happened because out of nowhere her younger brother appeared, and the reunion could not be described in words.

Maria told me all this, hot tears streaming from her eyes, and she finished the story with the chilling fact that at the end the woman said that her brother fell in the battle for Ramla in the War of Independence, at just sixteen years old.

Maria said that she would go to great lengths to meet this woman, who was almost certainly one of the people who had hidden in her and Ludwig's cellar, and I wanted to help. It was relatively easy to make contact with the interviewer from the radio program and through him to reach the interviewee, the good Mrs. Zisholtz, who indeed had been among those who hid in Maria and Ludwig's cellar. Maria met her, and told me later how this woman, despite everything she had been through, had rebuilt her life and begun anew.

I think I may have gotten somewhat off course from my diary, but obviously my past is full of pain and hard memories, and maybe something in this image has the power to numb the pain. Apart from that, I am already a very old woman, and that's how it is with the elderly: memories don't always come chronologically. In any case, it is important for me to note Maria's heroism again, and maybe this is the place to add that she is the one who always told me that the will to live must come above all else, and that maybe it is good that we forget at least some of the horrors, because if we don't, we won't manage to build a new life.

***

Avner sighed out loud. If his mother had lived according to Maria's wisdom and managed to forget even some of the things she had been through, maybe she would have been able to live a new life. It hurt him so much to see people who had been through horrors and were able to forget, while his mother never managed to.

He was absorbed by his private pain for several minutes, then recovered and went on reading.

***

The hardships on the boat did not end, even when we finally arrived on the shores of Israel. The British stopped the ship and exiled us to Cyprus. It wasn't bad there, at all. Even though it was a detention camp, food was scarce and medical services were lacking, after what we had been through, it wasn't too bad. Nobody shot at us, they didn't burn or abuse us, didn't even hit us.

Some of us received tents to sleep in. Every now and then strong winds would send the tents flying, but we would get up, catch the tent and rebuild it. Others among us, who were even luckier, got to sleep in a barracks. Love began to bloom there, big and small, and people divided the barracks into tiny rooms in order to give couples some privacy. Even though we were displaced persons and detainees, we felt a certain degree of freedom.

We had left the memories behind and some of us locked the pain away under lock and key, as I tried to do. Even then I knew, as I wrote previously, that pain had to be locked away, otherwise one could simply go mad. It was hard, at least at first. The memories of Anna never let up, but as weak I had been, skin and bones, I'd had the strength and will to live.

I think that nobody who went through such catastrophes doesn't feel guilt for wanting to live. But I wanted to. I had a need to laugh, to breathe, to eat, to talk, to live. Even then I thought, if I am the only one from my whole family to survive, I must stand on my own two feet. But I must tell the truth, to get the poison out, which is the goal of my writing at the moment.

**

Mrs. Reich's last sentences were so powerful to Avner that he felt he needed some air. The pain must be locked away, otherwise you could go crazy. So true and so hard to do. In his mind's eye he suddenly saw an image that he had repressed for many years.

He was a child, not more than ten years old. He had long since stopped asking his mother hard questions. Every time he had asked in the past, the answers had been increasingly frightening. He would look at the bluish vein that stood out on her forehead, and a crippling fear would pass through him that the vein would explode, his mother's translucent skin would tear and become a sticky mess of blood, like he had seen in a scary movie at the cinema by accident.

If he had known it was a horror movie, he wouldn't have gone. The monster in the film would enter the bodies of its victims and burst out of them, each time out of a different organ. In his imagination, he saw the monster burst out of the vein, and the image was intolerable, certainly to a ten-year-old child. That night, after seeing the movie, he snuck into his parents' room, lay down in their bed without waking them, and tried to fall asleep.

His mother had opened her eyes, and asked, "My boy, why are you not in your bed?"

"I saw a monster," he wailed.

His father, who had also woken up, laughed. "There are no monsters in the world, Avner, go back to sleep."

But his mother suddenly looked angry.

"Back to bed," his father said, and added, but this time unsmiling, "There are no monsters."

He went back to bed and heard his mother moan. He pressed his ear to the wall of their room, and heard her say, "Why did you lie to him, Nahum?"

Avner didn't remember exactly what his father replied, maybe he didn't answer at all, but his mother said out loud, "Don't lie to him, you know there are monsters in the world."

Afterward he heard her crying. She cried all night, and in the morning, when he woke up after a short night of sleep, she wasn't in the house. For years he blamed himself that the first time his mother was hospitalized was because of him, because of his crazy monster stories.

Now he read in the diary that fear had to be locked away, otherwise it could make you crazy. His mother had not locked away the pain, but neither had he. Was he going crazy too?

Avner got up, poured himself a glass of water, then realized that he had already poured himself a glass just a few minutes before and not had a sip from it. He took a sip from each glass, one after the other, and went into the bathroom. As he was peeing, he imagined a monstrous face inside the toilet. He flushed and in the small mirror over the toilet he saw his own reflection, a tired reflection, his eyes wild. He looked at himself again, from up close, and suddenly it seemed to him that his eye color had dulled over the years.

He remembered how when they had just met, Chaya told him, "You have such beautiful eyes, blue like the sea. Interesting. I heard that blue eyes are not a dominant trait, and you only get it when both parents have blue eyes."

He remembered how he had answered that his father had actually had brown eyes, but his mother's eyes were blue. Now he looked at his reflection again and his crazed expression, with the blue that had faded over the years, horrified him. What if he had inherited not only his mother's blue eyes but her crazy expression too? He dismissed his thoughts and smiled as he caught himself gesturing to himself.

He returned to the room, sat down heavily and resumed reading the diary.

***

On cold nights at the detainment camp I would lie in the tent, Maria beside me, and the two of us tried to keep warm, talking late into the night.

She said, "Your family was special. Your father was a special man. He was a shrewd but honest and decent merchant. Your mother was his whole world. We were true friends, heart and soul, even though I was younger than her by a few good years. You know, the only thing your parents ever argued about was your father's concern for all of you. Your mother worried too, but she was sure that her ethnicity would save you.

"Once I heard her asking him to get rid of any signs that gave away his origins, to take off his Kippah, and your father, who was such a gentle man, got really angry at that request. Your mother didn't let it go, and even asked him to shave his beard, but he was very stubborn. I think he knew that according to your religion it was forbidden for him to live with your mother, which was why he was extra insistent on not removing any signs of Jewishness, like the beard and the Kippah, or changing his name.

"You wouldn't believe it, but I read in the Holy Scriptures that even Moses married a Midian woman, and Joseph himself married an Egyptian woman. But your father must not have known those stories, and I think that it was very hard for him. He must have felt that he was living a major sin. They never had a Jewish wedding, nor a Christian one. Your mother told me that she really wanted your father to convert, but didn't dare say it out lout, and when she finally did, it was too late anyway."

***

Avner considered this. The religious education that he had received raised its head again: Halacha does not permit mixed marriage. They had desecrated the covenant with our father Abraham. On the other hand, who was he to judge? A Jewish man fell in love with a goyish woman, and love could have been victorious if what happened had not happened.

He picked up the diary again and went on reading.

***

I lay there and listened to Maria. The sound of her voice was pleasant to my ears, and even if I didn't understand everything she said, she spoke softly and lovingly, so that I didn't even care what she was saying, so long as she went on speaking.

"I know that your father would laugh and say that our quiet was what made our love last. Your mother even told me that he would say that we believed that luck only comes when it's quiet. The truth is, from everything that I saw in this hard world, I am certain that that is not true, that is, one cannot expect luck to arrive just because you are keeping quiet for its sake, right?"

I nodded my head and Maria went on, "I also think that quiet can't help maintain love, because if love is real, it doesn't really matter if there is surrounding noise. It is strong even in the face of powerful winds."

I didn't fully understand the depth of the wise things she was saying. I was young and inexperienced. But now, after almost sixty years with the man who was the love of my life, when I think of what she said, I understand how true it was. Even if the foundations of my house shake from time to time, like in any regular household, and even if strong, malevolent winds blow from outside, despite everything, and despite our delicate situation, our love was not damaged. I know now that many things that Maria said needed time to ripen and be internalized.

Maria said, "I'm not angry at your father. We really did keep quiet almost all of the time."

"But why?" I asked

Maria answered, "Before I met Ludwig, he worked in food distribution, which was what allowed him to move freely around the city. He kept up that work even after we met, in addition to running the shop. That was how he managed to bring food for the people in the cellar, until one day when someone reported him. Then I never saw him again."

There was so much pain in her eyes, pain that I could not bear. I hugged her, and a tremble passed through her. "Tell me nice things," I requested.

"The nicest thing in this whole story is what Ludwig did. Apart from that, it's not such a nice story, my dear Eva."

"Tell me anyway," I said, and she did.

"Underneath the rug there was a hidden opening that led to a cellar in the belly of the earth, and for days Ludwig organized the space so that it would be pleasant and comfortable in there, then covered the entrance with the rug. The hiding place was ready even before anyone really needed it because my Ludwig knew what was going to happen. He had that amazing quality, to always see a few steps head, and he was never mistaken."

I couldn't remember the cellar, but from Maria's story I imagined it as a crowded, but nice, warm room. "Ludwig had a family," she went on telling me with fresh pain in her eyes. "Before I boarded the boat to Israel I tried to contact them, but they refused to speak to me. I think they blamed me for his death; they thought that I was the one who urged him to help the Jews. But actually it was his idea, it came entirely from him."

Today I know that that was Maria's way of diminishing herself, to give credit to everyone else, but at that time I simply asked, "And what about your family?"

The sorrow in her eyes grew. "They were heroes," she said, her voice trembling. "After the Gestapo discovered our cellar, but didn't find me, they found them, all of them, my father, my mother, and both my sisters.

They tried to extract information about me from them, but they kept quiet. They didn't say a word. They were heroic. I didn't see them after I ran away, but I know that their fate was not good. They were real heroes." She sighed.

"Dear, Maria," I whispered. "Maybe now they are in a better place, where they aren't cold…"

"You are a smart girl," she replied. "Of course they are." She was quiet a moment, hugged me tightly. "Your father met your mother a long time before the war, and the pairing between their two worlds was a challenge to their families. Your mother said that your father's family was particularly perturbed, but their love triumphed, and that's what matters."

We were quiet for a moment then Maria said, "They brought Anna into the world, may she rest in peace." She had tears in her eyes as she recalled my sister. "Afterward, your grandmother and grandfather on your mother's side passed away, one after the other, which was very hard on your mother. But then you were born and brought so much joy into their lives."

"But none of that lasted long," I said in a whisper.

Maria said, "You know, your father really wanted a son, and they almost realized that little dream."

The last sentence of hers echoed in my ears for a few minutes afterward. "He wanted a son instead of me?" I asked, concerned.

"No, silly girl, not instead of you, in addition to you… but let's leave that alone for now."

This raised questions. I didn't understand what she was getting at, but Maria was stubborn. "Leave it be now, Eva, maybe I'll tell you some other time."

I tried to insist, but she got up and approached the entrance of the tent.

"Don't go," I said, and she came back and lay down beside me. "So tell me about something else." I cuddled up to her.

She hugged me tightly and said, "The things I know are not so nice."

"I'm not a little girl anymore, Maria, I'm asking you to tell me," I said.

"You had an uncle, Karl, and your aunt was called Alice, and they had two boys, Johann and Herman. Your aunt died of a terrible disease. I don't know if you remember how ill she was and how her death was the turning point in all of your lives. Until then you would play with Johann and Herman in the yard, but that was the end of that."

When Maria mentioned playing in the yard, it seemed to me that I clearly remembered jumping rope, and not just from Maria's stories.

"You would jump rope, and Johann, he was mischievous, always tried to bother you, you must remember that," she said. "But then Alice died, and Karl bought her a coffin laid with gold, ornamented with angels, really a special coffin."

Maria paused and with my eyes closed, I envisioned the golden casket.

Maria went on, "Sometimes people try to make up for something with money, but if you ask me, no money and gold could make up for anything."

"What do you mean?" I asked.

"Your uncle tried to make up for your aunt's death with a gold coffin, but no gold could cover over his character or make up for his behavior, even to his wife. In any case, from the moment that your aunt was buried, it was like the beginning of a new era. A hard, cruel, dark era, without even a drop of light. Everyone thought that your uncle Karl disappeared a few days after her death and took the two boys with him. But the truth is, he didn't disappear, which was a shame."

"You're not being clear!" I protested.

Maria shook her head. "There are things that are hard to talk about."

"But I'm old enough now," I said again, but she got up and left the tent. "Where are you going?" I called after her.

She replied without turning around, "I need a breath of air, I spoke too much as it is."

"But it's cold outside!" I tried to convince her.

She turned and came back and sat beside me. "Eva, my dear," she said. "Don't ask me to tell you things that I am still unable to deal with myself."

I was silent. I didn't know what to say. There was something in her expression that made me understand that it really wasn't worth interrogating her or trying to dredge up the details that she was hiding. It hurt me to see the sorrow in her eyes, and I said, "So, tell me more about my parents, okay? I like hearing about them."

Maria smiled at me sadly, covered the two of us with a blanket, and said, "You know how funny the holidays were? Imagine your mother's parents around the table at your family's Easter. It's funny to think about."

I realized that Maria was trying to make me laugh and herself too, to avoid the things she didn't want to say, but the smile was full of that pain of hers so I cooperate and smiled.

"There was one time that they invited us to celebrate with all of you. Your father tried to conduct that holiday as it was written in his weird picture book."

I remembered the Passover Haggadah, and even the pictures of the goat, the bull, and the dog. I also remembered the picture of the big sea split in two and the one of the butcher which always scared me.

"That evening, your father tried to do everything as it was written. You won't believe how much we laughed! And there was so much food on the table even before the meal itself, your aunt Alice said that it was crazy how much you could eat! Then your uncle said that all of this food was to cover up the taste of what you eat on this holiday instead of bread. What's it called, that cracker thing, tastes like sawdust?'

"Matzah," I said and could taste it.

Maria went on retelling that Passover evening, and it was as if the images got up and took on a life of their own before my eyes: potatoes in salt, the hardboiled eggs, the horseradish and *haroset,* the matzahs, and the big glass of wine for Elijah the prophet. Maria told how Dad tried to read the whole story out of his weird book, and how the wine that they drank lifted everyone's spirit and made them laugh uncontrollably. Then suddenly her face grew grim and she said quietly, "If we had only known that that was the last time that we would celebrate some holiday together, maybe we wouldn't have laughed so much. How lucky it is that we never really know what awaits us around the corner and what tomorrow will bring."

~

CHAPTER TWELVE

Our tents were replaced with shacks. Mine was small, but compared to the tent, it was a big improvement. One evening I fell down as I entered the shack. I remember that my head was spinning, and I can still recall the bad taste that I had in my mouth. A kind of sourness, like you get a moment before vomiting. A few seconds later I opened my eyes and didn't understand why Maria was staring at me looking so frightened. She sat on the floor beside me, one hand under my head and the other stroking my face.

I wanted to scream. I thought that they had come to take us away, that the war was not really over and soon our shacks would go up in smoke with the smell of scorched flesh, but Maria got me up from the floor, supporting me gently and walked me to my bed.

"You're burning up," she said. "Lie down and I will get medicine for you." A few minutes later she returned with a cup of hot tea and a pill to bring my fever down. She put a wet cloth on my forehead and sat beside me all night.

I hallucinated. Images and sounds raced through my mind at dizzying speed. I saw two girls playing in a yard and two boys joining them. I could hear my mother calling us to come to the house. I could see the bigger boy getting angry that he was forced to stop his game and the younger one crying for the same reason. I heard the older boy say to the younger boy,

"Stop crying, crying is for girls!" But the little one went on wailing.

I was feverish all night, and Maria stayed by my side stroking my hair, putting cold compresses on my face, and spooning tea into my mouth.

By morning I was much better. I sat up in bed, weak and tired, and looked at Maria with great love. That night she had been a mother, sister, and friend all at once.

"Maria," I said to her. "I dreamed that Anna and I were playing with my two cousins Johann and Herman."

"There was a time when you really did all play together out in the yard," she replied. "Anyway…" She smiled. "But you didn't dream it. I was sitting right here telling you!"

"Tell me again," I requested.

Maria sat at the edge of my bed and said, "Silly girl, there's no point telling you the same things over and over again, but after you fell asleep I suddenly remembered the wonderful smell of cooking from your aunt's house. She made meat in a cream sauce that tasted like heaven."

I didn't remember the smell, but I remembered the argument between my parents and asked, "Did my mother keep a kosher kitchen for Dad?"

Maria smiled. "You are asking smart questions," she said. "But I want you to know, your mother did everything she could to make your father happy, even things whose purpose she did not understand."

But I remembered them fighting and I had to ask. "They argued over *kashrut*,[5]" I said.

Maria shook her head and replied, "No. I never heard them arguing over that, but your mother was shrewd. She loved the meat in cream sauce and would sneak off to Alice's house to eat…"

I smiled. It made me happy that my mother was able to enjoy her short life.

Maria added, "But apart from that, she really did do everything for your father, and from the moment that she realized that he wouldn't leave his religion, she stopped trying to fight it, and even sent you to Jewish school. In retrospect, that might have been her biggest mistake."

The word "mistake" brought me back to the terrible image of my mother

---

5   Jewish dietary laws

being sent to the left and crying out "mistake, mistake!" Tears came to my eyes. Maria got up and left the shack. She returned with a warm, comforting bowl of soup. "Eat," she ordered. "There will be plenty of time for stories later, when you're well."

I was in Cyprus for almost a year. In July of 1947, after the British refused to send the thousands of Jews who were waiting in Cyprus to Palestine, the Jewish Agency organized two big ships to take us to the shores of Israel. I remember that period as particularly nerve-wracking. Thanks to the British barring our journey, we waited for over two weeks until finally one day we decided to go on a hunger strike. It's hard to emphasize the significance of that for people who did not have food to eat for years, but the strike accomplished its goal.

We boarded a ship called 'Atzma'ut,' meaning "independence." There was something in that name that warmed my heart. Members of the Jewish Agency organized places for us to sleep in almost every possible spot, including under the deck, and made sure that the voyage was as pleasant as possible. They even installed big fans, and most of all — made sure to have sick rooms and bring doctors and nurses aboard. Then we set out to the land that my father had dreamed of.

After we finally anchored at the Haifa port, we were brought to Kiryat Shmuel, in the outskirts of Haifa, where we were housed in shacks and warehouses. Although the Jewish Agency's department of children and youth immigration looked after our basic needs, poverty was rampant. But for people like us, who had come from years of scarcity and hunger, even a slice of bread and jam was considered plenty.

Throughout the day, members of the underground wandered around and taught us how to use weapons. It's kind of shocking to think of us children, some of whom not yet fifteen years old, holding rifles and learning to shoot them, but personally it gave me a great feeling of strength and power.

Maria, on the other hand, thought otherwise. "I don't want to learn to fight," she said numerous times. "I did not come here for that."

In the evening, when it got chilly, Maria would come home and say, "I don't understand, they told us that this was a hot country, with sun ten months of the year, so why am I so cold?"

When winter came and it became even colder, Maria suffered more and even though we should have been used to the cold, Maria couldn't stand it anymore but she needed money to get anywhere. We walked around Kiryat Shmuel and went into buildings to offer our services cleaning stairwells. A few places sent us away at once, claiming that they already had a cleaner or that they didn't need such services, but there were a few that were glad for the cheap labor.

Within a few days we had enough money to take the bus, and we went south to Tel Aviv. The city, even though it was not yet very big or bustling, seemed intimidating to me at first.

Maria was happy. At least for the first few days. "It's much warmer here," she said.

We had already figured out how to survive. Within a few hours we found a few buildings that agreed to give us cleaning work, and within a few days we found a place to sleep at night, in an abandoned shelter, with old furniture that people had thrown away.

But Maria's happiness was temporary. "I can't stand the humidity here," she said after a few days had passed. "I have to find someplace drier."

But I was tired of travel. I felt that I needed to try and make it work on my own. Maria tearfully went on her way. I did not know where she was for a long time, which made me very sad — after all, she was my only friend then. But I had to go on living. I continued to work cleaning stairwells. In one of the buildings where I cleaned, an older woman from among the building's tenants asked me in German mixed with Yiddish, "When did you last eat a hot meal?"

God must have loved me after all. If I was saved from the inferno, with Maria as my guardian angel, and then sent more angels in the form of these two, Zipporah Danziger and her husband Aaron, a couple with hearts bigger than their bodies, I must have done something right.

Eventually I realized that Zipporah and Aaron Danziger had had a single child, a girl who had disappeared one day and never been seen again. She had gone to visit a friend in a different city, and only three days later did her parents realize that she had never arrived but simply disappeared as if she had been swallowed by the earth. They searched for her for years to no avail.

She had disappeared and her parents were heartbroken, trying to go on with their lives without her.

Evidently something about me reminded them of their daughter, whose picture was displayed in the living room of their small home, which became my home that day. They were looking for a good enough reason to go on living, and I had mixed feelings about being the reason that they found. Once I even dared to raise the subject with Zipporah, but the pain that I saw in her eyes was so deep that I abandoned the subject at once.

In the evenings we would sit together and talk, and I told them about Maria and my need to know where she was.

Aaron did not waste any time. He turned to "Kol Yisrael" radio program the next day and published my name, new address, and that I was looking for Maria. He briefly described our experiences, as I had told them to him and asked for help in locating Maria.

Within a few days, an exciting surprise was waiting for me in the mailbox.

"I settled in Kibbutz Mishmar HaAliya." Maria wrote me in German. "There is wonderful sun here, but it is not humid like in Tel Aviv, and there are good people. I met one man by the name of Shimon."

I could picture the blush in her beautiful cheeks as she wrote that. "He has been a widower for a few years and he has two children. I am happy."

I wiped away tears of happiness. I didn't yet know that life would ultimately bring me to the same kibbutz.

During that time, Maria continued to write me, we would talk on the telephone as well, and even meet. "Shimon's children are wonderful," she said.

"Tell me about him."

She laughed out loud and replied, "He, how can I explain? He is simply Shimon!"

I laughed along with her and she continued to tell me about his children. "They treat me very nicely," she said happily.

I was blown away by her happiness and her journey, beginning from the days when she hid Jews in her cellar of her home with Ludwig, through to the connections that she used to come to Israel, to the way she restored her life.

There was one thing that bothered her over the years, which we talked about when she came to visit me in Tel Aviv.

We sat in a cafe in Dizengoff Square, and Maria said, "I tried to convert."
I was surprised by her wish to become Jewish.

"It would come full circle for me in my life. After all, Ludwig so loved Jews."

I looked at her gentle face, she was so pretty I thought, and I couldn't
stand her sadness. "So why don't you…?" I stated.

"I tried. They requested a divorce certificate from Ludwig, because
I told them that I live with Shimon, but when I explained to them that
Ludwig was dead, they asked for a death certificate."

"I don't understand," I said. "Where would you acquire such a certificate?"

Maria made a dismissive gesture with her hands. "Forget it," she said.
"They aren't bad people, just that this religion has rules of its own. Maybe
I could have managed to explain the situation to them but I gave up."

We met many times over the years. For a short time we even lived in the
same place — Kibbutz Mishmar HaAliya — and then we saw each other
regularly. She knew Meir before I did, and always smiled when I would say
how reality surpasses any fantasy.

"Who would believe that in the end you would find a husband from the
kibbutz, of all places?" she said.

But I am getting ahead of myself, and I will come back to that later.

At a certain point, Maria changed her name to Mira, and once even
told me, "Shimon, he insists that I take his family name, that's how he
is, stubborn. But what do you say, "Mira Levy." it sounds like a powerful
name, no?"

I remember that that made me laugh, how she approached life with a
smile. Each time we met she looked stronger and stronger and even more
beautiful and radiant than the last time.

***

Avner finished reading the section, then looked it over again. Mrs. Reich
had lived here in the kibbutz for a short while? That was interesting! He
probably wouldn't remember her if she had been here just a short time, and
when he was a child. But he actually remembered Maria and her husband
Shimon! Shimon had had livestock, cows and chickens. He remembered
Maria-Mira as a tall, thin, quiet woman.

On the kibbutz they had joked that she lived by the phrase: "Keep quiet and look pretty."

He closed his eyes for a moment, wanting to organize his thoughts. The fact that Maria, Eva's best friend, lived in Mishmar HaAliya, could further explain why Eva had chosen to be buried here, of all places. On the other hand, he felt that there was something more, that this choice of hers was more complex. And even if he already had enough reasons for her to be buried on the kibbutz, it still wasn't clear to him why she had chosen him as the person to read her diary.

He rifled through the chapter again and wiped a small, irritating tear from the corner of his eye. Eva still had so much optimism, despite her hard life. What strength one needed to always see the cup half full. Avner smiled to himself, thinking about how Nisim had once told him that one must always see the glass as half full, just that scientifically, one had to pass through the half-empty cup to reach the half-full point. This, said Nisim, was in the ideal case, when the glass was divided into two exact halves. What would happen if the person who had come up with the expression had said that we always need to look at the glass one-eighth full? But here before him was the account of a woman who had drained the empty part of her life, then fallen thirstily on the full part.

For the umpteenth time Avner tried unsuccessfully not to compare her to his mother. An image from his distant childhood came to mind. He had just gotten home from school.

Years earlier his father had shown him where the house key was hidden. "You know," he had told him. "Sometimes Mom is sleeping, and it's better if you don't disturb her."

On that day he took the key out from the fuse box and opened the door. His mother sat in her armchair, her back to the door, and did not respond as he entered. He approached and stood before her and was deeply shocked. His mother was wearing just a shirt and tights. He began to walk around the room, hysterical, trying to find her skirt, while his mother stared at him with an expression which seemed to say, "Remind me who you are." She did not wipe away the tears that rolled down her cheeks, but just pointed to the place inside the wardrobe where he found her skirt. The sight of her like that, in just a shirt and tights, had been etched in his memory since he was nine years old, an image which refused to be forgotten.

***

Zipporah and Aaron Danziger, my saviors, gave me a warm home, clothes to wear, a bed to sleep in, and plenty of food, without asking for anything in return. At first I offered to help clean the house, but I quickly understood that Zipporah did not want that. She would wear a robe and an apron, a yellow rag in her hands, and clean and polish every corner herself. I would follow her around the little house, amazed by the speed with which she cleaned everything. When she wanted to make me laugh, she would talk to the dust balls and suggest that they vacate the furniture before the dust rag caught them.

Zipporah was a funny woman who, despite the tragedy in her life, did not abandon her sense of humor, and she would act out the housework for me, so I could learn it properly but joyfully.

She would make me laugh to the point of tears when I heard her talking to slices of eggplant in the pan, "Please turn over, yes, I know that you're hot, but what can we do." She would chat with the objects and furniture while making faces that any comic would be proud of. "Move, now, chair — stand up straight!" On and on, endless, healthy humor, that one could only envy.

I don't know if something of her wonderful sense of humor stuck with me, but certainly I grew to be like her over the years, at least in terms of cleaning, order, and even the yellow rag.

On this subject, I must note that there is nothing like the color yellow for catching dust and not letting them get away. It's a strong, bold color, and dirt stands out on it in a way that is evident to any eye. I believe that the Nazis also chose the color yellow for the badge since it stands out. I apologize for the last statement. Amazing how everything I say winds up being connected to my past, one way or another.

Zipporah Danziger also loved to tell funny stories, and she herself often played the lead role in them. She had a big, well-ironed apron which she wore whenever she was doing work around the house. She told me how on one particularly hot day, she'd had enough of wearing clothes, remaining in just her undergarments and the apron over top. What happened afterward makes me laugh out loud to this day: one of the neighbors knocked on the door to ask for a cup of sugar. Zipporah went to the kitchen and brought him what he requested, and only when she saw him smiling broadly did she realize that from behind he would have seen her in just her underwear.

I loved Zipporah as if she were my mother, but still, at night I would sometimes cry into the pillow from longing for my family who had been lost. I am happy that my children were lucky enough to meet Zipporah. Her husband Aaron passed away before they were born, but Zipporah lived a long life, and my children called her Grandma Zipporah, even though they knew that she was not their biological grandmother.

***

Avner got up for a moment, then came and sat back down. Damn, he cursed softly, damn it with these memories of mine that keep popping up. Here he was as a child in elementary school, a few days after the Hanukah holiday. All of the children told of their visit to their relatives.

This boy had an uncle in Rehovot, she had aunts and uncles in Haifa, and there was even one boy with aunts and uncles in Eilat. Everyone had a big, extended family, and he was the only solitary child, without any real aunts or uncles. He recalled now how much he hated the fact that his mother forced him to call any older woman "Aunt" including all of their neighbors.

Sometimes he would sit and listen to the conversations between his mother and the neighbors, especially when they tried to whisper so that he wouldn't hear. Afterward he would ask his mother what they had talked about, and she would scold him without answering his question, "Call her aunt, not neighbor."

Suddenly, out of nowhere, came memories of fragments of conversations between his mother and those fake aunts, conversations that were whispered, and he had never understood why. He heard the word "hero" repeated. He would look through the keyhole and try to see his mother's face every time she said the word. Light would beam from her eyes, which he was not used to seeing. He recalled one conversation, the meaning of which he had not understood at the time:

"Converted?" He heard the neighbor asking. "But how, that is…" She was quiet for a moment, then went on, "What about that sensitive matter, what, surgery? Under anesthesia?"

He saw his mother smile, a rare occurrence, perhaps the reason he remembered the details of this conversation, and then replied, "Partial anesthesia."

He remembered the neighbor's stunned face, which made him smile.

"What?" She opened her eyes wide. "You're telling me that he saw everything?"

"Saw," his mother answered quietly. "But didn't feel."

"And that's not dangerous?"

"No. The doctor who did it is also a '*mohel*'[6] and a religious one at that; there were three rabbis there who oversaw the whole thing."

"And didn't it hurt him?"

"No. If you want something enough, it doesn't hurt."

Avner remembered this sentence — if you want something enough, it doesn't hurt. It made such an impression on him that he almost entered the room to hug his mother, but unfortunately for him, the door opened right into his face, and his mother looked at him angrily and said, "Say hi to your aunt, Avner."

***

In my adult life, I made the bed the way that Zipporah taught me, making sure that the distances between my blanket and the edge of my side of the bed, and Meir's on his side, were equal. I'm aware that that sounds like overkill, but there are habits that are stamped upon a person, and maybe the fact that for years I had no home, made it so that I internalized everything done in the home offered to me by Zipporah and Aaron. I liked to wear immaculately ironed shirts, and I wouldn't leave the house with unpolished shoes. They bought me clothes that I never dreamed of having, and filled my room with books.

---

6   The person who performs ritual circumcision

They were well-off. Aaron had a shop for eyeglasses, frequented by many satisfied customers for years. Zipporah worked with him in the shop until the disaster that befell them. They never spoke of that tragedy in my presence, and only occasionally did I hear bits of conversation in which they recalled their daughter who had disappeared. Unlike his wife, Aaron was a quiet man, but the kind look in his eyes would scare off Satan.

***

Avner set down the diary again. If he could, he would banish the memory that troubled him most of all.

"'*Shah, mein kind*,'" His mother would try to calm him in a language he didn't understand. "Don't cry, it's not good for your eyes."

He tried to stop, but he asked about his grandparents again. That afternoon, playing outside with his friends, they had stood in a line and mocked him, "Cry-baby Avner, doesn't even have a little brother," and, "Avner's family became fewer, when grandma and grandpa fell in a sewer." He stood there and cried, which only made them laugh harder.

That was the day he made up Hilik. His imaginary friend turned into the long-awaited little brother that Avner so wanted. Other kids in the neighborhood had little brothers and sisters being born. There was even a boy with new twin brothers, and he was the only one who was all alone. He remembered how he had tried to convince his mother to give him a sibling, and how he hoped for some miracle. That day that the other kids laughed at him to his face, he understood once and for all that the miracle he wished for wouldn't happen.

Hilik became a part of him, and he knew exactly what he looked like, what he liked to eat, and what games he liked to play. He thought to himself that Hilik was born in a land called "The Land of Maybe" and like him he was also an only child, lonely and miserable until he met Avner, and together they travelled in the land of maybe. They loved traveling together, but Hilik always had the feeling that he wasn't really him.

One day, while they were traveling, as usual, they met a tiger named "Doubt."

Hilik asked the tiger why he had such a strange name, and the tiger gave him an even stranger answer, "It isn't important what you think about yourself. What really matters is what others think of you, and if everyone is certain that you really are who you are, then you have no problem."

Avner never mentioned Hilik to his mother. The evening he invented Hilik, he asked her again, "Why don't I have grandparents?"

She stared at an invisible spot on the wall, her gaze narrowed and she said, "You must forget your grandfather, in particular!"

He didn't understand how he could forget someone he didn't know, but when he dared to ask that question, his mother got upset, and when she got truly upset, she would switch to German, which annoyed him, and more than anything, it frightened him. 'Fragen Sie nicht so viele Fragen' — "don't ask so many questions," from which he understood that he had asked too much.

Now, as Eva was describing a man with such a kind expression that even the devil would be scared off, he recalled thinking, as a child, that the body had a button for everything. A laughing button in the navel, or "belly button," which makes you laugh if you press on it, and a button on the left nipple, which makes you cry because it's the closest to the heart. Actually, with the crying button he wasn't sure if it was the left side of the body or the right. He would place his hand over a different side each time, trying to feel his heartbeat, to know which side to press, but his heartbeat deceived him.

One time, he felt it on the left side, the next time on the right. In any case, in order to cry he didn't need a button, because he cried easily enough without it, but he knew that the body had a button for it. He just didn't know where the button was for "forgetting" and where he needed to press for things to disappear. It frightened him that he wouldn't manage to forget his grandfather, but he already knew the answer from other times, so he didn't ask again.

~

CHAPTER THIRTEEN

My love of books, as I already mentioned, was planted in me by Zipporah and Aharon, with all of their heart and soul. They sent me to complete my studies at school during the evenings, and made sure I didn't want for anything. But each night I would see Aharon sitting slumped in his armchair, reading the Etzel's "Herut" monthly, his expression concerned.

Sometimes I would return home and find the monthly pasted to the wall in the stairwell. The "propaganda boys," as they were called, would walk the streets and paste it to stairwell walls and bulletin boards. Within a few weeks, the little neighborhood became a community of older adults. Underground operatives roamed the streets and recruited every young person to their purposes, because those were the days of the War of Independence, and they needed anyone who was strong enough. And so I, too, found myself on a truck, on the way between Binyamina and Zichron Yaakov, where the Etzel's central training base was located.

Zipporah and Aharon didn't oppose my getting involved. I imagine that deep down they might have preferred that I remain home. They had had enough loss and heartbreak, and certainly were very worried about me. But to their credit they were able to set aside their private concerns.

Along with me there were other young people my age and even younger.

In retrospect, it was clear that the ranks of the Etzel included many more new immigrants than Israeli-born youth. I soon developed a feeling of belonging and I filled with pride when I heard the Betar Song written by Ze'ev Jabotinsky.

I served as a volunteer in the training camp's clinic without any knowledge of medicine because that's what was needed. I soon became familiar with the medicines and pain killers and ointments for treating burns. I learned how to bandage wounds and how to measure blood pressure.

As much as this might sound prideful or out of place, I am aware that alongside the hard work at the clinic and the hard things I had to see as a result, it was a period in which I filled with self-confidence. I was blessed with a handsome figure and fine features, my hair grew long and I could easily have been a model for New Year's greeting cards. I apologize if what I'm saying sounds arrogant, but after all of the hardships I went through, I feel that I have more than earned a little self-pride.

After the war, I returned to live with my adoptive parents. I was their whole world, and they wanted the best for me. Evidently, even when it seemed like there was nothing left, some new light had arrived. They saved on themselves and gave me money so that I could study and move ahead in life.

I began studying Hebrew literature and linguistics at the Hebrew University in Jerusalem. The choice of the Hebrew University came from a sense of national pride. I wanted to study in the capital of our small, free nation. Since the usual building on Mount Scopus became an Israeli enclave within Jordanian territory, the studies moved to the Terra Santa College in the heart of the city, right in front of Paris Square. My adoptive parents were able to see me complete my Bachelor's degree, and Zipporah even saw me complete my Master's.

One day, near the end of my Bachelor's degree, I was chosen to go with a group of top students to an opening ceremony for the Tel Aviv University's Institute of Natural Sciences. It was during the Hanukah holiday and more precisely, the first day of December 1953. I remember the date well because it was one of the most exciting days of my life. There was something about this holiday, which always made me remember the good times back home.

Dad would light the Hanukah candles in a fancy menorah, and it seemed to me that I could really remember the special evening when Mom also invited Uncle Karl and Aunt Alice with their two boys to the candle lighting. (From what I realized years later from Maria, Uncle Karl never really liked Dad's traditions, but in my memory the holiday remained pure and beautiful.)

That same day, the first night of Hanukah and the first of December 1953, the course of my life changed forever. The group of students, myself included, arrived by bus to the Tel Aviv venue, where a group of local students awaited us. A big sign was hanging at the entrance to the hall with the words: "Welcome to the opening ceremony of the University Institute for Natural Sciences in Tel Aviv."

I don't know if I am managing to convey the national pride that I felt. An academic institute in the land of Israel, in the city of Tel Aviv, and me, Eva Reich, a twenty-three-year-old woman, among the guests to the ceremony. And I didn't yet know that my future would be determined that day... I saw him among the students who were waiting for us. He was almost a head taller than the rest of them, with a lock of hair across his forehead and a broad smile on his face.

I don't know if there is such a thing as love at first sight, but if so, that is what happened to me in those very moments. I almost didn't see the rest of the people, or hear the talking around me. I barely looked at the big stage, or heard the speeches, and I hardly tasted from the spread of delicacies set out on the tables outside. I was mesmerized by his sabra look, his strength, and even the smell of his body when he stood close to me.

I stared at him for a long time, at first from a distance, not daring to approach. I followed him with my gaze, and approached just enough that I could hear him speak. He was telling someone how he had just signed up for his first year of studies and I heard him say, "So there is a list on the dean's door to get a personal interview, and when I got there and saw that I was the tenth in line, I erased my name and wrote it first. Then a woman who was sitting there said, "What do you think you're doing?" But I asked her what number she was and when she said she was eleventh, I told her, 'Now you're number two.'"

I was fascinated by this cheeky native-born Israeli making everyone laugh, and I was smitten.

That same evening, at a small, pleasant coffee shop, he said his name was Meir Reich, that he'd been born in Germany and had arrived in Israel in 1933, at the age of four with his parents and older brother. He spoke a lot of his love of Israel and his parents' need to contribute to its creation.

"They looked for a place to live that would fulfill their desire to be a part of the Jewish settlement, so they finally chose a kibbutz, but my mother, how can I say it nicely, she couldn't get used to the smell of the cows and the chicken coop on the kibbutz, Mishmar HaAliya, so within a year they left and moved to Tel Aviv."

My breath caught for a moment. Mishmar HaAliya? Maria's kibbutz? I wanted to ask him if he knew her, but I stopped myself. I didn't yet know what and how I would tell him about my past, and if I were to mention Maria in that conversation, I would have to reveal details that I was still afraid to share. Besides, I was afraid that he would see me as an exile, a non-sabra, with a heavy past of terrible tragedy. I didn't want to be seen as pitiable so I decided to keep my story for another time when I knew him better and could trust him more.

***

A big smile rose to Avner's face. She was talking about the kibbutz again! Here was another reason why Eva Reich chose to be buried in this kibbutz, of all places! Because Meir, the love of her life, had roots here, and the kibbutz was sufficiently pluralistic. Good reason. But a moment later he caught himself and stopped smiling. To choose to be buried specifically in Mishmar HaAliya because of its pluralism and roots was all well and good, but that still didn't really explain why Eva chose him to read her diary. His curiosity grew from one moment to the next, and he went on reading.

***

Meir told me that he and his parents had moved to Tel Aviv when he was six years old. He studied at the Moriah school and continued on to the Herzliyah Hebrew Gymnasium. At the end of his schooling, he served in the IDF and was in the standing army for a while before deciding to study the geography of Israel at the new campus in Abu Kabir. I smile when I think of the size of Tel Aviv University today. At that time, the Natural Sciences department numbered just twenty-four students. My Meir was one of them.

Meir escorted me home late that evening. I didn't tell him much about Zipporah and Aharon, just that they were my adoptive parents and that my own parents had perished in the Holocaust. The next day I returned to Jerusalem and tried my best to go on studying. I had many exams and assignments, but the subjects were fascinating and I had first-rate lecturers and peers, some of whom had been born here in Israel and some of whom had come as immigrants. I had a certain envy of the long-time Israeli sabras, who spoke excellent Hebrew because they had been born into it, but that envy brought about good things. It made way for my great love for Meir.

Since he had grown up here, ever since he was four years old, he was tanned like a sabra, spoke excellent Hebrew like a sabra, bore none of the signs of coming from the diaspora and behaved like a free man, with only his European manners from his parents' home to suggest that he had not been born here.

On second thought, today I know that to be free is a matter of personality and nothing else. One way or another, that healthy envy of those who seemed free to me, pushed me to continue learning Hebrew well, both the high literary language and the spoken language with its slang and vernacular. Happily, I had no accent at all. I felt secret contempt for those who spoke only poor Hebrew or street Hebrew.

To this day it is not clear to me how it is possible to take such a wonderful language and spoil it. I remember saying out loud in one of my classes that those who are alienated from their language do not deserve it, which provoked heated arguments, as well as the anger of some students. I tried to not do that again. It was important to me to be part of the group, to belong, to not seem foreign and most of all — to not talk about my past or be the subject of pity.

***

Avner considered the last sentence. He couldn't ignore the feeling that again a mirror was being held up to him and that he had to consider himself more thoroughly, or like Nisim always said: to look into the whites of the eyes. He himself had often tried to connect with people, to be part of the group, but he was never very good at it. He had never been the life of the party and was always quiet, shy.

Now, reading Eva's clearly articulated words brought back memories of his childhood home, and for possibly the first time he admitted to himself that maybe for whatever reason his social skills had not developed was not because he was an unsociable child but because he hadn't wanted to have friends over to the house. And it wasn't that he hadn't had friends. He didn't even have to try hard to remember, he still knew the names of the children from school.

He remembered Eitan best, a freckled, skinny boy whose dad worked in the Foreign Ministry and every time he came back from abroad he would bring Eitan back toys that Israelis had never seen before. Eitan's mother was a teacher at their school. She was tall, with thick arms that always looked to him like they could protect you from anything. Eitan's mother spoke fluent Hebrew at school, which was replaced by slang the moment she left work. Eitan was proud of her. She was an unusual mother, who rode a motorcycle, and had the helmet and the attitude for it. She loved animals and got Eitan a formidable Rottweiler.

Avner would look at Eitan's mother, ashamed to admit that he was insanely jealous of Eitan, and that he wished his own mother was like Eitan's, including the motorcycle and the attitude. But Avner's mother did not ride a motorcycle. She didn't even drive a car. The word "dog" was forbidden in the house, and God forbid anyone mention a "Rottweiler." His mother would sit at home on her armchair, usually staring at an ambiguous spot on the wall. Sometimes he wanted to ask her why her fingers looked broken, but she would look at him as if she didn't even see him, and he lost his nerve time and again.

Luckily she didn't act that way all the time. When she took her medications properly, there were better days. She cooked, cleaned, ironed, baked, and even hugged her son. On days like that she talked matter-of-factly, almost like other mothers. But on other days she would say disturbing things.

Another memory arose mercilessly. He was talking with Eitan, inviting him to come over after school. He knew that he was taking a risk because he couldn't know ahead of time how his mother would be, but he so wanted Eitan to see that he also had a room full of toys so he ignored his fear. For many years afterward he never invited another friend over. Eitan came and, regrettably, his mother was not having a good day. She stared at her son and the strange boy he had brought with him and asked questions in an unknown language, "'Was ist Ihr Name?'"

When Eitan didn't understand that she was asking him his name and didn't reply, she didn't let it go but went on asking, "'Sprechen Die Deutsch?'" And when Eitan didn't answer that question either, because he didn't know German, she suddenly began to shout, "'Gevalt! Gevalt!'" And Eitan ran out of the house in time to miss her screaming, "'Raus' – "Out!'"

After that Avner kept to himself; he couldn't have a one-sided friendship. He couldn't be invited to his friends' houses without inviting them back. He gave up on a social life and didn't develop the necessary skills for socializing. Just like Eva, he hated the looks of pity, but unlike her, he didn't push his way into a laughing, noisy, lively group. Now, as he read the diary, Mrs. Reich's need to belong in society felt like a blow. He knew that he would never speak of this, not even with Nisim. Any explanation would have to come with too much exposure of his life's greatest pain. Suddenly he had a flash of an encouraging thought. Mrs. Reich had said a few times that pain must be locked away, otherwise you could go mad, which was exactly what he himself had been doing all his life. Somewhat reassured, he resumed reading.

***

My future as a literature lecturer was being formed during those years of study. I would observe and learn different professors' ways of teaching, and I learned a great deal from most of them. Here and there were those who it was better not to learn from, like for example, the lecturer for the myths of Israeli culture course. Now, writing this, I smile because the name of the course actually suited the instructor, who mostly addressed one such myth — that the Israeli man was supposed to love sports. That lecturer was primarily interested in international soccer games, which were broadcast on the radio and would manage his time and ours according to the soccer broadcast schedule. He would suggest that the lecturer before him finish his class fifteen minutes early, so that he could start and finish his own class fifteen minutes earlier, so that we all left happy: the lecturer before him, himself, and of course the students.

But apart from that, he left a real impression on me, because the myths that he spoke about touched my life in many different ways. He spoke about the myth of the Holocaust survivor as compared with the myth of the sabra, a topic that was very real then, and I myself taught those same myths years later. The sabra, according to common thought, was a masculine figure, rough, tanned, and authoritative; most of the time he was the officer of some patrol.

***

Avner felt difficulty breathing. He got up and opened the window.

He himself had never fit the sabra image. He even felt that he was the antithesis of it. He did not serve the military in combat or patrol, but rather doing clerical work; he didn't speak in a deep, bass voice, and he didn't drink or smoke. He was embarrassed to admit that he had been a virgin until a late age, while his few friends at that time had new conquests every day.

The day that he lost his virginity, with a woman whose name he didn't even know, he had completely erased from memory. Now he saw her in his mind's eye, dressed in a red bra and underwear, fleshy, and twice his age. More than anything he remembered the unpleasant smell of her breath of cheap cigarettes and alcohol. He had erased that day completely. He had not bragged to his friends about it, of course, because more than anything, he felt ashamed.

For years he bore that shame in his heart, not because of the particular woman or the place where the thing had happened, but because of his inability to meet girls, like the rest of his friends. They would hit on girls in every place possible. At the beach, at coffeeshops, on the street, even in the supermarket. He would observe them, wondering at their confidence in approaching unknown girls, and return home alone.

When he met Chaya, years later, he tried to impress her at first, so that she wouldn't notice his lack of self-confidence. He smiled to himself now when he thought of that first meeting. A friend had suggested that he meet her and he agreed, mostly because he was already despairing of ever meeting someone. He was so clumsy and heavy-handed in that meeting that he was sure that this pretty girl, Chaya, wouldn't want anything to do with him. But she didn't run away, not even when he spilled the juice that she had ordered on her dress, or when he was so shy that he remained silent for most of the evening. To this day he is not sure if he really fell in love with her or was just grateful to her for staying with him in spite of everything.

Within a short time he stopped trying to impress her and was just himself. Of course he didn't tell her about the day with the woman in the red bra. In time he opened up to her and told her about his mother. He even took her with him to visit her at the hospital. Chaya was pleasant, accepting, and understanding, but that only intensified the feeling that he had no spine.

The more she protected him, the more he felt trapped within himself, understanding how much he needed protecting, and concluding, then, that he wasn't a real man. Now, when he read about the myth of the sexy, masculine sabra, he felt that it must be a heavy load, to be like that, and was sure that even for those who lived up to it, it must be hard to maintain the image.

The existential need to embody that masculine strength, the hard road to earning the coveted title, and the daily war to hang on to your status, all of that seemed impossible to him. Now he wondered anxiously: why, out of everything that she had learned from her professors, had Eva specifically mentioned this? He took the diary, leafed back through it a little and took a deep breath. Here was the reason for mentioning the myth: Meir. She began with the fact that Meir was someone who lived on a kibbutz, a 'kibbutznik,' your garden variety sabra.

Avner even smiled when he thought of the kibbutznik-sabra, a smile of relief that helped him to re-close his Pandora's box. Until the next time.

CHAPTER FOURTEEN

Meir, the love of my life and my husband for nearly sixty years, always spoke proudly of his father as a hesitant, circumspect person. Throughout his life he considered every step and never acted recklessly, apart from the one time when he saw what was happening in the world and decided to leave everything and move his family to Palestine.

Meir always remembered his father's words, because over the years he repeated them again and again: "Sometimes you can afford to miss the train, but not in this case."

The family, as I mentioned, first settled on the kibbutz Mishmar HaAliya, then moved to what was then the small city of Tel Aviv, where Meir grew up. Back then the central square was a hill of sand; the city had not yet grown to its current, monstrous size. That was how he grew into a happy, loving man, with a hunger for life. A boy who grew up in a happy home with a warm family and played catch, dodge ball, "king of the castle," and jacks outside in the yard with other children.

He spent his childhood between school, the home on Dizengoff Street, and his parents' ice cream shop on the way to Allenby Street, right beside the square where the street curves west toward the sea. His parents' business flourished, thanks to the know-how and trade experience they brought with them from Germany. "Chocolate, mint, bubble gum!" — declared the lit-up sign over their little kiosk, as well as: "Ice cream? You came to the Reich place!"

Meir told how his parents stood there day after day, side by side, filling ice cream cones and betting amongst themselves.

"That boy, the one with the old lady on his arm, he'll want chocolate," said Mom. "You can tell from his face he has an appetite for chocolate."

"But the old lady, she'll want mint or some fruit flavor that doesn't exist." Dad would smile.

Meir's mom would reply, "Her? She doesn't eat ice cream; don't you know it isn't good for you?"

Meir was about ten years old when the first news arrived in Israel of what the Nazis were doing to the Jews of Poland. He remembered that evening as a kind of turning point in his life. His mother was dismissive of the broadcast on the big radio in their house.

"Rumors," she said to his father. "I don't believe that's happening."

His father listened but from that night on he developed a regular habit of sitting beside the radio to listen with great concentration.

Something of the happiness in the house never recovered. His father gathered information from the media and one day, at the beginning of 1940, he came home in shock, holding a booklet called, "The Holocaust of Jews in Poland," in which a leader of the Zionist movement had written that short of a miracle, there would be no Jews left on Polish soil, apart from the Great Cemetery. His father understood that his family who had remained in the diaspora were about to lose their lives in the most horrific way possible.

Meir's mother tried to keep up the sense of "business as usual" but nobody could deny what was happening when, three years later, the radio clearly reported the extermination of Jews in the Holocaust. The newspapers were also filled with hair-raising headlines about what was happening in the "enlightened" world. Meir believed that this was responsible for shortening his father's life, making him sick with severe kidney disease at a relatively young age.

The Tel Aviv municipality called for a large protest rally against the persecution of Jews in Germany and he remembered the demonstration as if it was yesterday. He was thirteen years old and stood there listening to the speeches. Most of them described the horrors in Europe. There were also those who still claimed that the whole thing amounted to a wave of rumors and none of it was actually happening, but the reality was a slap in the face. Representatives of the Joint arrived and told of tens of thousands murdered and of the annihilation of Jews everywhere.

In November 1942, when Meir was a youth, after his Bar Mitzvah, the Jewish Agency published an official report of the horrors, validated a month later when the Allied governments put out a joint statement on the extermination of Europe's Jews. That same night, Meir's father was taken to the hospital, and was only released a month later, blind in both eyes. Evidently the kidney disease that he suffered from had long been accompanied by diabetes, which affected his vision.

The happiness in the house was extinguished. Meir was growing up and engaged in what interests youths of that age: first loves, friends, first cigarettes, but all of that was overshadowed by the great sorrow and the news on the radio. Wanting to know everything, Meir asked questions and grew increasingly angry. Nobody was able to answer the big question, "Why?"

But all his father would say was, "It is just as I feared."

Meir rebelled. He was at that age when you stop accepting everything as it is, you ask questions and want to understand, look for a way and are unwilling to stay silent.

"Nobody is left there, no one!" he said to his parents, and was right. The family members, aunts and uncles and cousins and grandmother and grandfather from both sides, all of those who had covered their ears and eyes so as not to hear, not to see, and not to run for their lives, were tortured, burned, and suffocated.

Meir's big question hung in the air without an answer. "Where was God? What the hell was he so busy with that he didn't see the chosen people going up in flames?"

Meir heard conversations between his parents, who wanted to reassure their agitated son in light of the terrible news. Meanwhile, his older brother saw things differently. He refused to listen to the news, and every time the subject came up, he expressed restrained anger at those who had remained behind.

"You were still little. You don't remember how hard Dad tried to persuade them to leave." Almost every such conversation ended with his brother saying, "I can't feel sorry for fools."

Meir would listen to his brother but did not agree with him. For days he lingered at home, refusing to go to school and go on as if nothing had happened.

One day he heard his mother say to his father, "He will get a good education there, you'll see."

His father tried to protest at first, "What, let him go?"

His mother said that they had to think of the boy's future and that she knew of many families in crisis sending their children to the kibbutz so they could live a better life. "He already lived there for a year. They will be happy to have him back," she said and his father finally relented.

Meir actually liked the idea, but he wasn't so sure that the kibbutz members would receive him with open arms. He was afraid that they might be angry at his family for leaving to the city. But indeed the kibbutz welcomed him warmly, and perhaps it worked in his favor that the kibbutz was seeking young people to make up the community's next generation, and even sought out additional children to take in. So Meir returned to live at Mishmar HaAliya, as a newcomer.

Meir told me many times about his first days on the kibbutz and how he felt like an outsider. But he had a strong character, and his humor and intelligence made it so that the kibbutz kids soon accepted him as one of their own. For his part, he loved the communal lifestyle, the sense of brotherhood between people, and the direct connection with the land.

He grew up, enlisted to the military, and split his vacation time between his parents and his room at the kibbutz. His father held on for a few more years and died a short time after his brother was married.

For Meir, God had ceased to exist. His father's premature death broke his mother's heart and his brother's married life didn't work and disintegrated in an ugly way, and that added to his great anger at God who had ignored the pain of his family and people. Life on the secular kibbutz suited him very well.

***

Avner sighed so loud that he was sure Nisim could hear him from outside. He so identified with Meir. Exactly like me, he said to himself, exactly like me.

***

On the kibbutz, between the smell of the chicken coop, the cow shed, and the fertilizer, Meir learned to work the land, plough and harvest, milk the cows, and decided he wanted to study the land of Israel so that he could get to know the work better. He worked long hours in the sun, not thinking of its risks, and his light skin grew tanned. Maybe the seeds of his wild future had already been planted. His soft hands became calloused from the tools, his shoes took on the smell of the cowshed and the chicken coop. He learned quickly. He milked the cows skillfully, collected the eggs in the chicken coop, and became as much a kibbutznik as if he had been born there.

Then he met me that day of the opening ceremony for the Tel Aviv University Institute of Natural Science. Later on he left the kibbutz, and together we rented a tiny apartment in Givatayim, which we bought several years later.

As we grew closer, I knew that the moment of truth would come sooner or later. Until now, I hadn't even asked him if he had met Maria during his years on the kibbutz. I had also been there to see her there more than once, but I never saw him on those visits; I'm sure that if I had seen him there, I would have fallen in love with him then. But now that we knew each other well, it was clear that I had to do something, that it was no longer possible to avoid the truth and hide behind vague statements that reassured my uneasy conscience, the sharp pain, the blatant lie. I knew that there was no choice, I could no longer use the excuse of being a refugee. I knew that if I wanted him to stay with me, I would have to reveal my secret.

For many nights I couldn't fall asleep. In my nightmares I dreamed of Rachela, a freckled kibbutz girl with a long braid who wore shorts and a khaki shirt and looked like the perfect girl for my Meir. She returned to my dreams many times and I would wake up and feel a kind of emptiness in my belly. I felt that hollow growing and growing, as if someone was pulling at my guts and might soon tear at my liver and my kidneys and pierce my heart.

Until then I could easily justify my silence, but no more. I could not tie my life to that of this strong, tanned man with the constant smile and not tell him a thing.

I had no doubt that he would leave me.

For Rachela.

Because of the secret.

For days I planned how and when to tell him. The date came and finally it happened, but not as I had planned, suddenly and unexpectedly, like so many things in life. It was a pleasant, sunny day in mid-Spring. We went for a day trip with a little cooler filled with sandwiches, cake for dessert, drinks, a tablecloth, and disposable plates. We even took a mat to sit on the soft sand of the Nahariya beach to watch the sunset. We took the bus and arrived toward evening. Meir spread out the mat on the soft sand, and on it the tablecloth and our meal and opened a bottle of red wine he had hidden in the cooler without my noticing. In that moment it seemed like anything was possible.

He took a sip of the wine, and stopped my hand from reaching for the food. He pulled out a little box, and his eyes sparkled. "Will you marry me?" he asked, and hot tears of happiness streamed from my eyes.

As evening came on, the red sun's last rays of light glowed from the horizon, as if promising to return tomorrow, and then set. In the cover of darkness I shivered, both from the chill of evening and his burning touch. I trembled all over with the excitement of the first time, but also from what I planned to say. The moment of truth had arrived; I knew it was time.

I stroked his head, and asked him to wait, and I sat down on the mat, by the light of the moon. Quietly, with a downcast expression, I said, "Meir, I have to tell you something important. My dear mother wasn't Jewish… but," I hurried to add. "My father had an impressive beard, and I went to a Jewish school."

I was silent, afraid of his response. He stroked my head and did not say a thing, so I went on talking. I told him about Anna, our house, and the special neighbors we had. "Maria was like family to me, the only one that I have left," I told him. "I always wanted to ask you if you happened to meet her on the kibbutz… after all, she lives in Mishmar HaAliya."

Meir looked thoughtful. "Maria? I don't recall any woman by the name of Maria at Mishmar HaAliya, and the kibbutz isn't a big place, everyone knows everyone."

His response surprised me for a moment, but then I realized. "Of course! She changed her name from Maria to Mira. Maybe you knew her by that name?"

"Ahh, of course I remember her!" cried Meir. "A tall, thin woman with long, light hair, right?"

"That's her." I smiled.

Meir went on, "She lived there with Shimon Levy, he was a widower. The kibbutz was touched by how close she was with his family and how his children accepted her so warmly but they knew almost nothing about her, just that she had come with the Youth Aliyah, all alone…"

The conversation about Maria made me burst into tears again, and Meir gallantly pulled a handkerchief out of nowhere, wiped my remaining tears and looked at me with a kind smile. "It's not easy to expose a secret," he said. "Not easy at all. But now it will be easier for you, I promise."

Through my tears I whispered, "If you want to leave, if you go, I'll understand."

He looked me in the eyes, hugged me, and whispered, "Go? Where would I go?"

"In general… just leave… me…" I replied.

Meir burst out laughing. "Silly girl! That's crazy," he said. "I do indeed want to go, down the aisle, with you and only you."

"But I have no papers," I mumbled. "I have no identification. Just the immigration document with the number and name, and a picture that the man from the agency took, but no papers to prove who I am."

He kept on smiling and said, "Who you are? What do you mean? You're my future wife."

"But you must understand," I went on whispering. "Once I thought that a father with the beard of a rabbi was proof enough, but when I checked what the law says, I found out that…"

He stopped me. "You don't have to say anything. No need for any papers. I know who you are and I love what I see and nothing else matters."

I looked at him and a shadow of anger appeared in his eyes.

"Hell," he said. "You've been through hell while in the rest of the world children your age were playing kids' games, eating nice food, and sleeping in a warm bed. I don't need anything. What you have been through is enough for a whole lifetime of an entire people."

"But what about the wedding?" I asked. "How?" It's not that I hadn't thought of conversion, but Maria's attempts and struggles with the religious authorities, along with the fear that I wouldn't manage to learn everything that was required felt insurmountable. "I am afraid of being a refugee again. Maria, she also tried but couldn't do it…"

He listened to me and replied, "There's no need, it doesn't matter."

Today, looking back, I know that Meir didn't press me to do anything because he was angry at the religion and the establishment. He thought that every Holocaust survivor deserved to be accepted by the state. He didn't want me to have to negotiate with the establishment. He was also very angry at God, to the point that anything relating to religion put him off.

But today I can express remorse. Maybe I should have tried. But I was afraid. I suspect that I have grown more self-confident over the years. At that time I would look around and feel that I was not like everyone else. Today, in retrospect, I know that I could have relatively easily solved the problem. But I couldn't do it then. It must be understood that those who went through what I did carried pain, struggle, and fear in their hearts, and for most of them it is hard to describe in words.

Perhaps now, after so many years, I can release myself from the doubt and the need to keep this big secret, from you, Mr. Bock, and I thank you from the bottom of my heart that with your help, this will come full circle.

***

Avner reread the last sentence. She addressed him by his name. Coming full circle? Thanks to him? What was she referring to? Stirred up and curious he went on reading, hoping that the answer to his question would not be long in coming.

***

While we were sitting by the sea in the moonlight, Meir said to me, "Let it remain as it is; I don't care about having a religious wedding. We can do it some other way."

On my wedding day, in spring of 1954, I wore a white dress with no veil. Meir's parents really wanted to hold the ceremony in their synagogue on Ben Yehuda Street in Tel Aviv where Meir's father used to pray, but for obvious reasons we couldn't do as they wished: no Rabbi would marry us.

Meir's mother knew that her son was not a believer, but she claimed that it was what his father would have wanted and it was hard for her to accept that we had no intention of marrying according to Jewish custom. Meir had a long argument with her, beginning with the explanation that there would be no Christian ceremony just as there would be no Jewish ceremony, with the explanation that I was a solitary bride, who had lost her whole family.

"You have an opportunity here to do a good deed, to accept her and give her a warm home which she so badly needs," he said to his mother, and she finally gave in.

We rented the sports hall at the school not far from his parents' house for next to nothing, hired a photographer, and invited a few of our friends. Meir's mother wanted to invite a few friends too, and we honored her wish. Meir's mother prepared a casual menu, which included crackers, salted fish, and a few cakes she baked herself. We signed an agreement between us, without any ceremony.

A few years later, when Meir and I travelled to Romania, we ran into a friend of Meir's in Bucharest, who had become more religious when he emigrated from Israel and belonged to the local Chabad organization. Naively, he told us that the community's rabbi would marry Jewish couples without closely checking their "credentials." We decided to seize the opportunity and make our marriage official in light of the religion. This did not make me Jewish, but it made it possible for our children, born later, to present their parents' marriage certificate when it came time for them to register their own marriages with the rabbinate.

***

A cold wind blew lightly through the window which Avner had opened earlier. The great love which he was reading about now lifted his spirits. He thought to himself that if there was such love in the world, then anything really was possible. Outside the window he saw Nisim bent over the flowers.

"Hey, buddy," he called to him from the office.

Nisim turned to him, tucked his sidelocks behind his ears and smiled broadly.

"What's going on, what's up, what's happening?" Avner said imitating him.

Nisim laughed and said, "What's happening is that these roses, if I don't take care of them properly, will die."

"They look fantastic, leave them alone."

"What are you talking about?" Nisim replied. "They need fertilizer. It's the season for fertilizer. Yesterday I bought phosphorus and potassium, so I should give that to them now."

"You're amazing," said Avner, without a hint of irony. "You are so hard-working, you don't even rest for so much as a second."

"Listen," Nisim replied, modestly ignoring the compliments. "We also need to think about pesticides, you won't believe how bad the aphids are."

"You give them such dedicated care, nothing will happen to them," said Avner and thought to himself: the roses, like people, just need a little attention, warmth, faith — and the sky's the limit.

CHAPTER FIFTEEN

I didn't want to live on the kibbutz. Even though Maria lived there and the idea of living close to her was compelling, the thought of all the kibbutz members gossiping about us, knowing we were not officially married disturbed me. At first, Maria tried to convince me.

"Let them talk! What do you care?" she said, but I felt the need to start my new life in a fresh place where they didn't know us and where they wouldn't ask too many questions.

Meir also told me that people on the kibbutz wouldn't really care if we were properly married under Jewish law but I wanted to leave and he, as he would continue to do throughout the sixty years that followed, agreed. It makes me smile to recall the time that Meir told the kids that when he met me, he understood that from then on he would decide the big things, while all the smaller things would be up to me.

"What can I say?" He laughed. "Until now there simply haven't been any big decisions."

That was my Meir. Always willing to do as I asked, without so much as a word of argument. After we moved to Givatayim, Meir found satisfying work which made him very happy: he was an instructor at the "Avshalom Institute" in Tel Aviv and liked it not just because he was teaching his favorite subject — exploring Israel's flora and fauna, but also because the nature of the studies there did not include any exams or diploma studies.

Meir always told me that the young people who come to study at the institute were people who love our land with all their heart, and teaching them was what made his work so special. As the years passed he also joined the foundation for Israel studies and even wrote articles for the journal '*Kadmoniot*.'

Our little apartment in Givatayim was close enough to Meir's workplace and eventually to mine too, but that was not the only reason we loved living there. There was something special about the city, which was very close to the bustling Tel Aviv but at the same time quiet and stable. At that time we dreamed of owning our own home; I imagined a little corner, a curtain, a carpet, an oven and stove: a modest but thrilling dream.

In time, we saved up money and bought the place. It was just a two-bedroom apartment but it was our whole world. The little entrance was also the living room, where Meir hung shelves on the wall. Over the years those shelves filled up with my files, my writings, and extensive literature from every field. As a wedding gift from Meir's family, we received a big brown grandfather clock, which made the apartment look dignified. I loved that clock very much and I took it with me on the day that I closed the door of that house behind me for the last time. I will get to that yet. The kitchen was done in a light green Formica. There was a wooden table decorated with geometric shapes and just two chairs. Only years later did we add two more. Meir built our bed himself and covered our bedroom walls with wallpaper in soft colors. A small chest of drawers and brown wardrobe that we acquired inexpensively completed my vision. We left the other room empty, and it remained desolate for a long time. If it could have talked it would have certainly joined in the chorus of voices of those urging us to have children.

At the time I was ambivalent. Who would want to bring children into such a world? I thought to myself. I am not proud of it, but that was how I felt, true and painful as it may be. The world seemed to be a place where the adults could not protect their young, helpless children, and to bring them into the world seemed the most egotistical thing I could imagine.

I think that for years I believed that Maria did not have children for that exact reason. Only later did I understand that she simply was unable to. Me, I was deterred by my fear of bringing a child into the world and being unable to protect him. Anna had not been yet ten years old when my mother, apart from holding her and crying bitterly, could not do anything to save her.

Two years prior, on the 10th of September 1952, Israel and West Germany signed a reparations agreement, stipulating that the Germans would send Israel three billion marks as compensation for the suffering and material damage caused to the Jews in the Holocaust.

I remember listening to the radio and thinking that I couldn't be hearing right. Compensation? What compensation? If the money was returned, even so huge a sum, what about my sister? My parents? Would this dirty money bring any relief for the soul? How was it possible?

The two years that passed did not change my mind. But when I met Meir, he actually spoke favorably about the agreement. He claimed that it was time for the oppressor to pay, and to pay a lot. He said that this money could help to build houses, pave roads, and set the economy on its feet. There were vicious arguments in the house, and we never did reach an agreement. But the conflict between us was not just about the money. Meir wanted children and I didn't. As I already said, I'm not proud of it, but I couldn't live with the thought that I would have children and be unable to take care of them.

If I had been under the impression that only in the diaspora did disaster prevent parents from protecting their children, an act of Satan in March of 1954, proved that tragedy could strike anywhere. A bus was driving from Eilat to Tel Aviv carrying passengers returning from a celebration of five years since the flying of the Ink Flag.[7]

The bus carried men, women, and children, and even two soldiers who, tragically, placed their weapons on the upper shelves of the bus where packages were stored. At a bend in the road, on a route through the hilly Eastern Negev, terrorists opened fire on the bus, hitting the driver. The bus did not fall into the abyss but remained stuck on the side of the slope. The

---

7   The Ink Flag was a handmade flag raised in March 1949 marking a
     victory for Israel in the 1948 Arab-Israeli war

wounded driver managed to open the bus doors, allowing the passengers to escape, but everyone who got off was shot to death immediately. This story, told dozens of times on the radio, took me back to the ditches, the pits, the cold, the terror, and to the blood which flowed like water through the endless snow.

But in case that wasn't enough, the next day the newspapers told of a girl and a boy, brother and sister, who remained sitting on the bus and hadn't gotten out. Their parents, who were with them, had been killed. I remember the terrible thought: How were the parents killed? Did they try to escape from the bus and leave the children behind? I tormented myself with these thoughts but I couldn't get rid of them. The news gave no explanation and I never got an answer to that awful question.

What they *did* say on the news was that when it eventually grew quiet, the brother asked his sister, "Are they gone?" That very moment a terrorist got on the bus and shot him in the head. His sister, who saw everything, was saved because she was hidden by the body of one of the soldiers. The boy didn't die, but lost consciousness, which never came back. Years later I heard that he had died, thirty years after the tragedy.

I don't know if I am managing to explain myself well enough, and maybe it sounds bad, to not want to bring children into the world. But every time I thought of a helpless baby, completely dependent on me, the fear I felt was paralyzing. I did not believe that I could handle it. It's not something rational that can be explained in words. In fact, precisely because of what I went through I should have wanted to ensure the next generation, but fear is often irrational. In any case, I was considered unusual, strange, not a real woman. Nosy neighbors gossiped about me behind my back, pointed at me, and clicked their tongues. "That poor woman," I heard them say. "It must be because of the Nazis, that's why she can't have children."

I remember once, sitting on the bus on my way home, two neighbors sat behind me not seeing me as they spoke amongst themselves. They gossiped about everyone in the building.

"That one is hunched, one of her legs is shorter than the other, and that one is mean, she has a witchy face, and that one thinks she is twenty and dresses like a prostitute, and that one, the Holocaust survivor, I heard that the Nazis raped her, that's why they don't have children."

I can't express in words what a terrible memory that last sentence brought up for me. The kind of memories that I have simply erased over the years. For instance, when I was a little girl, maybe seven, my mother sent me to the neighborhood bakery to get a loaf of fresh bread. I really loved the little trips to the bakery, and more than once Mom scolded me for coming home with a loaf of bread that I had taken a bite out of because I couldn't withstand the temptation of that wonderful smell. That day, in late afternoon, it was already pretty dark outside. On my way to the store, I didn't notice the footsteps behind me. When I heard them it was too late. A rough hand grabbed me, and before I could scream, I found myself in an abandoned shelter. A man, not much bigger than Anna stood before me, but at that time he seemed huge and scary. He didn't do anything to me, just asked me to touch him and I refused and fled.

I never told my mother about it. Maybe in my heart I felt that I was somehow at fault, or maybe I was just afraid that she would no longer allow me to go to the bakery anymore. I suppressed the memory for years until hearing the gossipy neighbor saying that I must have been raped. The other neighbor replied, "No, I heard something else; that Meir of hers, he just looks like Paul Newman but he's not much of a man, if you understand my meaning."

That evening I called Maria. I needed to consult with her about this matter, to hear her opinion. In retrospect, if I could have undone that conversation I would have. What kind of silly nonsense came over me, to ask Maria, of all people, such questions? I should have understood by then. But she was like a mother to me, and my despair was so great that I wasn't thinking clearly.

"It's kind of funny to ask me such a question," she replied. "Even a little ironic, no?"

I apologized from the depths of my heart. In my stupidity I had thought that she didn't have children by choice. I apologized again and again and even added, in my defense, "I didn't know, my dear Maria, I am so sorry."

"It's all right," Maria reassured me. "You couldn't have known. And truthfully? It's complicated… on the one hand it really is a crazy world, but on the other, if I could have children, I probably would, happily."

"And the fear?" I asked.

"Fear and parenting come together but in the end, the laughter of children is the answer to everything. Their laughter could heal the pain of the entire world."

A short while later I became pregnant for the first time. To this day, I think that being a mother, apart from being the best feeling that exists on the face of the earth, is an almost impossible mission, an unwritten commitment to protect them from everything. But every time I heard them laugh, it felt like a victory. I think that I managed, at least partially, to protect them, because I made sure they lacked nothing and kept them from unnecessary knowledge that could disturb their peaceful lives. But it is hard for me that I will die without telling them the whole truth.

I hope, Mr. Bock, that you will find the right words to do so. I imagine you think that I am selfish and that I am asking you to do what I could not manage. There is truth in that, Mr. Bock, however, I have two responses. One is that the truth, as hard as it will be, will no longer have so hard an impact on their lives now that they themselves are already married and parents to children. The second, and more important of the two, is that I believe that after you finish reading you will understand why you were chosen for this task, and may even be happy to do it in the spirit of atonement.

***

Avner leaned back in his chair and breathed deeply. Even after everything he had read until this point, a lot remained unclear. He was surprised. Along with the surprise he asked himself: what did she know about me that I don't even know? Though he did not yet have a satisfactory answer, it was clear that this was no coincidence. If until now he might have plausibly explained to himself why it was that Mrs. Reich had chosen him specifically, now it was clear as day: this was no random choice.

This was surprising, bordering on alarming. Atonement? What was it he needed to atone for? Had she come to teach him a lesson because of his problematic relationship with his mother? He immediately dismissed that crazy idea. After all, Mrs. Reich would have no way of knowing about his relationship with his mother. So what atonement was she talking about?

He took a sip of water from the glass on the table. Why torment himself with guessing? He had been trying to figure it out for two days now even while it was very likely that the answer was written in the diary, black on white. There was no point guessing. He just needed to go on reading through to the end. With a heavy sigh he read the last lines and his heart ached for this woman who, to the end of her days, was unable to feel whole, just like him.

***

My eldest, my daughter, my pride and great love, was born three years after Meir and I moved in together. I called her Hannah, my darling girl, Hanna'leh, and soon enough we shortened it to her nickname, my little Hani. I very much wanted to name her after my mother, but I didn't want to give her a name with a foreign sound, so I called her after my beloved sister. I worried greatly at first if there might be bad luck in it, God forbid, to name her after my sister who was killed at a young age, but Meir reassured me, "Hannah is not exactly Anna, it is in memory of her, but it isn't the same." Three years later I gave birth to my son, a charming, lively child full of constant energy. I called him Yosef, after my dear father.

I worked hard to raise them calmly and with confidence and, as much as possible, to avoid the anxieties frequently associated with being a mother. Sometimes there were reasons for my maternal concern, regarding their health. Yossi was a healthy, happy, and smiling boy, but was short and thin, so I took him to the best doctors when I was afraid he might not be growing properly. But there was no reason for concern: Yossi might have been a bit short, but not unusually so.

The specialist doctor who checked him said, "He is a smart, perceptive child, and healthy. He will grow at his own pace."

So I tried to relax. I managed to get over my fears and let them visit their friends and go on activities and trips with the school. But I paid a heavy price for it, a price of worry that ate away at me. Every time they went out I would remain awake for hours, listening to the sounds of the house, praying that I would hear the key in the door already and know that they had returned home.

When Yossi enlisted to the army and chose to serve in a combat unit, I was haunted, lying awake at night, consumed by worry. I would listen to the news on the radio every hour, finding myself smiling when the newscast began with some mundane crime: some corruption or another, robbery, tax evasion, or best of all — reports on the latest heat wave. Anything so long as it wasn't: "In an incident involving IDF soldiers…"

Hani was a wonderful girl from the first moment, mature and independent, with opinions of her own and a strong artistic side. Yossi, on the other hand, was a mischievous boy, always pulling pranks. He put that energy into playing and fell in love with sports. Today, he is a journalist and sportswriter. Meanwhile, Hani now has a clay and plaster studio of her own with dozens of regular students. She sculpts and draws and many of her works have been displayed proudly in our home in Givatayim.

I often joked with her about how much mess her work creates. Sometimes they would leave bits of clay on the floor, but my Hani didn't care. I was worried that the dirt would bring germs and disease with it, but she would laugh out loud and say that nobody had ever died from a little dirt. Her laugh reassured me and I relaxed.

After Meir passed away, I moved to live in an assisted living facility and put one of Hani's sculptures on the dresser in my room. It is a sculpture of half a woman. The first time I saw it, it gave me shivers. There was something in it that cried out but at the same time had a kind of pure beauty. I remember my granddaughter Alma looking at it one day and asking her mother why the sculpture wasn't finished.

Hani looked at her lovingly and said, We are never entirely whole, are we? We are always incomplete…"

~

CHAPTER SIXTEEN

I, Eva Reich, Holocaust survivor, was accepted as an employee at Bar Ilan University's department for Israeli literature. It makes me smile to think what Hitler and his friends would say about that. I think it fair to assume that they would not particularly love the idea of teaching Jewish students Hebrew literature at an Israeli university. If that isn't a victory, I don't know what is.

I loved my job: I loved to teach, I loved my students, and more than anything, I loved the Hebrew language. My students knew to speak proper Hebrew around me including getting the male and female subject pronouns right. Still, sometimes when I heard them using slang, I would just smile to myself and not say anything. I would look at them with great affection, sabras born into freedom, and just try to share my love of the Hebrew language.

In my opinion, it's a language of triumph, and we must be deserving of it. I taught my students to discern between different forms of literature, we discussed poetry and prose, and together we learned to differentiate between the hero and the antihero, between fantasy and reality. I devoted a whole section to teaching them about allegory, which typically involves unanswered questions and symbolic meaning.

My life story is, to some degree or another, a kind of allegory.

∗∗∗

Avner smiled at the comparison. A life story with unanswered questions? Hey, Mrs. Reich, he said to himself with a broad smile, get in line, I practically invented that!

∗∗∗

I was very attached to the young students, Israeli-born and post-military, who came to study literature. I have no doubt that a large number of them were themselves writers and I was sure they would have a wonderful future. One of the most talented among them was Oded. I didn't know who he was at first, but when I found out, I was moved to the point of tears.

Oded wrote short stories and funny pieces, and from time to time he would bring them to me to read and give my opinion. He had wonderful ways of expressing his ideas and I was delighted to read them. For example, he once wrote that poverty is much more common to human reality than economic stability. I always had to read and reread his words in order to understand them fully.

If I may stray from the sequence of events for a moment, I would like to relay a funny incident. In one of the classes we read a passage which included mention of a man as "lame."

One of the students, who was not born here, raised his hand and asked what made the man uncool.

I didn't understand his question, but Oded explained, "It's not a judgment of him, the man is *lame*, as in disabled, can't walk."

I was happy for the young man who, even though he was not born in Israel, had managed to learn the slang. I was also pleased that it gave me the chance to teach him proper Hebrew.

Ultimately I discovered who Oded Levi was, and it moved me immeasurably. He was the grandson of Shimon Levi, Maria's partner. She had told me of him more than once and was as proud of him as if he were her own grandson.

I remember her telling me that he studied at Bar Ilan, but it had never occurred to me that he was my own student.

I have more to say about Maria and the wise things that she told me, thanks to which I wound up following up on parts of my past, but since I already mentioned Oded, I will say that I met him at Maria's funeral one year ago. She was very old, ninety-six when she died. I myself will not die young, obviously. Maybe it is true what they say, that what doesn't kill you makes you stronger. Here I am, an old woman of eighty-five, and apart from the memory difficulties starting to show signs, I feel good.

At Maria's funeral, as I said, I met Oded. We had both loved Maria, and she had been a unique figure person for both of us. She was buried in Kibbutz Mishmar HaAliya, where they permit burial of those for whom Judaism is in the heart and soul, if not on paper.

***

Avner felt slightly light-headed. "So not only did she live here for a short time and I don't remember her, she was right here, not so long ago," he said to himself.

He tried to recall Maria's funeral but could not. He reread the last sentence and tried to think, but the picture did not become clearer. He thought to himself that there had been a lot of funerals in the past year. No wonder it was hard for him to remember a particular one. He considered asking Nisim if he remembered something like that, after all, Nisim had a fantastic memory.

He smiled to himself remembering how he had once told him Chaya's birthday, and to remind him every year so that what had happened once would not happen again. Should he bother asking now? After all, Nisim was not willing to help bury non-Jews here. Maybe it was better not to re-awaken that old argument between them?

Avner decided not to say anything and opened the folder in which the funerals from the last year were recorded. He didn't find anything there, so he looked for the file from the previous year. Within a few moments he found Maria's name, which had been changed to Mira, along with her partner's family name, even though they had never been married, Mira

Levi. He looked at the date. One year and one month ago.

Suddenly he had a flash of memory, clear as a window from which someone had just wiped away many years' worth of dust. He recalled visiting his mother the following day. He paid so few visits to his mother that he could remember the details of each one. But it wasn't a coincidence that he had gone to visit his mother then; he had gone to ask her again.

That day, a year and a month ago, he had carried out the ceremony for Maria-Mira Levi. Heavy rain fell all morning and he was worried that it would complicate things. Luckily, it stopped a little before the funeral and the skies grew clear. At the end of the funeral, an older woman approached him, complimented him on the dignified service, told him that she had known the deceased very well, that she had been a Righteous gentile, without medals or certificates, and told Avner that he had done a huge mitzvah. He thanked her wholeheartedly.

She had turned to leave, and rain began to fall again. "The rain here is unexpected," she said. "One moment the sky is clear and the next it is crying along with me."

He had wanted to reply but the rain grew stronger and he didn't run after her. He smiled at her and turned to go back to his office, when suddenly she turned, right by the gate beside the words "petting zoo" she called after him, "You look just like your father!"

He wanted to ask her how she knew his father, but she had already gone out through the gate.

The next day he had gone to visit his mother.

He found her sitting on a bench, warming her bones in the warm sun during that season of confusing weather. On the bench beside her sat two nurses dressed in white, one fat and short, the other very old, and Avner heard them talking about the weather.

"It's really impossible to know what to wear in this weather," said the fat one.

The older one replied, "Yes, just yesterday it rained, not even rain, hail! And today it's a heatwave."

The fat one got up from her seat and rearranged the plaid blanket over Avner's mother's legs. When he approached, she said, "Good that you're here. You should come more often, or she may as well be completely finished."

He smiled faintly at the nurse, and as the two of them walked away he heard the older one say, "She's done for as it is."

Avner sat beside his mother and she looked at him dimly. "You got thinner," she said. "There's bread under the mattress in the room."

Avner did not reply. He knew that there was no point in answering, and that she offered bread to anyone who sat with her. At first, when he visited her regularly, the nurses would tell him about the moldy bread that they would find underneath her pillow and that she would offer it to all of the other residents. His heart would fill with a kind of pride then, that she shared her treasure with others, but with time the pride turned to pity, and finally a kind of painful acceptance of the situation. Now, too, he didn't reply, only took her hand in his and went on sitting quietly beside her, thinking if and how to ask her in spite of everything.

Two young men were walking on the path in front of them. "What a waste it was yesterday in Eurovision," Avner heard the dark-haired one tell his friend.

"Yes," replied the redhead. "What shits. They just hear "Israel" and don't even listen to the song. Shits, I'm telling you, everyone is antisemitic. If there is a reason I moved to Israel, it's that antisemitism, even in the United States."

Avner didn't hear the rest of the conversation, because the two got farther away and approached an old man, who rejoiced. Avner wondered if they were his grandchildren, and how strange that one had red hair while the other had dark hair, and he felt a sharp pain in his heart when he thought how he had never brought his girls to meet his mother. He hadn't even told them about her state. Only his wife Chaya knew, and from time to time, at least at the beginning, she would encourage him to go visit.

It touched him that Chaya seemed to care, but even she said that it was better not to tell the girls. Avner knew that Chaya was afraid of "what will people say," and the truth was that they'd never ever had a deep conversation about it. He knew that she would rather not tell anyone, maybe even feared that the madness might be contagious. Now Avner saw the two boys kiss the old man on the cheek and he smiled warmly at them. His heart ached.

Avner turned to his mother, raised her chin in his hands and looked into her eyes.

"There was a woman who came to my work yesterday, Mom," he said.

"Great," she said.

"You understand me, Mom?" he asked, amazed, and was sure that she was nodding her head. Somewhat encouraged, he went on, "The woman said that I looked like Dad, do you remember Dad?"

A shadow of happiness flashed momentarily through her blue eyes and she mumbled something unclear. Maybe she said Nahum's name?

"I really am similar to him, at least on the outside," he said. The thought crossing his mind that if he really was like his father he wouldn't be such a coward, and would check the facts properly. He knew that he was just asking his mother these questions now to reassure himself that look, here he was, asking and checking. But he knew that he wasn't making a real effort to investigate his origins because he was afraid of the answers.

He looked into his mother's eyes again and saw a lingering shadow of happiness there. He thought that he should not spoil the moment, that this was a rare moment, but did not stop himself. "Do you think I look like Dad?" he asked quietly, and indeed the moment faded.

His mother's face flushed and her expression became hazy again.

The fat nurse suddenly appeared behind him and with a half-smile said, "Don't upset her. When she's upset, it can take her hours to return to herself. We don't want her all disoriented, do we?"

***

For almost forty years I worked at the university. It wasn't easy to adapt to innovations and technology, and it took me a long time to manage to move from a chalk board to a slide projector and eventually, computerized presentations, but Meir helped me as best he could and sometimes my children and later my grandchildren, as well as my students helped too. I learned to use the computer, and in time I even learned to surf the internet and I have more to say about that later on.

Things at home continued on as usual. Meir was happy with his work, the children were growing and developing, and our little nest was warm and cozy. But I still had my secret, and there were days when I felt tortured by it.

In the evenings, when the children were small, we would sit together in the living room and listen to the radio. When they played the hit parade, we would guess which of the songs would make it to the "listener's choice" segment and cheer when Hani guessed right, time and again. When the kids got bigger and there was television, we would watch our favorite shows together, and Yossi would ask Hani to guess who the killer was in the series/show "Columbo," even before the detective in the trench coat had set to work.

We had many of these little customs that make a family. Apart from listening to the radio or watching television together, Meir would also play "memory of the week." According to the rules of the game, once a week, we would sit, all four of us and each one had to tell something nice from the week, ideally something related to the whole family.

I feel tears of joy spring to my eyes when I recall Hani, a little girl with two long braids, sitting on the couch and telling us that the sweetest thing that had happened to her this week was a flute party. Hani wasn't especially musical, I must say, but as part of her school program she participated in the flute club. That same week, the teacher had put on a flute concert in the little hall beside their school. Hani stood on the stage with the rest of the children, and I am afraid she was faking it for most of the performance, but she looked so sweet to me that I really didn't care. Hani went on to say that she was happy to see us in the audience.

Meir smiled proudly. "Your mother sat taller than everyone so that no one there would miss that this amazing girl is her daughter."

We all laughed when Yossi imitated me, sitting in the hall at the edge of my chair, upright and looking around to make sure everyone saw me.

Yossi also had endless things to share, like the time he said that the sweetest thing that had happened to him that week was when I took them to the sea in Tel Aviv. I didn't have a car or a driver's license, but I made sure my children did not miss out on anything. I took them to shows, to science exhibitions, and to the beach.

"There were sand in my sandwich." Yossi laughed, and I, so touched by the fact that he had chosen that trip to the beach as the sweetest thing of the week, didn't bother to correct his Hebrew.

One time, when it was Meir's turn to tell something sweet, he looked at me with a smile and said, "Your mother, she is always worrying about you. For example, she makes sure that you won't be hurt by germs, like when I saw her put a fork into a loaf of bread, lighting the stove and burning all the germs from the bread."

That's how Meir was. He saw my fears and extreme worry as the sweetest thing that happened that week. "You are amazing," I told him, "You make every bad thing good."

When the children asked that I, too, say something sweet from the week, I didn't know what to choose. There were so many things but I was also afraid that it was all fragile and might suddenly fall apart.

Finally, I chose. "You know how happy you made me this week?" I asked. "The other day I sat down to prepare for the class at the university and I heard little footsteps behind my back and I felt you looking at what I was reading."

The children looked at me in embarrassment. "You heard us?" they asked. I smiled.

"And you aren't mad?"

"Not only am I not mad," I replied. "But I choose that as the sweetest thing this week. You know why? Because you are curious and smart children!"

I remember their happy faces, but also Meir's expression which said: you also transform everything into something good, Eva'leh, you too.

The four of us accumulated many hours of contentment and pleasure and I felt a twinge in my heart when I recalled the time when I had not wanted to have children.

We also had a custom in which every night before sleep, one of us would tell the children a story. Meir loved to tell them stories from his past in the once-small city of Tel Aviv. He would tell of people from the city, the little shops which became big businesses, the plaza that had been sand, and later, grass and then the fountain, and every one of his stories was seasoned with a smile and his limitless good humor.

When it was my turn to tell them a story, I would usually take a book off the shelves from our collection and read them various fairy tales. In truth, there were stories which I didn't see as suitable for kids, so we didn't acquire such books, but rather other legends and adventure stories in abundance. I always looked for a story that they might learn something from, but most of all I wanted to find ones we could enjoy. I really loved Alice in Wonderland by Louis Carroll and from time to time I would be amused by the thought of my aunt Alice in the title role.

On particularly cold nights, when there was nothing on TV that we all wanted to watch, we would sit and chat with the children. Each of them would tell about something from school and occasionally read us a story from their reading. One evening, we were all sitting, covered by a blanket, and Hani got up and took out the family photo album. We leafed through it, laughing over chubby baby Hani, and proud of Yossi in his elite soccer uniform. In older pictures, my children looked and exclaimed.

"Wow, Mom, did you really hold that crooked tower in your hands?"

I smiled at them. "Anyone who's ever visited Pisa took that photo," I said.

"And here is the Eiffel Tower," said Yossi.

"And this is Big Ben." Hani surprised me with her knowledge.

"Mom, is this a synagogue?" Yossi asked about a photo of me inside a church.

I was quiet for a moment but Meir answered for me, "That's a church. It's like a synagogue, but for Christians."

"What are Christians?" Hani asked and Meir answered her instead of me again.

"Christians are people whose religion is Christianity, just like the Jews practice Judaism and the Muslims practice Islam."

"Mom, who are they?" Hani asked, and I told her about her grand-mother and grandfather and of Anna.

"You are named for her, my dear," I said, hiding a tear.

"But why did you name Yossi after your father and not me after your mother?" she asked insightfully.

I was prepared for such a question and replied, "Your grandmother had a foreign-sounding name. I didn't want you to have a name that would be a challenge at school."

Yossi got up and brought over a different album. For a moment I wanted to ask him to put it down but I didn't say anything.

"Oy, Mom, here's Mira," he said.

My children knew Maria well. She was Mira to them, a distant aunt from "back there" who had come to Israel and married Uncle Shimon. I spared them details of Maria's life, and as is the way of children, when you tell them something clear, they accept it without asking questions.

"Here are Uncle Shimon and Aunt Mira together," said Hani. "Aunt Mira is so pretty in this one!"

The children went through the album until they got to our picture in the gym of the Tel Aviv school.

"Did you have a nice wedding, Mom?" Yossi asked.

In the photo, Meir and I could be seen sitting on chairs one beside the other. "Very." I replied.

"You were a beautiful bride," said Hani, and I was touched. "Mom, where is your veil?"

I was quiet with embarrassment. It was hard for me to lie, but in those moments I couldn't find the strength to tell the truth. My children's questions did not come as a surprise, but they still hit a sore point. I was angry at myself, even angry at the world and I sent them to bed. "That's enough for today," I chided them, though they hadn't done anything wrong. "Now, to bed!"

For many years I recalled that image of my children, not understanding my sudden anger, going to their room with expressions of surprise. Years later, they sat with us in the living room. Hani was already married and pregnant with my granddaughter Alma. Yossi was about to get married too. They came to visit me one afternoon. I don't remember why the album was there on the table, but they looked through it with great interest.

"Oh, Mom, here are the photos from the secret party," said Yossi. "Do you remember how we weren't supposed to tell anyone?" I remembered well, of course. Meir insisted that we celebrate our twenty-fifth anniversary together so we had a small, family celebration.

Meir bought me a gold ring, which I have been wearing ever since.

I remember how Hani looked at the ring in amazement and suddenly said, "Look, Mom, Dad had it engraved for you" She held the ring up to the light and read out, "Eva, 'Harei at li', "You are mine," Meir."

"He forgot a word," said Yossi. "Why didn't Dad write 'Harei at me-kudeshet li,' "You are consecrated to me," like in the wedding ceremony?" This time too, the words stuck in my throat and I froze, embarrassed and silent. They weren't little kids anymore that could be sent to bed without explanation.

It was Meir who found the way to answer them without revealing anything. "You don't write 'mekudeshet' — "consecrated," at your twenty-five year anniversary. That's something you say only once in a lifetime," he told them.

A tremble passed through me. How did he always know how to find the right words, this man of mine? What a dear and wise man he was.

Sometimes the children would bring a bible story from school that they had been studying. One day Hani reported that they had been learning about Joseph and his brothers, and with her well-developed sense of justice, she was upset by the lie that the sons told Jacob.

"How could they?" she asked with the innocence of a ten-year-old girl.

I told her that the story is to teach us what we shouldn't do.

She was not satisfied with my answer and asked, "Is it allowed to lie to Dad?"

"No," I answered her, without thinking. "No. my dear. Sons may not lie to their fathers."

Hani laughed and said, "But I am a girl, can I lie?"

I smiled at her wordlessly, but that whole evening I was again tormented by the fact that I was teaching them not to lie while not following my own rules. It sent me into a period of insomnia in which I couldn't manage to fall asleep. I would argue with myself, tormented that I had not done a thing. After all, I knew that I could have gone through a relatively simple process and correct what was not sorted out. Although the establishment had made it difficult for Maria, ultimately, conversion during the early years of the state was a simple procedure, lasting a few days at most, so why could I not find the strength to do it?

I would try to justify myself, that it wasn't so simple and moreover, as a refugee, a survivor, I could not then manage these things. I didn't even know about the conversion proceedings. There was no one to guide me, and anyway, for a long time I wasn't even sure that I needed to convert.

And if that wasn't enough, I would remember Edgar, the son of the bank manager, who I had seen on the boat talking with his friends, and his words echoed in my ears again and again, "Raped, beat, those scoundrels. Her daughters died, her husband was murdered, their shop was taken. There was valuable merchandise there, probably silk, not just your average fabric shop. It was a flourishing business, scoundrels, they murdered her too, just because of him."

Those rumors, that I did not examine, were so hard to consider that I suppressed them for many long years. I had to survive, I was looking out for my survival and I couldn't go digging in the past. But now, what excuse did I have for not checking? One night, while I was lying in bed, tossing and turning, I came to the conclusion that I must investigate. I decided to check what Maria remembered. I would see if there were any remaining relatives or refugees from among my extended family. I had no doubt as to Anna's death, who had died before my eyes. My mother's death was also certain to me, as she had been sent to the wrong side of the selection.

But my father? He had disappeared; what if he was still alive somewhere? And what about the rest of my relatives? My grandmother and grandfather? Even if one of them had survived, they surely would have died by now. But I had also had cousins, no? And what if one of them had made it? How could I live with these doubts all of these years? I had to check it out, whatever may come of it!

✳✳✳

Avner set down the diary with a particularly heavy feeling. The picture that the diary painted made him examine his own past and face what he had suppressed for years.

He remembered the endless arguments between his parents. His mother had wanted to check, to investigate the past, but his father refused. The subject came up a number of times in the house, usually in a whisper, when they thought that he was sleeping, and occasionally at full volume, in a foreign language so that he wouldn't understand. He didn't understand the words, but he understood the tone, and knew that the same argument had arisen again.

Various times he heard his father say, "Let it go, Sarah, there's no point."

His mother would reply, "No, there is a point, it's important." Then she would cry.

Dad would try again more gently, "For what, Sarah? It won't give you anything!"

But she would answer him, "How can you erase the past, Nahum, how?"

His dad would try to say, "Exposure will bring explanations, unnecessary explanations, things we might prefer to not know."

At a certain point his father's tone would grow angry, as if he had accumulated years of anger, and he would tell her, "I am ashamed of them, of my family."

Avner's mother would be quiet for a few minutes but would come back and implore him.

The anger would spread through his body and he would say, "The past is dead, Sarah, dead. Got it?"

"You were a hero," she would whisper. "The world needs to know!"

But his father would reply, "No, Sarah, nobody needs to know. The past is dead... dead!"

Then his father would go inward, shut inside himself and the house filled with an oppressive silence such that Avner wished they would go on fighting just to put an end to this horrible quiet. He recalled how his father would speak proudly of the Jews and quote phrases from books he had read.

One such sentence that he quoted echoed now in Avner's mind, "Israel is like the sun."

He searched the phrase on Google and found it almost at once. He was quoting from a book by Werner Sombart: "Israel is like the sun — at its coming, new life bursts forth; at its going, all falls into decay."

Now, as though someone had cleaned the glass window of his past, he recalled his father's speaking tone. He was filled with pride and a powerful longing for his father gripped him. He remembered how after that argument in which his father got angry and said that the past was dead, the silence lasted an extended time, and he didn't hear any more such arguments. At the time it struck him, because he knew his mother and she was stubborn.

Now, with the glass window of his past polished clean, it pained him to think of the big brown envelope labelled: "Sarah Bock, documentation, Yad Vashem Museum." He knew that despite his father's refusal, his mother had not let go of her searching the past.

~

CHAPTER SEVENTEEN

I don't know why happiness cannot last forever. I shouldn't complain: many people are not blessed with so many long years of sweetness. But we had almost sixty years together, why not a little more? I suppose that even if our happiness had lasted a few more months, or even years, I would still struggle with its end. Everything that I went through in life was peanuts next to the death of Meir. My tall, strong, tanned husband died suffering, swollen from medication and unable to move.

Now, a moment before dementia takes over what is left of my mind, I must put down in writing some of the hardest images etched in my memory and I will start with the painful day that we learned of his illness. That morning when he got up, I saw a strange lump on his neck.

Meir was a healthy man who never took so much as Tylenol. He was not the kind of man to go to the doctor. He always joked that when he was really sick, he only went to the doctor because, after all, he had to make his living somehow, then to the pharmacist to buy medicine, because the pharmacist also had to make a living, and finally he would throw the medicine away, because he needed to live too. But that morning he went to the clinic, and the doctor sent him to get tests right away. The results were unequivocal. My Meir, who had quit smoking forty years earlier, who ate well and exercised, had a tumor on his right lung.

At first it was hard to believe. What did the bulge on his neck have to do with a lung tumor? Of course we sought a second opinion with a private specialist right away. But he was equally certain about the terrible diagnosis. Along with that he was optimistic.

He looked at Meir's medical history and the results of his last tests and said, "The tumor is small and it's isolated. A few treatments, surgery, and you should recover."

We soon realized that it was an idle promise. We did as the doctor said, and Meir started getting chemotherapy. My strong man did not give in to nausea, pain in his bones, or self-pity. He walked tall to the hospital, where they put a needle in his arm, and slowly dripped poison into his veins. After three rounds of exhausting treatments the doctor informed us that the tumor had shrunk and that we could proceed to the next stage — surgery.

Meir went to the hospital determined and confident. He was the one to reassure me and the kids, instead of the other way around.

"Don't worry, Eva my darling, just a little more and oops... it'll be over," he said.

He was operated on by the private doctor and left the operating room with just one lung and torn vocal cords, leaving my smart man unable to speak.

The doctor came to talk to us with a grave face, explaining things we did not want to understand. "Sometimes it eludes us, betrays us, we think it's small but it turns out stronger than it appears."

For three months Meir tried to rehabilitate. He kept up his daily walk outside, and I joined him every day. He made sure to eat well despite his diminished appetite, and more than anything, maintained high spirits. He did not let any of us sense how sick he was. Around three months after the surgery, the two of us went out for our daily walk. We went down Yad Mordecai Street and turned up Eilat Street toward the pool where Meir had taught our children how to swim. Meir loved that place with its tall cypress trees and the merry cries of children jumping in the pool.

We stood there for a few minutes and turned to go back when suddenly I noticed that Meir was not walking straight but in a kind of zigzag. "Meir!" I cried out in alarm. "Why are you walking like that?"

Meir did not understand what I was talking about. He did not feel anything unusual. The tests confirmed the fears that had crept back into my heart: the cancer had metastasized in Meir's head. The treatments, hair loss, weakness, the swelling all over his body, the struggle — all of it had been in vain.

I think that even Alzheimer's won't erase the memories that I will now describe.

We sat down one evening in our little living room. Meir was swollen from his medication, but managed to whisper, "You know, the metastasis was overkill."

As if the illness itself was welcome and only the metastasis was not.

To hear such a sentence from a man who had never complained, whose love of life was essential to him, could break even the strongest spirit.

Meir was a vital man. He had a healthy appetite for everything you might call "living." He loved to travel, to eat, to listen to classical music, to read, to visit friends, all of it. He so wanted to live to the point that even that terrible disease did not defeat his will.

At first the awful metastasis was almost completely eliminated. He went through a series of radiation treatments; his eyes sank into his head and his body shrank, but he did not lose his will to live.

The doctor said that the radiation would cause memory loss. In the visit following the end of the treatment cycle, he turned to me and asked about Meir's medicine as if Meir himself was not in the room.

In a whisper, Meir said that he could ask him, and answered the doctor in great detail about the medicine that he was taking, in what dose, which medicines he should take in increasing quantities from one day to the next and which to decrease.

The doctor looked at him in surprise and said, "My dementia is worse than yours, Mr. Meir."

Later, the metastasis returned full force. Again we went to the doctor, but he said that if Meir received further radiation, it would melt his brain, literally.

We went home, and it was the hardest night that I remember from that period. I played Meir his favorite album of Mozart's symphony, I sat beside him and we cried together. At the end of the symphony, Meir asked me a question from which I understood both the strength of his will to live in spite of everything, but also that he knew that his death was approaching.

He asked, "So what, I don't get any more radiation?"

In his last days, Meir lay helpless in the hospital. When he wanted to go to the bathroom, I asked for the nurse's help but she replied that she was drinking coffee just now, and anyway, he had a diaper. God in heaven, what kind of humiliating treatment must an old man endure in his final days? Why treat him like a sack of potatoes? I feel like I cannot complete this section of my diary with this enormous pain and with that terrible image.

I believe that my Meir is sitting up above, smiling, because he never stopped smiling. I have a particular moment of happiness in mind now that I wish to share, so I can stop crying.

Meir was the one who put the kids to bed at night. It was a kind of unwritten but regular arrangement. Most nights he got them to bed with a smile because he believed that whoever went to sleep with a smile on his lips would dream pleasant dreams and wake up happy. So he had a ritual in which he and the kids recited the children's song, "La, la, la leprechauns."

The three of them would make a line: Meir, then Hani in front of him, and Yossi in front of her. Meir would hold Hani's hand and she held Yossi's. Then they would march like a centipede to the children's room. All the while, Meir would tickle them and the sounds of their happy laughter rose to the heavens.

When they reached their room and got into bed, jaws aching from laughter, Meir would cover them with a blanket and declare, "And now, ladies and gentlemen, the song which won first place at the leprechauns' festival, La la la leprechauns: today, today I had a fever, then I went to play, then I drank juice and farted, today, today, today."

I relished their laughter, scolding Meir for teaching the kids bad words, but I wasn't really mad. His laughter and theirs was worth everything. Their laughter could heal the sorrow of the entire world.

***

Reluctantly, Avner turned his thoughts to the death of his father Nahum.

TZVIA GOLAN | 159

He had a strong memory of the shock of his death, the suddenness in which things transpired, his inability to accept reality just like that, without warning or preparation. Even then the thought had crossed his mind how cruel it was to die like that in the middle of the night. It is cruel not just to the deceased but to the family members left behind, stunned.

He could still hear his mother's broken cries when she couldn't wake Nahum and then touched him and found him cold.

He could still recall the voices that accompanied the funeral procession, "Nahum died a merciful death," said the Rabbi. "He earned his place in this world, a man full of kindness, and has a place in the world to come."

Someone else got up and said, "He lived a full life, just too short. It was too soon to be called back to God, he was not yet fifty years old."

Avner's heart ached remembering how he had not even had the chance to say goodbye to his father. He had been so young, and had not had his father for many years. Now he read about a full life, sixty years together, and a death for which there had been much preparation. Meir and Eva and the children knew that his death was coming, and still there was so much deep sorrow, pain, and grief.

He came to the conclusion that there was no difference really between death that was expected and death that came suddenly. Either way, it is brutal.

He groaned so loudly he worried that perhaps it could be heard outside. He got up, restless, felt that he was hungry, and looked in the small refrigerator for something to eat. He found Nisim's container of vegetables, took a couple pieces of yellow pepper and crunched on them.

This section of the diary made him think not only of the pain of his father's death, but also his musings on love. Mrs. Reich had had so much love, love that made him appreciate her, on the one hand, and envy her on the other.

He tried to think if he himself was a good father to his two adolescent daughters, and reassured himself that he, too, had rituals at home: once a week they all watched a movie together. Here, he was also doing good things for his kids. Only he couldn't recall the last time he had heard the sound of real, liberating laughter in his home. He had not laughed for years, laughing out loud, the kind of laughter that's a release, that comes from the heart. What a shame it was that he couldn't manage to laugh like that. Pensive and sad, he picked up the diary again and resumed reading.

***

Meir died exactly two years from the day that I discovered the mass in his neck, in the hospital where he spent the last days of his life. Though I tried to bring him home so he could die in his own bed, his condition did not allow for that. In his final days he was hooked up to tubes in every place possible and spent most of that time sleeping deeply. I remember thinking to myself that perhaps it was better for him to sleep and not feel pain.

For long hours I sat beside him, reading to him things I had written out of pain. I held his hand, not expecting any response. The day before he died he opened his eyes for the last time and asked me what time it was. I was beside myself with emotion and sorrow all at once. I replied that it was six fifteen in the evening.

Meir looked into my eyes and whispered, "Time isn't passing for me, each day is longer than the one before." Even in his state he still spoke clear, perfect Hebrew, and these words, in his crisp language, hurt my ears like knives. Then he closed his eyes.

That night my kids forced me to go home and lay my head down for a few hours. They made sure a nurse was at his bedside, and reassured me, like a little girl, that everything would be fine. I returned to the hospital early in the morning in time to see him breathe his last breath. Hani arrived five minutes too late. Yossi, who came from Haifa, arrived two hours after his father left this world.

Meir was buried in Holon. Yossi bought two plots, one beside the other, and when Hani was alarmed at the sight of "my" plot, I told her that nobody had ever died from purchasing a plot. Yossi even said that it promoted longevity. If it were under my control, Meir would have been buried someplace else, like the cemetery at Mishmar HaAliya, which is more pluralistic, so that I could be sure that I could rest by his side for eternity. But unfortunately I could not express those thoughts to my children.

After Meir passed away, I would lie in bed at night with hot tears streaming from my eyes. I was aware of every tiny sound in the house, every movement of the wind outside. I could hear Meir breathing regularly beside me, quiet and pleasant to my ears like wind in the trees, like Mozart's symphony that we always listened to together. I spent my nights tossing and turning and overwhelmed by memories: the four of us traveling by bus to a vacation in Eilat. I recall how I said that maybe we didn't have enough money for it.

Meir pulled his brown wallet from his pants' pocket, poured its contents onto the table, the small coins scattering noisily. "You see, Eva, why do you say that we don't have money, look how much money we have," he said and smiled.

So many memories haunt me at night: we are sitting in the living room, it's cold outside, all of us are covered with plaid blankets and the sound of the children's laughter fills the house. Another memory, I am walking beside Meir, tall and strong, the eyes of all the girls we pass lingering on him, and he holds my hand so softly it surprises even me, how could such strong hands be so gentle?

And another memory, we are walking together to the opera house, I am dressed in my best, and he is in a suit, a prime specimen. They were showing "The Tales of Hoffman" by Jacques Offenbach. On the way, Meir regaled me with information. He always knew so much, like a walking encyclopedia. "You know," he said. "Offenbach was born Jacob Eberst. Yes, he was Jewish, born in Cologne, Germany. His father was a cantor, and Jacques loved music from childhood."

I'd turn over, unable to fall asleep, and again hear breathing beside me. I turned on the light but there was no one there. Loneliness is so hard for me and the pleasant images change as if the director of my life decided that I'd had enough fun and a small lump on the neck, practically invisible, would turn the tables entirely. Now in my mind's eye I see Meir is sick, undergoing surgery, he could hardly speak, his upright walk disappears and in its place is a hunched body, first aided by a walking stick then transported by wheelchair. The difficult images do not let up.

On one such night I decided: tomorrow I will ask the children to help me move to a retirement home. I don't want to stay here alone. I turned off the light, the tears continued to flow, and just then, in the moment that I hoped that blessed sleep would finally come, the doubts returned along with my argument with myself, which ate up the rest of the night. How could I, I asked myself, how could I live with the idea that I hadn't thoroughly investigated, and how could I let Meir live with me without arranging matters properly?

In these moments I lied to myself so much I thought of Dan Ben Amotz's story collection and imagined myself the queen of lies. I feel my whole life is a collection of poor excuses, of a refugee who made a profession of her misery. I try in vain to answer the big question: did I tell Meir that I was not Jewish because I did not want to live a lie with him or because I knew that the rabbinate would make problems for me? My anger with myself swelled, grew, and intensified.

Here you go, I said to myself, now you can't be beside him forever. I can't go on cheating the whole system. A bitter smile rose to my face: I lied all of my life and I can't go on lying after my life is over. For one moment I thought to myself, actually, why not? After all, if I managed to lie all my life, why not go on lying after my death?

And maybe, a terrible thought entered my mind, maybe I wanted to marry Meir, not because I loved him so much but because I knew that he was from a kibbutz and I hoped that he would not care so much? Maybe I knew, deep in my heart that he was never so invested in religion? Was I just looking for a simple solution? I tried to tell myself that was stupid. After all, I couldn't have known that his kibbutz was so secular, but that is the nature of nighttime thoughts, not always rational, but more like a kind of waking nightmare.

On nights when those thoughts haunted me, I would sit up in bed and recreate my experiences over and over, listing the excuses one by one. At first I hadn't known that I even had a secret, I was a little girl, and children accept reality as it is without asking questions. It's only adults that raise questions later on. As a girl I thought that that was how it was for everyone, that you eat an apple dipped in honey at one holiday — and a huge turkey for another.

Later, everything fell apart and all that mattered was survival. Was I supposed to torture myself, if later in Israel, my life was pretty good? I tried to comfort myself, but it didn't really work because I could still hear my mother saying '*Fehler*' and tormented myself for lowering my head and not trying to clarify what the mistake was.

I felt that I was slowly going out of my mind. Suddenly I didn't hear Meir's breathing and the quiet hurt my ears to the point that I practically asked out loud to go on hearing him breathing beside me. But instead of his breathing I continued to hear a voice of reason, without a drop of emotion. I know that I have not told the full truth, I know that that was more comfortable for me, and I know that I dragged those closest to me into that lie.

* * *

Avner was overwhelmed with pain. Sleepless nights were something he was very familiar with, to the point that he sometimes wondered if he had ever slept long and deeply. Whole nights he tossed and turned in bed. He, too, was tormented by hard memories from his childhood, as if etched by someone into his mind.

Unbidden, a tough image came to him, one of many: he returned home from school on a day when he had received a high grade on an exam. He knew that his mother would be pleased, and he was excited and happy. In the stairwell he already smelled the terrible smell. He didn't know where it was coming from, but at the entrance to the house were people in white cloaks and masks on their faces who did not let him in.

He recalled how he shouted at the top of his lungs, "Mom!" And how he had pushed through the legs of the people and burst into the house.

When he woke up, he saw his father, who looked like he had been crying, standing beside him. He had never seen his father cry. He always taught Avner the importance of toughness and restraint. Avner recalled that his father hurried to dry his eyes and smiled at him. Beside him he saw a few unfamiliar faces. He looked around and saw big, white beds with children lying on them, some of them attached to tubes. He felt a pain in his hand and was afraid to find that he was hooked up to a tube himself.

For a moment he was sure that he was dead and thought that surely this was what hell looked like. Certainly he had committed bad deeds. Later, people spoke to him in a quiet, calming voice, asked him how he felt, and his father stroked his head until he thought perhaps he had actually gone to heaven.

Afterward, he heard the people talking outside the room. One of them said, "This poor kid is very lucky."

Another replied, "Yes, the amount of gas in the house could have killed an elephant."

~

CHAPTER EIGHTEEN

Avner tried to return to the diary but it felt so heavy. He was bothered, disturbed by the feeling that Mrs. Reich was holding a mirror up to him, reading his thoughts and aware of exactly what he was going through.

"It's too much for me," he said to himself. He glanced at the first lines of the next section of the diary and the words "coming full circle" caught his eye. Indeed, he had just been overwhelmed by memories of a difficult period of his life, which had ended abruptly and here she was talking about coming full circle.

He already knew that Eva Reich was a determined woman while he, to this day, was not. Nor had his own personal journey come full circle; he felt he had not even begun. It always struck him as too intimidating, too sad, too much torment. Grudgingly, he recalled how he would walk in the street and envy the passersby. They always looked happier, less troubled than him.

He once saw an old man walking slowly down the street, carrying a plastic bag with herbs and cucumbers poking out. He must have been on his way home from the market. Avner was even jealous of this old man, that his life was so straightforward — get up, go to the market, come home, eat, lie down for a nap, while his own life was so full of painful memories. He knew that these thoughts were stupid, that undoubtedly this old man had hard memories of his own and still, something in the sight of that shopping bag seemed to represent a complete contentment with life, something he himself had never managed.

He rose and opened the office window. He saw Nisim standing by the petunia bed, bent over, pruning and removing the dead flowers.

"Exquisite colors you planted here," he said through the open window. "A real spectacle, the red, pink, and orange, magnificent!"

"Unbelievable," Nisim replied without turning his head. "It isn't even June and the petunias are already drying up. What kind of summer have we got coming, God help us. By the way, if I trim them now, they'll grow dense and healthy, we'll have a meadow of petunias."

"Lovely," Avner marveled. "I don't know what I would do without you."

"I don't know what I'd do without me either." Nisim laughed. "But thank you!" He stood up and turned to the window. "You know, people always want what they don't have. They're always asking for Gerberas, which need a ton of water and partial shade, but petunias? They're so hardy." He held up a tanned fist to illustrate the strength of the flower. "And they make do with watering just once a week."

"Amazing," Avner replied. "Your knowledge of flowers amazes me every time."

He closed the window and sat back down. He felt like Nisim was reading his mind too.

"People always want what they don't have." He suddenly felt a bit ashamed, that he might be ungrateful for his own life. He really had a very reasonable life, after all, with a wife, two daughters, a nice apartment, a livelihood, and still he lacked peace of mind.

"You don't have time either," he chided himself. "It's late already, finish reading!"

$$***$$

When Meir died, something within me died too. My zest for life shut down almost entirely. I also sensed my memory betraying me here and there, which made me feel more than a little panicky.

I found myself getting on the bus in the wrong direction, forgetting my wallet at home and positive that it had been stolen, leaving a pot on the stove without turning it off, and other little signs of memory problems, which led me to acknowledge that the day may not be far off when I could no longer tell or write anything sensible.

It's not easy to accept that an entire chapter of your life has simply ended, but I knew that there were some things I must do before the curtain falls. I knew that I had to go to Berlin at least once, to fulfill the unwritten will that Meir had left me. I knew that it would be hard, but I was determined. When I returned from Berlin, I had troubling, sleepless nights until I reached a decision. There is something very comforting with the fact of making a decision, and suddenly, once again, I could sleep peacefully, as if a heavy weight had been lifted from my heart.

On the one hand, the decision to leave the house in which we had lived for nearly sixty years was not at all easy, to say the least. The decision was very painful, and terminal as an illness. On the other hand, I felt that there was no point in remaining there alone.

The morning after I decided, I got up, made myself extra hot coffee but skipped the usual toast and butter because I had no appetite. I sat down in the little kitchen, cup of coffee in my hand, and looked around. We never had expensive tastes. We always made do with what we had.

My son would sometimes tell us about new innovations and inventions, but he knew that we would always smile at him, Meir and I, and stay with what we had. Meir would refer to these as "those modern modernities" and Yossi would smile and wave a hand dismissively.

The kitchen cupboards were covered in greenish Formica, faded over time, the sink was cracked and the tap was old, but everything was so clean it sparkled. The table in the kitchen where I sat that morning was ornamented with diamond shapes, also green, with four simple wooden chairs around it. On the countertop, leopard spotted with light brown stains was the electric kettle, which was modern relative to the other objects nearby.

I got up and moved around the rooms of the little house and couldn't articulate what I felt. In the small hall stood an ancient sofa, one solitary, comfortable armchair, and a huge bookcase so crowded with books that the shelves sagged in the middle, alongside old binders from my years of work, notebooks in which I would record my thoughts, as well as photo albums.

On the wall was the clock we received from Meir's parents as a wedding present. To the right of the hall was our bedroom, which had known endless love. I found it almost impossible to open Meir's clothes closet, so I did it at a later stage when I was functioning on automatic. I gave all of his clothes to Yossi and closed the closet as if closing another chapter of my life.

The day before I left, I did one more little tour of the apartment and almost fainted when I found a single, orphaned tie that had been forgotten there, like a painful souvenir from better days.

Hani and Yossi had mixed feelings about my decision. I sat with the two of them at the kitchen table and they looked at me with pain I didn't know how to handle. I tried to reassure them with words, even with jokes, but they didn't laugh. I suppose that for them, this marked the definitive end to their childhood in the home in which they grew up. Hani cried and it pierced my heart with a new, unfamiliar pain. But there was no choice. Gently, I explained again and again why I had to make this hard move and in the end they both understood.

I asked them to take whatever they wanted from their childhood home. Hani took a few household appliances, a vase or two, and mostly photograph albums, and a notebook in which I would write my musings. At first Yossi didn't want anything, but in the end he took a wine goblet, his father's clothes, and a few books.

I offered that they take the grandfather clock, but neither of them had space for it. In the end I took it with me to the retirement home and for days I thought about what I could do with it. It reminded me of home, but it was too painful to be reminded of it all the time. Ultimately, I reached a decision what to do with it and to whom I would give it, but I will get to that later.

My children moved through the house teary-eyed, opening and closing drawers, and even though they understood, they asked a thousand times if I was sure about this move. At a certain point the three of us sat in the hallway on the sofa, which we later gave to a needy family, and Hani opened my notebook. She read some of my thoughts quietly to herself, alternately tearing up and laughing, and Yossi sat and looked at me with an expression that broke my heart.

When she shed a tear, he did too. When she laughed out loud, he asked what was funny. She read him a few sentences that struck her as particularly funny and wiped away her tears every few moments.

"I had a student who wrote better than me," I admitted to them. "Oded Levi, Shimon's grandson, remember?"

They remembered Maria and her husband Shimon of course, but Yossi gestured dismissively. "You write great, Mom, no one compares to you."

I dropped the subject. I knew that no matter what I said, Yossi would always think I was perfect. For whatever reason, that thought pained me. Perfect? I was so imperfect!

"Oy, Yossi," said Hani. "Grow up. Mom didn't really throw a stone into the heavens, and it didn't fall the next day." We burst out laughing.

All of us remembered Meir's exaggerated stories. "You won't believe it," he said to them once. "Your mother knows how to tame animals." The two of them looked at him in amazement.

Meir told them how I had once been in the forest and came upon a big lion, but I looked him in the eyes and the lion simply lay down on the ground and swished his tail.

I listened to the story and smiled to myself. It's true that I was in the forest, walking for long days. I even saw the lion more than once, only I didn't dare look him in the eyes, which were usually blue and not really the eyes of a lion, and he didn't really submit to anything, because he had a rifle in his hands. But my children would listen to the imaginary heroic stories that Meir came up with and Yossi would believe every word.

The three of us recalled how he came home from nursery school crying one day because the kids didn't believe that his mother had thrown a stone into the sky and it only came down the next day.

"Grow up, little Yos," Hani said. I quietly enjoyed hearing her nickname for him.

I sat with my children for a long time, and between tears and laughter we read more and more. I can't explain how my daughter, my eldest, my smart girl, overlooked the sentence which included the word "lie" as if it wasn't even written there. Obviously I had lots of musings on that subject, but she skipped over all of them.

I moved to live in senior housing in Ramat Gan, right beside Ordea Square. I made pleasant connections with the manager of the place as well as fellow tenants, many of whom shared my circumstances: a little forgetful, a little confused, but positive and physically independent.

I started writing this diary in the second year that I lived there, with the understanding that the curtain would fall not too long from now, my memory would become a sticky porridge, and it would no longer be possible to distinguish between fact and fiction. In truth, at first I didn't know what I would do with the diary once I finished writing it. The need to write it sprang out of some desire to commemorate my family, my parents, my sister, Maria, my Aunt Alice, Uncle Karl, and my cousins. But throughout the writing, things arose, which ultimately led me to decide to whom to hand over the diary, which shook me up.

Funny how people can't know if the thing that they decide to do is right or not. I think that in this I acted from emotional motives with all that that implies.

***

Avner considered this last sentence for a moment. What was she trying to tell him? After all, it was already clear that it was no coincidence that she had chosen him to read her diary. It's interesting, he thought to himself, that she says she began writing for one reason, and the initial purpose of the writing shifted with time. His curiosity overcame the worries that nagged at him, waiting for the right time to pounce.

***

Life in the senior living facility was pleasant, but I had a lot of free time open up. I no longer cooked for myself nor cleaned my room on my own. I ate in the dining room, and my room was cleaned once a week. I filled my time with lectures that I would attend, like the one I'll describe momentarily, because it was thanks to that lecture that I finally decided I had to investigate my past and not hide behind uncertainty any longer.

The lecturer that day was named Leah. She was a relatively young woman, put together, light-haired, with a pleasant face, short and full-bodied. All of us raised an eyebrow. She looked so young. No doubt that even if she had been in the Holocaust, she would have been a baby and there was no way that she would have memories from that age. She got up on the stage and explained: she was not a holocaust survivor but rather a nurse at a psychiatric hospital, and she wanted to tell us about a chilling story that had happened recently, to one of her old guys. That was what she called them "my old guys" and there was something maternal and compelling about her.

The old guy, as Leah told us, had been hospitalized in her department for many months already. He had come to the hospital following a request from a neighbor in the building where he lived. The worried neighbor had called the ambulance, saying that the man had not left his house for a few days and that neighbors had knocked on his door to bring him food, but he didn't answer.

The medics, accompanied by a locksmith, came quickly and found the man lying helplessly, dehydrated from lack of food and water. He was admitted to the hospital's internal medicine department for a few days, where they stabilized his condition, but when, after a few days he hadn't spoken so much as one word, and looked disconnected from his surroundings, he was sent to the hospital where she worked.

Nobody had ever come to visit Mr. Leibovitch — that was his name. The nurse told us how the hospital management tried to look for his family, but all that his neighbors knew was that they had never seen a soul come to visit him. The hospital director did not give up and even made a request on the radio program for locating relatives.

Finally, as the nurse told us excitedly, the efforts bore fruit. Relatives were found: a cousin of his mother, who lived in Cleveland with her children, her grandson who lived in Israel, as well as a cousin of his father's who lived here in Israel, married with children and grandchildren. The nurse wiped away a tear as she told how the father's cousin came to visit

Mr. Leibovitz, and how after the visit it looked as though the old man had been brought back to life.

He resumed eating and began to take an interest in the world around him. The man continued to visit him relatively frequently. One day two youths even came to visit. One introduced himself to the nurses in the department as the grandson of the cousin from the United States, and the other boy said that he was the grandson of the Israeli cousin.

The nurse Leah finished telling this touching story, describing how happy Mr. Leibovitz was when the two young men came to visit him together, and told how the rest of his family members from Israel now came to visit the lost and unfortunate uncle regularly. Before getting off the stage, she said that Mr. Leibovitz was about to leave the hospital soon and return to live in his home and his family members were finding him a caregiver so that he could live with the dignity that he deserved.

**

Avner had never believed in mysticism. He wished to remain connected with reality and believe only what he saw. Was this even possible? Could it be that the two youths and the elderly man from Leah's lecture were the same ones that he himself had seen when he visited his mother? Was it possible that the redheaded boy and the dark one who he had seen at the hospital not long ago were right there, in this story that Eva Reich was telling?

He tried to shake off the troublesome thought, and was even a bit taken aback by himself: What is this, was he crazy? No, no it was impossible that these were the same youths, it must be a coincidence. And yet, as he tried to reassure himself, the bigger question arose in his mind: was Eva Reich hinting that she knew where his mother was? Did she weave the whole story, or at least its end, to make him finally investigate his roots properly? Was this related to the turn in her reason for writing the diary that she had mentioned earlier?

Avner checked the time and was slightly startled. It was already two in the afternoon. Another hour and a bit and the relatives would come, and he hadn't finished reading or formulated what he was going to say. He had to go on reading. He flipped through the remaining pages, two sections in total, and was suddenly gripped by fear at what he was about to discover.

~

CHAPTER NINETEEN

"Perhaps in the next century doctors will learn how to mend a broken soul and give us a better life," I said to Maria at the end of that conversation, when we sat together at her house in the kibbutz.

"There are psychologists who try to do that," she replied. "And sometimes they really do God's work."

"Have you tried?" I asked.

Maria sighed. "Of course," she replied. "It's stupid to not try to help yourself."

I was moved by this. More than once I had thought to seek help from a professional but every time I put it off, coming up with various reasons. Usually when I was having a really hard time I spoke to Meir or Maria, and I suppose I didn't really believe that a stranger could help. I justified myself by claiming that a broken soul could not be healed. Still, I wonder if it is possible.

In truth, I only once really tried to get professional help. It was after a hard night when I dreamed that my lie was found out in an ugly way and that everyone I love was angry at me, even those who knew the truth. That day I went to a health center on my own. I was sent to a serious-minded man who sat across from me, a table separating us. He asked me tough questions and wrote down every word that I said. I felt suffocated and distant.

When I got up to leave at the end of the meeting, the man asked, "Would you like to come back?"

"No," I replied without thinking twice, and I told myself: to hell with all these professionals. Why would he ask me if I want to come back? Since when does the doctor consult with the patient? I left, and what I remember most of all was the feeling that I had been right all those years: a stranger couldn't help me.

***

Avner moved uncomfortably in his chair. If a stranger couldn't help, it seemed to suggest that he himself was not a stranger to her. Scary, he thought to himself. Scary and equally intriguing.

***

Maria's simple living room had a pleasant, clean smell. An old brown rug made the place feel warm and a brightly-colored curtain covered the big glass door which led to the garden. The garden was well looked-after, with date flowers surrounded by green grass, and it was clear that someone was putting in gardening work and ongoing professional maintenance. From the living room you could see the kitchenette, simple white wooden cupboards, an oven and stove, a little Amcor refrigerator, a table of natural wood and a few chairs.

The little apartment had one other room, Maria and Shimon's bedroom, or as Maria once said to me with a wink, "That's the love room."

We sat together in the living room, sipping hot tea with Petit Beurre biscuits and had a pleasant conversation. Although she was already quite old, Maria's mind was totally clear and her great beauty well-maintained.

"You know…" I said. "Hani's daughter Alma is already studying for the university entrance exams."

Maria smiled at me. "The apple doesn't fall far from the tree. In fact, in this case, the apple didn't fall at all — it's still attached to the tree!"

"Stop." I smiled in embarrassment. "You always find something good to say about me." I went on telling her about my two grandchildren and she listened and did not stop smiling.

"Look how things all worked out in the end," she said. "Yossi's son is already enlisting in the army. You must be so proud!"

"And how are you, my dear Maria?" I asked, knowing that she was no longer well, but she waved a hand dismissively.

"At my age you have to thank God every morning that you open your eyes and manage to get up."

She rose and poured us more tea. "You're still as thin as a rail," she said to me in a concerned, motherly tone accompanied by a worried expression. "Take a cookie, nothing will happen if you put on a little weight."

I embraced her warmly and told her anecdotes from my years of work. She always loved hearing me talk about work and once told me with a smile, "I am like someone on a diet who cooks every day. If I can't eat, at least I can touch the food."

When I didn't understand what she meant, she explained, "I love hearing you talk about your years of working with young people. It keeps me young somehow."

That was when I told her about my students and about Oded, Shimon's grandson. "He was a brilliant student." She smiled again.

"Do you know if he's still writing?" she asked proudly.

I knew for sure that he was writing since he brought me things that he had written on more than one occasion and we would have discussions about them in class. Some of the turns of phrase that he had written are still in my memory to this day.

I told Maria, "He once wrote that every part of the body has its attribute: lightness of the feet, sweetness of the lips, strength of the arms, goodness of the heart, appetite of the eyes, and integrity of the spine. Which leaves nothing for the mind."

Maria smiled momentarily, but it turned vaguely bitter. "The memory..." She sighed. I looked at her quizzically and she explained, "The mind is left with the memory, Eva. In fact, if you think about it, all of the parts together support the brain's role, the role of "remembering," you see?"

I understood very well. Our feet help us to remember where we walked, or, unfortunately, from where we fled. The lips help remember the taste of things, and so on. And the brain, of course, commands the body.

I looked at her again. "What?" she asked me.

"You owe me a few stories, for years now, Maria, maybe now is the right time?"

Maria sighed. "All right," she said. "Maybe the time has come. If I don't tell you now, there won't be anyone left to tell you later."

"Don't talk like that," I scolded, but I knew that she was right. Maria had suffered from diabetes for years now, and recently there had been a decline in her liver function. She was getting treatment from the best doctors but knew that her days were limited.

"I am realistic, Eva," she said. "There are facts that one must come to terms with." She got up again, and suddenly appeared more hunched.

"Where are you going?" I asked.

"To get us something to eat," she replied. "I'm hungry."

From the little kitchen came a smell of fried omelet and the scent of fresh bread, which to this day reminds me of the little bakery on our street in Alexanderplatz.

"Come here," called Maria. "The eggs are getting cold."

We sat in the kitchen on the simple wooden chairs at the little table, eating a late breakfast — it was already afternoon by then — on blue plastic plates, drinking tea in red plastic mugs, and I felt like I was eating caviar in a five-star hotel.

"Very tasty," I said, and bit into the omelet with enthusiasm.

"Thank you," said Maria. "It's nothing, really. My kitchen skills begin and end with eggs and salad."

We finished eating in silence, and Maria sighed again and began to speak, as if the dam had been breached all at once.

"Do you remember your cousins?" she asked.

I remembered them well. Johann, the older of the two, was tall like Uncle Karl and had his blue eyes too. Herman, the younger one, was a thin boy, and I remembered that my aunt was always concerned that he was weak and unwell.

"Very well," I replied. "We played with them in the yard almost every day."

The image of us all playing was clear in my mind. "Do you know what I remember?" I asked with a smile. "Aunt Alice would say that she was afraid Herman would fall apart in the bath."

"Amazing that you remember that," Maria replied. "He was born with a small heart murmur, but the doctors said it was nothing and that he could live with it without problems."

"I didn't know that," I said. "I just remember that he was always really thin."

"True," said Maria, "He was thin, but very tall, and by the way, your aunt was particularly anxious. I guess that she was really worried about what would happen to her boys after she..."

"Yes," I said. "And maybe I inherited her endless worrying."

"You remember that day when an ambulance showed up downstairs and took your aunt?" Maria asked.

"Of course," I replied. That day was forever etched in my memory.

"Your mother wanted her sister to die at home, not in some cold hospital, do you remember that?"

I remembered that at home we heard Mom crying more than once and telling Dad about the stages of her sister's terrible illness. I remember that as a girl I didn't understand what she was saying. I didn't know what cancer was. Anna and I would visit her with Mom, until Mom stopped bringing us along. Later, she returned home from the hospital.

"He was an awful man," Maria said suddenly.

The harsh statement surprised me. Maria never said bad things about anyone. "Who?" I asked, stunned.

"Your uncle," she replied quietly. I was stunned. It was my uncle, of all people, that she spoke so harshly of?

"He was meticulous and strict," I replied. "And sometimes would get mad when we ran wild, but not so awful? Why would you say that?"

Maria looked at me with a sad expression. "I was a close friend of your mother's. She would tell me everything," she said. "About her life with your father and how his extended family banished him, and also about Alice, who suffered at the hands of her husband."

This new information made me very sad. I vaguely remembered how as a girl we never went to visit my grandmother and grandfather on my dad's side. I even remembered that Mom would sigh when we asked to visit them, and wouldn't explain why we couldn't, but I didn't know it was that bad. "Banished?" I asked.

"They never got over the fact that your mother was not one of their own," Maria replied without a hint of judgment. "You must understand, for them it was terrible, that their son chose to live with a non-Jewish woman. They were ashamed of it."

I was filled with anger at the thought that family members, our own flesh and blood, cast Dad out just because of his love for Mom. How was it possible to banish a son when the enemy's knife was at their back? My anger was evident to Maria, and she tried to defend them.

"The customs are so different, and they didn't invent that hatred between Jews and Christians."

Maria got up and cleared the dishes from the table, setting them down in the sink. She stood with her back to me and said, "But it didn't break your mother, it maybe even made her stronger. She needed to prove to them that it wouldn't help, she would remain faithful to her parents' house."

"And Dad?" I asked. "Did he try to convince her to convert?"

"Your father was a stubborn man, but very smart," Maria replied. "He knew that there was no point in trying, but he did not agree to change his ways either, as you probably recall."

I remembered clearly how Dad, with his impressive beard and wearing a Kippah, prayed and said the blessing over the food every day, wrapped in his prayer shawl.

Maria turned and, as if reading me like an open book, smiled and said, "It makes me smile today how the two of them, both your mother and your father, would bless the food, each in their own way."

"Their great love overcame almost everything," I said with pain. "It's just too bad that Mom…"

Maria looked at me sorrowfully. "At first your mother was stubborn, wanting to prove to your father's family that despite what they were doing and even though they didn't even want to meet you or your sister, your family would only grow…"

"What?" I asked. "What are you talking about?"

"I mean that, at first, she wanted to prove to your father's family that she would win, and later she believed that she would also be able to defeat all of the evil in the world too."

"She was wrong…" I whispered. "Maybe that was the mistake she was referring to…"

"Maybe," said Maria. "But if the family had grown, who knows what would have happened…"

"Maria," I said quietly, "Please explain what you're saying."

Maria turned back toward the sink and whispered, "Your mother knew that your father really wanted a son, you remember that I told you that?"

I remembered well those sleepless nights in the shacks in Cyprus and Maria's stories that were like a sweet melody to my ears. "I remember that you told me that my father wanted a son, but not instead of me," I said.

Maria nodded and replied, "Correct. Not instead of you. In addition to you."

"What are you saying?" I asked in alarm.

"Exactly as I said," she replied in a whisper. "Your mother was pregnant when everything happened."

I tried to digest that terrible information, and thoughts, some logical, most not, rushed through my mind. I could hear Edgar again, on the migrant boat. Raped, he said, maybe they really did?

"Maria!" I raised my voice. "Edgar, he said that she was raped."

Maria turned to me quickly, her face grave, "Nobody touched your mother! She was pregnant by your father, but then she was sent to the other side, to her death, you remember that?

Of course I remembered that, all too well, but now I tried to remember more, whatever I could. I tried to recall how my mother looked, her facial features, but especially her body. It was so cold then, a freezing cold had come over everything. Mom was wearing a long coat most of the time. How could anyone have seen anything?

"But Maria, how come I didn't know?" I asked and tears welled up in my eyes.

"You were a little girl, dear Eva, a little girl," she replied and turned back to the sink to wash the plastic plates.

I recalled the one picture that I have at home, the one that I dug out of the ground. Even in that picture Mom was wearing that same long coat and it would have been impossible to see that she was pregnant. I thought of getting up and going home. Or to block my ears and not hear any more but I was unable to leave. As if glued to the spot, I asked, "Are you sure?"

Maria was not quick to reply. She finished washing the dishes, then turned and said, "They murdered her and the fetus together. I am sorry, but you asked me to tell you, and I thought that maybe you knew about it."

"I didn't know…" I said in a whisper and stood up. "But I am glad you're telling me. It's time I know."

Maria gestured toward the chair and when I sat back down, she sat beside me. She held my hand in both of hers and said gently, "The memories are too painful. Maybe we should stop here?"

"No!" I practically shouted. "I want to know. I am not willing to go on living like an ostrich!"

"You were always a smart girl," Maria said with tears in her eyes, "Always."

I smiled faintly at her and said, "You also said that Mom told you that Alice had a hard time with Uncle Karl?"

Maria looked at me for a long time, as if deciding if I could bear the reality, then replied, "Your uncle was a difficult man, you don't remember that?"

Suddenly I had a flash of Aunt Alice kneeling on the floor, picking up the pieces of the vase that Anna had broken, and blood running from her finger. "I was a child," I said. "Children don't come to conclusions from one incident."

"That's true," said Maria. "I don't know which incident you are talking about, but there were many. He was a very hard man. I think that everything that happened suited his strict character, someone who thought that the race should be pure."

The last sentence echoed in my head for a few moments. "Pure?" I repeated.

"Yes," she replied, "He believed everything that was said in the news. He thought that Hitler was a demigod."

I couldn't remember the mood in Alexanderplatz then, and Maria

added, "They believed that the Aryan German was superior in every dis-
cipline. Even in sports, in the Olympics that took place then, their athletes
were light-haired and muscular, the manliest of men, and your uncle — he
was obsessed with collecting these bits of information, he saw himself as
a superior man."

Maria's words filtered slowly through me. I did remember Uncle Karl as
a tough man, but I didn't really know how tough.

"After Alice died he disappeared. Where did he go?" I asked, hoping to
get an answer to at least one of my many questions.

Maria did not answer. She sipped from her tea and got up to add hot
water to her cup. "After their mother died, your cousins changed," she
said. "Johann in particular. He was angry. After that he was angry all the
time. Herman just cried. He practically didn't stop crying for days. Only he
wouldn't cry in front of his brother because Johann would yell at him that
only females cried. You know… sometimes we are angry and we don't have
any way to let that anger out. I think that that was what happened to poor
Johann. He was so angry and he took it out on whoever he encountered.
Once I even left the house to forcefully prevent him from burning a street
cat's tail. I got the cat away and Johann threw a stone at it. He became an
angry boy, and he expressed it in a destructive way."

I tried to recall all of this, but all I could remember was that after the
funeral they disappeared, all three of them. "And Herman?" I asked, hoping
that some bit of information would help me piece it together so I could
remember. "What about him?"

"The angrier Johann became, the more compassionate Herman grew,"
said Maria. "You wouldn't believe how much power there is in compassion… Herman would stand on his tiptoes, making himself taller beside
his brother and shout, 'No! Not a chance! You will not touch this cat!' He
would run home and bring a bowl of milk, that's what he would do."

I had no recollection of these details. All that's left is to imagine the
image of the two boys, one angry and the other merciful.

"And my uncle didn't try to address Johann's issues?" I asked.

"Your uncle was a hard man, Eva, a very hard man," she repeated and
shifted uncomfortably in her chair.

"Come, let's go back to the living room," I suggested, knowing that a long, difficult conversation at least deserves comfortable seating.

We sat down on the sofa and Maria said, "Like I told you before, your father's family never accepted your mother, and they never stopped mourning his choice until the end of their days. Your mother's family actually came to terms with the situation pretty quickly. It was rather surprising, but I think that your mother's father was a very smart man and understood that he would lose her, which distressed him all the more given his other daughter's terrible illness.

"So they were all respectful toward your father and did not say anything about your mother sharing her life with a Jew. Everyone, apart from Karl. 'That Jew,' he would call your father, or 'that Yid.' He refused to say your father's name. He harassed Alice constantly. He claimed that this Jew was desecrating the purity of the German race. He devoutly bought 'Der Stürmer' and would look at the pictures on the front page with obvious disgust.

"I even remember your mother telling me that Alice asked him to stop buying that terrible paper, and how he would show her the caricatures of the greedy, murderous little Jew with the hooked nose that would be the downfall of the proud German people."

Maria was quiet for a moment. "Maybe we'll stop here?"

But we both knew that we wouldn't. She straightened the cushion behind her back and wiped some imaginary dust from the armrest of the sofa with a finger. I could tell that she needed a break from the story, but she went on, "Truthfully, I think that he was simply jealous of your father. Yosef was a rich man, and his fabric shop was doing well while your uncle was having trouble finding work. He was unemployed for a long time, which drove him mad. And jealousy, you know how bad that can be."

"But he was a doctor!" I said. "How could it be that he didn't find work?" I even remembered the little hospital where he worked at some point. I remember getting a checkup there one morning when my temperature was very high. Uncle Karl received my mother and I with a smile and checked me thoroughly. I remember the white room with no curtains, my uncle's white robe and the stethoscope which hung around his neck.

Maria looked at me sadly. She didn't want to ruin the picture I had painted in my mind, but despite herself she said, "He worked in a little hospital but it shut down when the budget ran out. In fact, the director there was Jewish himself. Your uncle blamed him for the hospital closing. He would say that Jews were supposed to be great businessmen but the hospital director was lousy at business."

In my memory we were an attractive, happy family until Aunt Alice died.

"Memory…" Maria said as if reading my thoughts. "Memory plays tricks on us. Sometimes we want to remember something good and convince ourselves that that's how it was, but reality was otherwise. Your uncle hated your father, maybe because he envied him or perhaps simply because he was Jewish."

Maria grew quiet, evidently deciding whether or not to go on.

"What?" I asked her.

She smiled. "No, nothing," she said. "I baked some cookies, want some?"

I smiled at her; just a few minutes ago she had said that her kitchen skills amounted to eggs and salad. I knew that her whole life she had diminished her accomplishments, as I have already written, and didn't give herself credit in any area, but I didn't say anything about it and wiped the smile off my face. I didn't want to let her change the subject. "But after Aunt Alice died, my uncle disappeared with Johann and Herman," I said. Maria sighed deeply.

"Not exactly, dear Eva," she said. "Unfortunately. Maybe you don't remember when I told you that they didn't disappear. Our memories really do have an amazing capacity for forgetting what is best forgotten."

In a quiet voice she went on, "After the funeral, Karl withdrew into the house with the two boys and I would hear shouting from inside. I couldn't hear what they were shouting but sometimes, in the first months after your aunt's death, Herman and Johann would come out and play with you two."

"Interesting," I said contemplatively. "I really don't remember that."

"You were a little girl, it's no wonder your memory is a little vague," she said and sighed again before continuing, "From the window of my house in Alexanderplatz you could see the schoolyard. To this day I am grateful to the good Lord, who gave your mother so much intelligence that she didn't send you to school that day. In fact, even before then I wondered more than once why she sent the two of you to the Jewish school. After all, you could have been safer at a different school, and would have been accepted, but your mother respected your father so much, and maybe wanted to make up for the way his family treated him. In any case, that terrible day, when she left you at home, I am grateful to this day. The other children were not so fortunate."

"What happened?" I asked as a heavy feeling came over me.

"From the window of my home I saw the officer," Maria went on, speaking quickly, like she was afraid of losing the courage to tell me. "He was armed and wore boots, and beside him was a second, younger officer who looked just like him, like peas in a pod. Other officers accompanied them, but those two walked at the front of the line and really stood out. I was transfixed at the window until I heard shouts from inside the school. I went out. The closer I got the better I saw the two officers, and God knows why their eye color is so clearly etched in my memory. Maybe because blue is supposed to be the color of serenity, like the sky, and their eyes lacked any humanity.

"In any case, I couldn't not go and try to maybe save someone, even just one child. But I didn't manage to. If I could go back in time, if I could have known what was about to happen to them, maybe I would have tried harder, but I couldn't do anything. Most of the children were caught and sent to the other side of the school fence where they were loaded onto waiting trucks like a bunch of poultry. There were children who resisted. They kicked, scratched, and spat in the faces of the officers who laughed at them through white teeth. But none could withstand them. The trucks left, and not one of them returned."

Maria went quiet. The terrible image of the children being forced onto big trucks was disorienting to me, an image I had repressed for many years. We had heard those shouts plainly that day. The next day we did not go to school, and in fact from that day on we never returned.

Maria went on speaking as if to cleanse herself of the pain she had witnessed that day. "To one side of the schoolyard, underneath a small awning, sat a girl, maybe twelve years old, not more, in a thin dress, just socks on her feet, and a much smaller child on her knees, with his head in her hands."

Maria was quiet again and whispered that she was very cold. I got up and brought her a blanket from the bedroom. I covered her legs and sat back down. I don't think I had ever seen her like this, on the verge of breaking down.

"Sometimes, there is no accounting for luck. It comes and does at it sees fit. Otherwise, it is impossible to explain how that little girl managed to avoid the trucks. But I will never forget what I saw then until my dying day. The tall officer and the young officer beside him screamed at the frightened girl, 'Raus! Raus!' But she did not get up because of the little boy on her knees. Maybe she didn't understand why they were yelling at her to get out, after all she was outside. I think that they were yelling "Out" to anyone standing nearby.

"They must have meant that she go to the trucks, but she protected her little brother's head with her hands and did not get up. The older officer pulled out his gun and shot in her direction. The girl jumped up and began to run, leaving a trail of blood behind her — and the body of her brother, with an open wound in his head where the officer's bullet hit."

Maria was quiet, hot tears running from her eyes. "Herman…" she added drily. "Didn't have blue eyes. He had his mother's brown eyes."

For a moment I didn't understand why Maria was recalling Herman's eyes just then, but the next moment I realized what she was alluding to and why she was emphasizing the blue eyes of the older officer and the younger one who looked just like him. Something inside me resisted. How could it be?

"Are you sure?" I asked, and she nodded sadly. We both knew I wasn't asking if she was sure about Herman's eye color.

~

CHAPTER TWENTY

I didn't go home that day. It was already late afternoon and a heavy rain was falling outside. The paths around the kibbutz were filled with deep mud. Through the window of Maria's little house I could see the dairy farmer in a raincoat and boots hurrying to finish his work. He brought the cows into the barn, urging them affectionately. The cows lowed and I sat transfixed by nature in all its glory. From the window you could see green, almost infinite fields, the heavy rain made them look washed clean as if in defiance of the things Maria had told that evening.

"I must rest a bit," Maria said and did not make any further comment about Herman. "I am tired to death." That gave me chills. She got up with an uncharacteristic heaviness and turned to the "love room."

She still called it that, even though no real love had happened in there for a long time now. I knew how much she mourned her Shimon, and I identified with her. Only someone who has lost their beloved can really understand.

I remained sitting on the armchair, facing the window, and evidently I dozed off. With my eyes closed, I had visions of my childhood landscape, combined with the nature scene outside the window. I saw the courtyard of our home in Alexanderplatz had green grass, where the rain was washing the leaves until they were shining except that in Alexanderplatz there was also heavy snow, and that day it was very hard to leave the house.

Mom stayed home with us, and Dad went out alone, as usual, in the early morning to the synagogue on the corner of the street. Dad wore a long coat and had a prayer shawl around his shoulders. I heard Mom say to him, "Yosef, put that prayer shawl in its bag, don't go out like that!"

Dad replied, "I am a proud Jew!"

I also heard Mom's broken cries when he returned with his beard almost completely shaved off.

"I told you," she wailed, "You are proud and they cut your beard, that's what you get!"

I remembered the look of him standing before the mirror, wiping his eyes with his prayer shawl, and quoting, "You make us a reproach to our neighbors, our heart will not back down."

I didn't know then what Dad said. I didn't understand his words and I didn't know how much strength there was in the Book of Psalms. I remembered how Mom ran to the stairwell, then outside, screaming. I thought then that she was going to hit whoever did this to my father. She looked so strong and protective. But what actually happened was the complete opposite.

Mom fell, unconscious, out in the courtyard of the building. I saw her through the window and Maria ran to her, lifting her up and supporting her back to the stairs and from there to the house.

Maria rose from bed about an hour later. I looked at her and my heart ached for her. She was always thin, but now she was skinny all over. Her shoulders were stooped and her eyes were sunken. She still looked as beautiful to me as a princess, but that even she, the powerful one who supported all of us, who never broke under the load of pain, suddenly looked so fragile to me was unbearable.

She looked at me in embarrassment and said, "I got old, dear Eva. Old and tired, and I haven't even told you everything yet."

I did not know if I had it in me to hear more, but at the same time I knew that I had to find out what I needed to know before dementia set in. Maria went into the small kitchen, put the kettle on the stove and made us coffee.

"It's practically evening, are you hungry?" she asked.

"No, just coffee is really enough for me for now."

She sat before me on the flowered armchair and said, "Shimon loved this armchair. You know how it is, everyone loves his own armchair."

I smiled at her and tried to repress the image of my Meir sitting in his armchair at home, and not managing to get up from it on his own for the first time.

"I want to tell you something else," she said. "I think you should know everything."

I looked at her tensely, she took a sip from her cup of coffee and went on, "After the hospital closed, Karl was a frustrated doctor, without work. He was unemployed for a long time. Go figure, maybe the idleness drove him out of his mind, maybe it could constitute what they call in court "mitigating circumstances.""

Maria was quiet, then sighed. "Nonsense," she said out loud, as if answering herself. "No mitigating circumstances would explain what he did afterward."

I looked at her inquisitively. "He finally found a job, your uncle, at the Hadamar Hospital." I had never heard of it before, but from Maria's tone I understood that this was not a normal hospital.

"What was that place?" I asked.

Maria sighed and then said, "People whose luck had run out, those with serious mental retardation, or patients with terminal illnesses, they were hospitalized there, only..." She fell silent.

"Only what?" I probed.

She whispered, "They put them to death, a kind of "mercy killing" for those not deemed worthy of life, by their standards... which is a euphemism for murder."

Hearing the words "hospital" and "murder" together was chilling. I was well aware of German doctors who carried out inconceivable crimes and conducted experiments on humans under the guise of medical research. I remembered hearing of the trial against the doctors in Germany, which began in October 1946, and went on for a year and a half. It was in all of the newspapers but I couldn't bring myself to read the shocking details described there. Trembling, I realized that for years I had suppressed the thought of my uncle, the doctor with the blue eyes, and that maybe he was among the accused. I couldn't bear to read the details, the names of the accused and the atrocities that they committed.

Now I could no longer hide behind the silence of doubt. I asked her directly, "Was my uncle among the accused in the case against those doctors?"

Maria looked at me as she replied, "No, I think that he was killed in battle before then, in Russian shelling. He was not among the defendants, but his son, Johann, was."

"Johann?" I asked. "But he wasn't a doctor!"

"True," replied Maria. "But he was the sorcerer's apprentice to his father."

In a moment Maria had taken me back many years. The image of the Brauchtzigan couple, who had hung themselves in the living room of their house with Bach's music playing in the background flashed before my eye.

"Stupid people!" Mom had fumed when she described the horror to Dad. "Bach and Beethoven's music!"

At our house we listened to classical music regularly. You could almost say that I grew up on Mozart, Beethoven, and "The Sorcerer's Apprentice." But the phrase "the sorcerer's apprentice to his father" left me breathless. "What did he do?" I asked anxiously.

Maria did not reply at once. She got up, took our empty mugs to the kitchen, and from there asked again, "Are you hungry?"

"Maria, come here!" I called out. "I don't want to eat!"

She returned to the living room, her expression hollow, and said, "Being hungry won't change what happened."

She sat down before me. "Johann was an angry child, I already told you that, but his anger was the bad kind, not pained anger, there is a difference, as you must know."

Maria's way of explaining behaviors and discerning between the causes and consequences of each was remarkable to me. To be angry out of pain or to be angry out of evil — either way the result was anger, but the differences are enormous.

"Johann was malicious. One can be angry without abusing animals, without beating one's younger brother and shouting at him afterward that he's crying like a girl, without accompanying his father to the clinic where they did experiments on living people, and to see what happens to a person that... I've said enough," she said. "I don't know what got into me that I decided to tell you all this."

She got up and went to make us dinner. I knew that there was no point in my trying to question her further. I also wasn't sure I could take anymore. "After we eat, I'm going back to sleep," she said. "But you are welcome to stay over."

We ate in silence, a quiet that hurt the ears. Even the hot soup that she made did not warm me. "You know," she said suddenly. "Oded, Shimon's grandson, bought his grandfather a computer for his last birthday. Shimon didn't really get around to learning how to use it, unfortunately. And generally, it's funny, these young people think that us old people will manage to learn to work with all of this new technology. But the computer that he bought is still here in the entrance and it has internet."

Maria got up, took a decorated tablecloth off the small table in the corner and said, "I put it here. The young people say it has everything you could ever want to know. Do you know how it works or are you like me?"

It's not as though I had real knowledge on the matter, but as I already said, my children and grandchildren taught me enough for what I needed. When I was working at the university, I had also used what they taught me, but now this gave me an opportunity to use this know-how again.

"My grandchildren taught me to use it," I said. "I am no great expert, but I know how to search for things." Maria smiled a tired smile, and I knew that she was smiling because I understood her intended meaning without her having to say it.

This undertaking lasted that whole night and did not end until I found information and verified it at the Yad Vashem archives a short while later. I started out by reading stories of survivors as documented on various Holocaust memorial websites.

"I'm not seeking revenge," wrote one survivor. "I am seeking justice." I stopped reading for a moment and thought to myself about what the word "justice" means to me. I didn't find a suitable answer, but I was sure that as I saw it, looking for justice was to seek the truth.

From one moment to the next, my need to find testimony grew as well as my desire to find remaining family members. I continued to peruse the various sites, looking for my father's name, Yosef Berliner. I found no direct sign of him but I found his name among a list of those who perished in the extermination camp at Auschwitz. I clung to the letters of his name as if I had found him alive and whole and warm tears flowed freely down my cheeks.

The name Berliner, I learned, was a very common one in Berlin at that time. So I found myself browsing long lists of Berliners and I wondered if any among them were related to my father. I felt anger bubbling up at his relatives who cut him off just because he fell in love with Mom. He never ever spoke of his family to us. I assume that it was too painful for him to remember them. Just once, I heard him mention his grandfather, who had been born in Berlin.

Dad then said to Mom, "Indeed, I am as much of a Berliner as you, even my grandfather is buried here."

I don't remember what Mom replied to him, but sitting before the screen, in this quest to find blood relatives, I had a flash of memory from an old Berlin cemetery. I looked among the gravestones, at the tiny letters, which were barely decipherable, and thought that I recognized the name "Abraham Berliner." It was impossible to really see the dates written on the gravestone, and I thought that I didn't know much about my father's grandfather anyway. I didn't know when he was born, and certainly not when he died.

I continued this hard endeavor, of searching for proof from the trial that Maria told me about. Most of the details that I found online were hard to read and digest. I also came upon the website of Shimon Weisenthal, whose life's work was to bring war criminals to justice.

"Amazing," he quoted in one letter. "How even these days, with the wonders of technology, it's hard to find people." He explained that while the world was becoming a global village, those who wished to disappear could do so very easily. This remarkable man had located about a thousand war criminals through meticulous work, gathering information.

He died of old age in 2005, after saying, "I found the mass murderers and lived on after their deaths."

I took a break from reading on the computer and contemplated this unusual man who chose to make such hard, important work his life's purpose. I felt a little ashamed then, that not only did I repress things, but I never even checked the facts of my personal life before now.

Determined in my aim to find evidence, I continued to search for it.

I found horrific descriptions of "medical" experiments done forcibly on humans without a single drop of mercy.

I found information about horrific experiments intended to see how humans survive at high altitudes, under stress and lack of oxygen, horrific information about exposing the human body to dry and freezing cold, shocking documentation of causing severe and deliberate infection to test drug efficacy, breaking prisoners' limbs, and experiments with various healing methods and other terrible things, which even the page can no longer tolerate.

Not one of the awful descriptions mentioned my Uncle Karl, nor my cousin Johann, although a number of atrocities were attributed to a doctor and sick officer who went unnamed. It was also written that no doctor worked alone. Every "doctor" was accompanied by "junior" doctors — like Uncle Karl von Bock, and perhaps his son? I wondered.

For a moment the thought crossed my mind that perhaps the younger son, Herman, had also come around to join his father and brother. I stopped reading for a moment and tried to make sense of my thoughts. Indeed, Maria said that Herman was a compassionate and merciful child. There was no way I would find his name among the criminals.

As I continued looking at various sites, my breath caught. A pair of blue eyes with a blank expression appeared on the computer monitor below the name: Johann von Bock, war crimes. There was no exact documentation of the trial, but the case summary was enough for me.

The trial took place in June of 1947, while I was in Cyprus, before arriving to Israel. I don't know if I can express here in words the extent of the horror described there in just a few lines. I didn't know that Johann studied medicine like his father, but he was too young to have been a lead doctor. The person who would have conducted the experiments was someone else, possibly even his father.

However, Johann won the case because of lack of evidence that he himself carried out mass sterilization of Jews, men and women, with the aim of exterminating them and purifying the race. But he was there, I no longer had any doubt about that.

I continued to read about experiments involving sterilization. The website mentioned that sterilization of a thousand women could be done en masse and quickly if one doctor and ten assistants worked together. In fact,

194 | THE BERLIN GIRL'S DIARY

the methods were fast and inexpensive and included injecting a chemical into the prisoner's body that completely destroyed the lining of the uterus. It was further written, to my horror, of poor women who were operated on by the Nazis and their ovaries sent for testing the treatment's efficacy.

Meanwhile, many of the defendants tried to deny everything. "Maybe we were there, and maybe not," some of them said.

There was an entire page on the site describing Nazi ideology: to eliminate those that were not deserving of life, a great privilege already approved by two respected professors in 1920. The experiments were carried out with compassion, and the women of Auschwitz's Block 10, the block chosen for experiments, were actually allowed to live, while the rest of the women in other blocks were sent to the gas chambers. So, too, the Nazis claimed in their defense, did the men in Block 28 benefit. The accused claimed that their actions were within the context of patriotic deeds, in service to their homeland. But at trial, the plaintiffs, ex-prisoners, women and men alike, said that they had been the lab rats of Auschwitz.

Ultimately, the claimants were unable to prove that Johann von Bock took an active part in the actions. Maybe his youth also worked in his favor. After all he was older than me by just a few years. A quick calculation suggested that he must have been about nineteen at that time. He won and disappeared the day after his trial, as if the earth had swallowed him whole.

I stopped reading. I got up and stumbled into the bathroom where I puked my guts up. I stood and observed my reflection in the mirror. I was as pale as plaster and couldn't stop crying.

I placed my hands on my belly and was grateful for my nosy neighbors, who gossiped about me until I was persuaded to have children. The laughter of children can heal the sorrow of the whole world, I heard Maria's words in my head, the sorrow of the whole world.

I don't know if anything has healed my sorrow since. Of course, I never told my children about any of this. I continued to talk with Meir at night undisturbed, but no more than that. My sorrow grew deeper, along with the difficulties of memory, which were closing in on me.

Sometimes my imagination would interfere with reality, and the sad result was that I could no longer always distinguish between them. It was clear that I needed to write everything down, so that my children would know in the future who I am and where I came from, but also that I would have to find someone from among my extended family, so I didn't grow old with the thought that only Karl and Johann von Bock were my remaining living family.

Maybe, I thought, I could find the other cousin, Herman. And maybe, I hoped, some other uncle might turn up, from my father's side, or a cousin, even a second or third cousin, the main thing was to find someone from among my relatives.

I felt that if I didn't find anyone I would die feeling regret. Logically, I knew that I was not guilty of anything, but it is hard for me to explain how soiled I felt, like a mark of shame stuck to me. The image of my childhood, which I had thought was happy, had shattered like a big wave crashing on a rock. I felt I had to clean up the stain before I died.

That night I didn't close my eyes or even lie down to sleep. Tired and hurting I sat in the armchair. When Maria got up with especially slow steps, she went to the kitchen and made us coffee. With trembling hands she handed me a cup and sat down heavily before me.

"Good morning," she whispered. "I think that I will go back to bed for a bit, I don't feel so well."

I wanted to call the doctor, but Maria smiled and said, "Nonsense, there's no need, I'm just a little out of sorts… it's too bad I told you so much yesterday… after all it won't accomplish anything…" She got up and went back to the love room.

I followed her and asked, "Are you sure there's no need to call a doctor?"

Maria covered herself with a blanket and smiled at me. "I'm fine, just a bit tired." She closed her eyes and I got ready for my trip home.

A moment before I left her house I entered her room once more. She was lying in bed with her eyes closed and I was sure that she was sleeping. I left the room on tiptoe, and then I heard her say out loud, "Forget everything, Eva? It doesn't matter anymore… I shouldn't have told you."

I turned to her and she opened her eyes. They said the total opposite: Search, Eva, search.

∾

CHAPTER TWENTY-ONE

I want to write down everything here: my whole truth, all of my feelings, even the hardest things. Maybe I will preface this by saying that I know that every truth, even the purest, can be multifaceted, with more than one side to it.

And my truth is incomplete, which might be the one thing which allows me to continue to breathe despite the things that I am putting down in writing right now. In my search for the truth I read a lot of material about topics and deeds that I never knew about. I learned, for example, that there was much research done on those who experienced the Holocaust as children.

Moshe Sanbar, for the Chairman of the Center for Holocaust Survivors' Organizations, for instance, sought reparations for those who were small children during the war. When I read the research, it gave me a kind of permission for the fact that to this day I have never talked about these things with anyone because, like many Holocaust survivors, I have tried to suppress it all my life. Now, as I grow old, my memories are stronger than my ability to forget them. But maybe there are things that the mind refuses to remember just like there are events that the mind refuses to forget.

For years, since realizing that I was not Jewish, I was operating on an incorrect assumption. When my mother said *'fehler,'* I understood that to mean "mistake," because she tried to tell them that she was actually "one of them." But today, having done extensive research on my past, I am no longer certain that that was the mistake my mother was referring to.

There had been an anti-Jewish atmosphere in Germany long before it was too late. Long before. My father recognized this, as did Anna, and even me. I have said too little about Anna and I am sorry that my memory betrays me so much lately that her upright figure is disappearing from me. What I remember is that she was extraordinarily beautiful and danced ballet. It is shameful to say that I remember my envy for her even now. I was not sent to learn ballet, and I even remember Mom saying that I was better suited to drawing or playing an instrument. I didn't do any of those things, because time was not on my side. First, I was too young, and then it was too late.

If I consider what actually came to pass, I had an amazing opportunity to do what many in my situation were unable to accomplish. Even though my formal education was disrupted, I had the great fortune to make up my studies later. But I know today that my good fortune was practically a miracle. Many people in my situation were not so lucky, as a result of which many survivors remained uneducated. Not only was my beloved sister unable to complete her schooling and advance, she did not get to live at all. But she learned classical ballet. I remember her wearing her ballet shoes and dance outfit and dancing to Swan Lake in our home. I would watch her with unabashed envy. I thought she was perfect. She also danced in the school dance troupe and I believe she was among the better dancers there, with a dazzling future ahead.

But in our city they thought differently. Even though we went to the Jewish school, where discrimination only seeped in during the later stages, around the horrific time of Kristallnacht, there was discrimination against Jews in the education system long before then.

In my search for my relatives I investigated that too and got to know the facts. Already by the time I was three or four years old, restrictions were placed on Jewish children whose primary aim was humiliation. We were forbidden to participate in municipal sporting events, made to sit on the back benches in class like lepers, and exposed to mental and physical abuse on the part of their Aryan contemporaries and even the school teachers.

As I said, there were things that are etched in the memory that no dementia will ever erase. The day that I will describe is like that. I even remember that it was a Sunday, the weekly day off from the Christian schools, and the day after our Sabbath at the Jewish school. That day there was a big sporting event in which children from several schools in the city were meant to participate. The general event was meant to demonstrate children's athletic abilities in all kinds of sports. The big show was supposed to open with the classical dance troupe, which was made up of children from several schools. Anna was one of them. She was seven years old, and mature for her age.

I remember the event well because there was a big argument in our home on the Saturday, the day before. Anna wanted to play Stravinsky's "Rites of Spring" on the gramophone, the piece chosen for the show. The mood in the house was tense. Dad wanted to prevent the desecration of the Sabbath and I think it was the first time that Mom argued with him about religious matters in front of us. She demanded that he let Anna listen to her music. But he refused and Anna cried for almost the entire day. The worst part was that the fight, and Anna's crying, turned out to be for nothing anyway, because the next day, when we arrived at the event, our school principal approached Mom and uttered a single word in a cracked voice, "'Nein' — "No."

I remember that I did not understand what he meant but Mom did: Anna would not be allowed to perform because she was considered a Jew. The irony of it all was that she wasn't even Jewish. Mom tried to argue, but the school principal silenced her.

Anna was devastated for a long time afterward and she refused to be comforted. Yohanan Ronen described it well in an article that I mentioned earlier about children of the Holocaust. At the age when children learn to stand tall, run, fly, the children of the Holocaust learned to crawl and disappear, he wrote. In his article, he describes the extent of the harm done to the children who experienced the horrors on their own. He talks about how the personality of the man is constructed during his childhood. One's future, what that child will do with his life, depends greatly on his childhood.

Anna was forced to leave the ballet group, and I think with that she lost much of her desire to live. It gives me chills to think what would have happened if she had survived like me, and been granted the chance to grow up. Would she have become a dancer or would she have remained a bird with a broken wing?

I don't know what part of all this affected me the most, but I carried the thought of Anna's dream, which shattered into pieces, for years. With my own children I insisted that they never give up their dreams, that dreams are meant to come true and that even if the road is hard and bumpy, you must stay the course.

When Hani discovered her talent for art, I had mixed feelings. I was worried that she wouldn't be able to make a good enough living as a sculptor, but I also knew that I would support her and help her to make her dreams come true, which is indeed what happened. I could see how happy it made her to live her dream. When Anna's dream burst, something broke at home, and Mom's fighting spirit dwindled, but did not break. Not yet, that is.

When I mentioned how we learned to crawl and disappear, that evoked another incident that won't leave my memory. I don't remember which day of the week it was, but I remember the knock on the door all too well. I hate to say it but to this day, if there's an unexpected knock on my door, my heart skips a beat.

Meir joked about that more than once. "That's how you *yekkes* are." He would smile. "No one can come to visit without warning you in advance." More than once I told him that he was a *yekke* too and we would laugh about it, but for me, a knock on the door from an unexpected visitor was and still feels to me like a bad omen.

That day the knocking was stronger than usual. It was evening already and there was classical music playing in the living room. The knocking on the door sounded agitated, loud, jarring. From the entrance to my room I saw the officer. He stood tall and serious. I didn't hear exactly what he said but I cannot forget Mom's cries no matter how hard I try.

Dad and Anna were called to come out of the house and go with the officer. Mom lay on the floor weeping bitterly. I tiptoed out and asked, 'Wo ist papa?' Mom didn't answer. She cried for hours and I sat beside her on the floor crying too. Late that night, a miracle happened. Dad and Anna returned, safe and sound.

Anna told us that they were taken to the synagogue where there were lots of Jews from our street. "They didn't do anything to us," she reassured Mom. "And in the end they told me and Dad to go home."

"What happened to all the rest of the people?" I asked, but Mom shushed me. She probably knew that the rest of the people did not fare as well as Dad and Anna, who were saved, probably, thanks to her.

A few days later they cut Dad's beard. Mom probably understood then that she would no longer be able to protect us, and I don't know why she didn't listen to Dad's pleas. He wanted to leave. For days he repeated his entreaty, and Mom, evidently, would quiet him. Afterward there began talk of "kinder transport."

At the time I didn't understand what it meant but today I know that tens of thousands of children, Jewish and non-Aryan Christians were sent on their own to the UK, which had a solution for refugees to Israel as it was. Children were chosen for transport based on the parents' request to the national representatives of German Jews. Anyone considered an urgent case was approved pretty quickly. Maybe we were not considered urgent but Dad at least had to try, and "kinder transport" was heard many times at home, especially after the sports show on that terrible Sunday.

I remember Dad taking us out one day. He told Mom that he was taking us for some fresh air. Anna was a bit sickly, with frequent attacks of heavy coughing. Looking back, I think that those coughing fits got worse from the day her dream was shattered. But then, that same day, Mom shut herself up in her room along with Maria, and did not oppose us going out.

Dad dressed us in warm coats and I didn't understand why he was putting our clothes in a suitcase. Today I know that he was attempting a desperate act, to bring us to the train station where the children chosen to be sent to Britain were gathered, and beg for our lives. He probably knew that it didn't work like that, but he was so desperate that he was willing to try anything.

When we arrived at the train station, I saw a few dozen families. They all had suitcases and it looked like they were all going on a trip together. When I read, years later, about Jewish children being sent across the border, I learned that many parents did not tell their children until the last moment, letting them think that they would be traveling together. I stood there transfixed by crying children, holding onto their parents' clothes. Many parents had a hard time maintaining their composure.

As I was standing there, I heard the announcer calling out the names of children and checking their identification. Dad approached the announcer and talked to him for a while. From afar it looked like he was listening to Dad for a moment until he waved his hand. Dad went on talking to him.

The man lost his patience and shouted so loud that even we heard, "Get out of here before I call the police!"

Dad seemed frightened by the threat and knew that if the police showed up it would not turn out well for us. He turned back to us with tears in his eyes.

At night I heard Mom shouting at him, and him trying to justify himself. "I thought…" he said. "Since you…" I didn't hear the rest of the conversation. I must have fallen asleep. Dad tried to convince her for a few more days, but it seemed that the more he tried, the more Mom stood her ground.

What I will tell now I remember in detail, probably because it was done with great secrecy. In fact, I also remember the incident because of the anger in the house afterward, and because Anna told me about it when our house nearly collapsed with Mom's rage. Even now when I think of my dear father who did not give up, and did desperate things to try to save us, I feel proud. At the same time, I tried to manage my anger at Mom, who refused to see what Dad saw, but I tried my best to understand her.

In any case, a few days after the train station, an announcement was published in the British-Jewish newspaper, the "Jewish Chronicle" calling families in the UK to foster "two good-hearted little girls, an extremely urgent case." For years afterward, when I investigated things, I understood that Dad acted from a place of utter despair; he knew that we would have no chance of crossing the border of Berlin anyway, but the description "two good-hearted girls…" was a great description, because evidently the British Jews preferred to take in girls, the younger the better.

Mom heard about it by chance. I don't know which of the neighbors told her, and anyway it doesn't matter. When she heard, she responded with restrained anger.

Anna told me that at night, after I had fallen asleep, Mom said to Dad, 'Fertig.' "She said just one word," said Anna. "Just, "it's over." And that's it." I didn't understand what was over and I remember the fear that gripped me.

After that Mom gave him the silent treatment. I think that she did not talk to Dad for at least a month. Anna and I would watch them from the side, hoping to see a smile, to no avail. At night, we would press our ears to the wall we shared with our parents' bedroom, hoping to hear speaking, maybe laughter, maybe a sigh out loud, but we heard nothing. One morning we got up and Dad tried again to convince her.

Mom remained quiet most of the time and finally said, "I will never ever leave Alice's grave behind. Understand?!"

Today, I know that we could have been sent, like many children were, to another country to be saved. Most countries preferred child refugees to adults, since children posed no risk to the labor market. They evoked humanitarian responses and were thought to be more adaptable. I smile bitterly as I write this, thinking how Maria would say that all the countries who saved children preferred them because their laughter heals the sorrow of the entire world.

I know that Mom refused to send us because she trusted her homeland, and thought, "It won't happen to us." Then she couldn't bear the thought of being separated from us.

I don't know how many children like that found their parents later on, but I do know that many of them were saved and lived full lives after they were torn from the arms of their families. Not Anna.

With mixed feelings I sit now, big tears filling my eyes. How can I even think that we were not sent away? Why don't I consider my mother, who would not have been sent to another country to be saved? But then I envision my two children, and me, when I was in that hell, and I can wholeheartedly say: I would sacrifice my life to save them. I wouldn't stop to think twice. Maybe that was the mistake Mom was talking about?

CHAPTER TWENTY-TWO

Since the visit with Maria which, sadly, was the last time we met at her home, I was ill at ease.

Maria was taken to the hospital a short while afterward and she was in bed attached to tubes and machines when I visited her there, only able to communicate with her kind eyes. I was angry with myself that I had not insisted on calling the doctor during our last visit, that I didn't see how difficult it was for her to get up and how she sat down so heavily.

I was so preoccupied with the stories she was telling me. I still torment myself for that. In any case, both at her house and again at the hospital, her eyes seemed to hint to me not to leave any stone unturned. I think that she knew I would find relatives and that it would be worth the effort to do so.

***

Avner tried to read between the lines of the last sentence. She seemed to be suggesting that she had found relatives. What did that mean? He suddenly had that feeling as if he was sitting in a public place and someone was staring at his back. He turned in alarm to see who was staring at him. "Idiot, there's no one else here!" he said out loud to himself.

He needed some fresh air. He got up and opened the window and saw Nisim sitting on a bench with a prayer book in his hands. "Hey, what's up?" He tried to speak in his regular voice.

Nisim looked up at him from the prayer book and gestured that he would respond momentarily.

"Sorry," Avner apologized. "I didn't notice that you were mid-prayer."

Nisim got up, took three steps back and three steps forward, bowed toward the east and prayed silently.

Avner watched him with a feeling of barely hidden envy.

'O-seh shalom bimromav, hu b'rechmav ya'aseh shalom aleinu ve al kol yisrael, ve'amru amen,' Nisim recited the end of the prayer.

Avner smiled gently.

"Afternoon prayer," Nisim said. "It's after two already."

Avner looked at the clock in dismay. There was just one hour left until the funeral. Close family members would probably arrive within half an hour. He had to get himself together and go on reading. Again he felt as though someone was watching him. If Mrs. Reich got to the truth one way or another, what would it say about him? The panicky feeling that Avner knew so well bothered him. He did not like feeling out of control and something in his usual defenses: the mask he wore, the protective shell, had cracked.

He suddenly recalled overhearing a conversation between Nisim and his wife Bracha once and how much strength his friend drew from his belief and his ability to find help in those close to him. Avner no longer recalled the reason why Nisim lost faith in something, but remembered the innocent conversation as if it had happened yesterday.

"What do you do when doubt is eating away at you?" he heard Nisim ask. "What do you do when you lose faith in someone?"

He couldn't hear Bracha's reply, but a moment later Nisim said, "No, my dear, I'm not talking about you, God forbid!" A moment later he added heaven forbid, to be safe. "No, not you, God <u>and</u> heaven forbid!"

Avner smiled to himself as he recalled the conversation and how he felt that Bracha must have been smiling too. Even without hearing her answer, he understood that she was asking about the details, and when the conversation was over, Nisim said, "So much wisdom in one little woman!"

Avner remembered his friend's happy expression, like now, as he finished praying and asked with a smile, "Are you finished now, or do you need us to stretch out the next hour?"

∗∗∗

It took me time to recover from Maria's death. Throughout several long weeks I oscillated between the almost uncontrollable need to explore further, and the wish to finish my life in peace without knowing any more. Perhaps what tipped the scales was that I felt my memory problems getting worse.

I no longer remembered the birthdays of my children and grandchildren, and even more shocking was that I was forced to look at a picture of Meir so that his face would not be erased from my memory. I understood that I had to follow through. A few months after Maria passed away, I picked myself up, went to the Yad Vashem Museum and headed to the archives. The woman working there was very gracious. She is almost as old as the stories that she documents, but she is as attentive and open-eyed as a much younger woman. Her coworkers say that her generosity in her work is what keeps her so alert, even though she is close to eighty years old. She is a diminutive, almost miniature woman, who busies herself from morning to evening with documentation. Soon enough there will be no one left to tell, or perform this sacred duty.

The little woman received me brightly. "My name is Elisheva," she said, and shook my hand warmly. She led me to her tidy office. There was a big bookshelf, a brown sofa, a desk, and a few vases of flowers filling the room.

She gestured to the brown sofa. "Sit," she said kindly. Then she told me about how back in the 1940s, people from all over the world who were searching for survivors came to her. Maybe a lost brother had been found somewhere in the world, a sister who had disappeared, an uncle, people who had made it through the inferno, seeking solace. She used flowery turns of phrase here and there, but it was a pleasure to hear her speak.

"People sent me their names, the country where they're living, their birthdates, family members names, and waited. Maybe someone from their family would also turn up. They knew that the chances were not great but it was worth the effort. And me? I've been sitting and documenting and double indexing the names of the applicants and the names of the people they are looking for, for years. I write everything on a typewriter. I'm not one for the wonders of technology. But I have a huge inventory from all these years, an endless repository of pain."

I looked at her in admiration. She had dedicated her whole life to helping others.

"My young colleagues type up the details in the computerized database," she said with a smile. "They give attention-grabbing headings, like "Who knows who" or "Near or far, we are seeking family, wherever they are," — and people get in touch, from all over the world."

I was amazed by the intensity with which she spoke. It was clear to me that without her dedicated, uncompromising, and inspiring work, there would be no such database and many families would not have found each other.

"People come to me from all over," she declared proudly and pulled a few sample stories out of a bulging binder:

"Abraham, born in 1919, in a small town in Czechoslovakia, whose parents bought him and his brother Hungarian birth certificates and smuggled them over the border, is seeking his brother Isaac who disappeared. Maybe he is still alive somewhere, because Avraham never found his brother among the bodies that floated on the river.

"A woman born in Leiden, Holland, in 1926. She was sixteen years old when her father was forced to hand his prosperous business over to the Germans, and told the family that they had to find a hiding place. Her younger sister fled and disappeared, and maybe she was alive somewhere in the world?"

"I knew a woman who helped Jews during the war and hid them in her cellar," I told her sadly. "She told me of a woman named Tova who found her brother, but later he was killed here in Israel."

Elisheva shot me an understanding look. "I've seen a lot of pain and suffering here, along with indescribable happiness. Who was that woman who helped the Jews during the war?"

I told her about Maria and Ludwig, the fabric shop, the cellar, everything.

"That's amazing," said the little woman. "It's amazing to hear about people like that."

"There *were* people like that," I told her sorrowfully. "She died."

Elisheva looked somber. She leafed through another file and said, "I'm really sorry to hear that, but I have many heartwarming stories, too. Here, I'll show you more samples."

She told me about Mordechai, who had been a very thin boy, and was thrown out of the train window to freedom by an anonymous man who had been standing behind him, and saw an opportunity for him to survive. Mordechai was looking for the man who had thrown him out and saved his life, and the anonymous man had also come to look for his own relatives. "Reality can be stranger than your wildest imagination," she said. "The man came to look for his family and told me how he had thrown a skinny boy out of the train. I can't describe how moved I was to connect the two, nearly sixty years later!"

I looked at the many documents. She had written down every detail: physical appearance, dates, precise places, and many pictures taken in the ghetto, when everyone was still alive. "As the years pass," she said sadly. "There is less chance of finding anyone living, but the documentation is still here. At this point I work as a volunteer. Sometimes children come, the next generation, even grandchildren, and talk about a grandpa, an uncle, a relative, and look for documentation. It's my life's work. But truly?" She smiled at me. "I think that if I stopped doing what I do, I would miss it terribly. After all, it's been forty years that I've worked here, I couldn't stop as long as there might still be a chance of someone finding a relative. It's like an earthquake, there's always a chance of finding someone under the rubble."

"Yes I understand," I told her. "I felt a similar feeling when I left my work and retired."

Elisheva nodded. "In any case I didn't stop recording, indeed since the Martyrs' and Heroes Remembrance (Yad Vashem) Law was enacted in the Knesset in 1953, many people have been working to document every bit of evidence and every piece of information on what happened. They even documented the years before, while Hitler was still deciding who was worthy of living."

208 | THE BERLIN GIRL'S DIARY

"Good for you," I said, and she waved her hand dismissively.

"I couldn't manage without this, it's part of my life," she said. "I record the lives of survivors and gather information on the murderers, the murdered, and the heroic people who saved and helped, sometimes even risking their lives to do so. Those who gave refuge and some food, stood guard, took care, and did their best. There is a separate database for each category. There's a whole one on the good people who saved Jews, like the woman you told me about earlier."

"She died last year," I said quietly. "But she really was a special woman."

"It's so heartening to know that there were many like that," she replied. "But not everyone is on record, unfortunately. There were many reasons that people didn't come to document their stories, but the main one is probably the fear of probing in the past."

"Yes," I said pensively. "The fear of poking around in the past, and maybe also the wish to erase it, as if it never happened."

"That's impossible, of course," she said. "People cannot erase what they have been through, though I must say that if it was possible, it would be much easier on a lot of people."

"You really are amazing," I said.

"Thank you," she replied, embarrassed. "I don't think I'm so amazing. To this day I haven't even managed to learn to type on the computer."

"That doesn't diminish the magnitude of your work," I said, and she smiled again.

"The truth is that over the years I also documented by making recordings, and I have the help of a photographer who takes pictures and puts together documentation videos. I can't tell you how chilling some of the stories are."

I was quiet a few minutes, leafing through the stories written in round, neat handwriting and she asked, "Who are you looking for, Mrs. Reich?"

"Please, call me Eva," I replied. "My mother was not Jewish, but my father was. They were killed in the Holocaust, along with my older sister. I survived by chance but I never looked for anyone who may have survived from my extended family. I think that it's time for me to do that."

I did not know the names of my father's family members, just the surname.

"Unfortunately that isn't enough," she told me. "Berliner was a very common name in that city. Without first names it will be hard to find anything."

I looked at her sadly.

Maybe wanting to comfort me, she asked, "And what about relatives from your mother's side?"

I could feel my cheeks heating with embarrassment, but I gathered courage and gave her the names of Karl and his two sons. I did not stop to think if one of them might still be alive. Maria had told me that Karl was dead, killed by Russian shelling, but would I be able to look in the blue eyes of my cousin Johann? Could I say anything to him? Would finding my cousin Herman help me to come full circle?

Elisheva looked at me with great interest as I told her about my uncle and cousins and promised me that she would check the databases and get back to me if she found anything.

We parted ways, and I left her office with mixed feelings. I felt that I had to know, but I was afraid to find out more.

A few days after my visit to Yad Vashem, the phone in my room rang.

"Would you be able to come to my office?" Elisheva asked me, and my heart skipped a beat. I was overwhelmed with emotions.

"Did you find someone?" I asked.

She replied, "I think so. I am not sure, but maybe. I think you should come here. It isn't a matter for the phone."

Within an hour I was already on the bus on my way to Jerusalem.

Elisheva received me brightly. "Good for you to just get on a bus like that, at our age, that's no small feat." A moment later she apologized, "Sorry that I dared to say "our age.""

I laughed. "We're a similar age," I told her. "No need to apologize."

She led me into her office. There, as she was offering me to sit down on the brown sofa, she said, "I'll let you read what I found. It's pretty long, so I suggest that you get comfortable."

She pulled a large brown paper bag out of a binder and said, "One of my young colleagues helped me find these. Without his help, I don't think I would have found anything."

I took the bag with shaking hands, and she said, "I really hope that I didn't make a mistake and that there is indeed a connection to your family, because unfortunately I did not find anyone left from the Berliner family. According to the sources that I have access to, nobody from your father's family survived, but I think that there is something here about your mother's side. Is the name "Sarah" familiar to you?"

I racked my brain, but couldn't think of anyone by that name in my family. "No," I replied.

"She looked at the bag in my hands. "Sometimes I get the names mixed up, let me check again." I handed her the bag.

She leafed through the pages for a moment and handed the bag back, saying, "No I didn't make a mistake. The woman's name is Sarah. When I asked the young man who helped me to look for names like those you gave me, he found this."

I tried to recall if I had ever heard the name Sarah related to anyone from my family or among my relatives. "Do you remember this Sarah?" I asked.

She thought for a moment, then said, "There was a woman who came here once, she got to the entrance to the offices, and then did not know where to turn. You see? Usually people who come here know exactly what they came for, but she looked so lost! If I'm not mistaken, she said that her name was Sarah."

A moment before leaving the room, she added, "Last night I flipped through those records. At the time, when I sat with her, I wrote down everything she said, word for word, as I do with everyone who comes to give testimony. Sometimes things are so hard and said so directly… in any case, I made a few comments in brackets." She sighed deeply, smiled with embarrassment. "Okay, I've talked enough… take your time, read those over, and then we can talk a bit."

She turned and left the room, and I looked at the first page. The subject read: "Sarah Bock," With that, I entered into the world of this woman of whom I did not know until then.

✳✳✳

Avner dropped the diary. A cold sweat broke out on his brow and he felt like he might faint. He took a sip from the glass of water on the table and along with fear, he was filled with terrible anger, mostly at himself. He had ripped up that brown envelope to shreds. How could it not have occurred to him that he was just ripping a copy, and that the original was saved somewhere?

Should he read the pages now? His instincts told him to throw it all in the trash beside the table. He looked at the bin, amusing himself with the idea of going on as an ostrich and not reading the pages where his mother's words were recorded.

He tried to comfort himself: maybe it wasn't even his mother? How did he know for sure that this was the same Sarah? After all his mother barely left the house. How could she have made it to Yad Vashem on her own? But the next moment he brought his fist down on the table. "Enough!" he heard himself shout. "Enough!"

He knew that he could not hide anymore, that he was no longer a helpless child, the solitary boy with no siblings apart from the imaginary Hilik. If Hilik was here now, he thought bitterly, even he would scream, "enough!"

Avner picked up the diary, leaned back in his chair and read the document until its end.

***

So I sank into the world of Sarah, written with great feeling, and I am including a copy of it here:

I don't know if the devil will come if I tell the whole story here. He comes whenever he wants. He doesn't ask me permission and maybe I am now making a huge mistake and inviting him here myself, but I am already here, so I will say everything,

I was the oldest in my family. I had a little sister and a little brother. Mom told me to look after them, not to let them out of my sight. I had aunts and uncles and grandfathers and grandmothers, but none of them are alive anymore. Many years have passed. I want to tell about that day, but I don't know where to begin. I would like to tell a bit about how it was at home before the devil came, but I don't remember so well, just that day, that's what I remember. How my sister and brother and I went to school that morning, like every other day, and Mom shouted after me that I look after them and not take my eyes off them, as I already said.

When we got to the school, we saw the truck from a distance, and my sister ran toward it happily. She must have thought that there would be a trip. Before that day, we had gone on school trips on trucks. So my sister ran quickly and I ran after her to stop because my little brother couldn't run that fast, but she didn't stop.

A soldier stood beside the truck, and he caught her and threw her into the truck, and I still didn't understand at first what exactly was going on, but when I heard shouting and crying of children, I realized that something bad was happening and I knew that it was my job to look after my younger siblings, and now only my brother was left. So I ran away with him, and my shoes fell off, probably the laces had come undone as had happened many times, but I didn't stop to put them back on, and I sat in the corner of the yard. I didn't want to sit, just to keep on running, but my brother was small, he had no strength to keep running, and if I kept going I would have had to leave him behind, which was out of the question.

So we sat there for a long time, in the corner, where they didn't see us. My brother lay across my lap. From a distance, I saw officers approaching us and I knew that we would have to run, but my legs couldn't manage to get up. I felt as if I was glued to the spot, frozen. My brother began to cry and I stroked his head and held it between my hands.

(*Sarah cupped her two hands, to show how she held her brother's head, and spoke in a whisper, in a grave tone. I could not help but notice that two of her fingers were crooked.*)

I did not manage to do as my mother said. First, I didn't take proper care of my sister, and now I failed to save my brother from the tall officer. He stood before me and laughed. Can you hear him? (*Sarah let out a sharp, terrible laugh.*) I looked at him as he laughed, he had shiny black boots and blue eyes. I don't know why I remember his eyes, I can't seem to forget them to this day, that blue, and I saw another officer behind him, smaller but also laughing, and with those same blue eyes. See? I looked at them, at their blue eyes, instead of protecting my brother. Get it?

(At this point I suggested to Sarah that we film her. That way there would be longer-lasting documentation, it would keep better, but Sarah quietly asked not to, and I let her go on, to get her pain out, which she had held so close for so many years.)

No need for a video, the devil can come back any moment, if he sees, it will be bad.

(I tried to tell her that she was safe, that the devil would not come, and that a film would last better, as living testimony for her children and grandchildren, who would come and learn and read and know, but she was alarmed and vehemently refused.)

I have a son. He is handsome and small like my brother. I have to take care of him, that nothing bad will happen to him. He has the name of a military man, because only the strong will survive.

(I comforted her, if she doesn't want her son to know of the horrors, the information will not be sent to him, unless she approves it, and she relaxed, as if an opening had been breached in the protective wall she had been hiding behind.)

He shot him, you hear that sound? He shot him in the head, my hands filled with blood. I didn't protect him well enough. Maybe there was a hole in my hands? How could it be that a bullet passed between my fingers, just scratched them a little, but passed through them and hit my brother's head? I don't know how, for years I've been thinking about how it could have happened, but I have no answer.

Then my hands were full of blood, suddenly my legs were no longer glued to the spot. I got up and ran. I ran faster than a speeding bullet. Faster than his shiny boots. My hand hurt terribly, but that's how it is, you know, when something hurts more, you don't feel whatever hurts less, and my heart hurt so badly, and it hasn't passed to this day, that great pain.

(Sarah went on talking and blaming herself, I tried from time to time to stop her, to tell her that none of it was her fault, but she didn't listen.)

I ran. I didn't even wait. I don't know if my sister came back, and my mom must have looked for me, but I ran away, I didn't believe it was possible to run so fast. I don't know if those blue eyes followed me, because I didn't look back, not once, just ran, and I heard shouting, but I didn't stop, until I had no strength left. I saw a door to a kind of shed, and thought that maybe if I went in there I could hide because I had no strength left to go on running. So I opened the door to the shed, and there were people there who said there was no space, get out of here.

I was so tired, that's what I remember most, how exhausted I was, and suddenly someone came back and opened the door to the shed and said that I could come in, but I heard his accent, like the officer with the blue eyes. I was so scared, but I looked in and saw that his eyes weren't blue at all. He looked at me and said again to come in, but his accent was really frightening. I looked down for a moment, he had boots on, and then I must have fainted.

(I looked at her as she spoke. She spoke quickly but haltingly. Blue veins stood out on her forehead, and her skin looked completely transparent. I stopped her more than once, brought her a glass of water, but she didn't take so much as a sip and went on telling her story.)

I don't know how long I was unconscious. I think that it was better for me that way, much less painful. And quiet, finally quiet. The noise in my ears was hard, you know? To this day I hear something, like whistling. I can't seem to stop hearing it. Even then I wanted to forget but couldn't. But then I woke up, and he stood there before me, and I thought that maybe he really was looking out for me. I saw him holding a bandage which was all red, but he said, "I know a bit about medicine. I checked your fingers and it looks as though someone shot you and the bullet just scratched your fingers and passed between them. You are very lucky."

I wanted to tell him that I wasn't lucky at all. If I was, that bullet wouldn't have passed between my fingers, but then I thought that there was no way he could be looking out for me, he must be another liar, like all of them, even Mom said that it would be fine and it wasn't, and Dad made promises but none of them came true, so this man must have been lying too. Then he said to me, "Everything will be okay."

Even though he had that accent, I suddenly believed him, you know how it goes, sometimes we believe what we want to, and he told me not to worry, he would protect me.

***

Nisim poked his head through the door of the office. "Avner, it's quarter after two, are you ready?"

Avner felt as though Nisim was bringing him back to reality. He knew that he could no longer entertain the idea that this wasn't his mother telling these terrible things. Indeed, it was clear that she was speaking of him, her son with the military name. But then who was that anonymous savior that she was talking about? And what did he have to do with all this? There was no doubt that Mrs. Reich was very interested in his mother's life story but still, why him?

"Avner, is everything okay?" he heard Nisim ask again.

"Okey dokey," he tried to answer with a smile. "I'm almost done reading."

"Okey dokey, huh?" Nisim asked. "Because you don't look so good, if you don't mind my saying so."

"Listen," Avner said impatiently. "I only have a few pages left to read here. I'm almost done and then I'll come out, okay?"

"Fine, fine," said Nisim. "Just telling you the time, that's all."

Avner sighed, he didn't mean to offend Nisim, but he had no choice. With trembling hands he picked up the diary and went on reading.

***

He really is a good man, he told me about his father, who was an officer, and he believed that the Germans were better than the rest of the world, so he went with his truth, even against family members, and took his older son with him, and the two of them enlisted in the SS.

He said quietly that he heard that hundreds of children had been forced out of the school, and they didn't have parents or relatives or anyone. And I told him about my little brother, who my hands did not save. I told him how they laughed and how I could still hear the command 'Raus' ringing in my ears.

"Then I didn't know what to do," I told him. "Your family, that's not good, that's a big problem."

He replied, "My family is not me."

I asked him, "Do you have a mother?"

"Mother died a long time ago," he answered. "She was very sick. They made her a golden coffin, with angels."

I so wanted to believe him, maybe he really was different, and I believed, and I stayed with him in that shed for a long time, and he protected me that whole time. He would go out early in the morning and come back in the afternoon with food for all of us, and sometimes even bring medicine for those who were not feeling well. The Nazis thought he was one of them and they believed him that he was only looking out for other Germans with all that food and medicine.

Sometimes, he would even take me to the house of friends of his and introduce me as his cousin, but afterward we would go back to the shed. He was always afraid that someone would see that there were people inside, so we kept the lights off and stayed in the dark and quiet, just waiting for it to all be over.

But then one morning he went out, as usual, and didn't come back in the afternoon. I don't know who turned him in but he told me after that suddenly three officers from the Gestapo came up behind him, when he was standing in line at the store and asked him, "Who is all this for?" Because they saw that he was buying a large amount of food, that was suspicious to them.

He told me that they took him to their station and interrogated him but he didn't reveal anything and they ordered him, "Swear that you are loyal to your homeland." They wanted to see if he really was loyal to his homeland and the Nazis, may their memory be erased. He did, so as not to arouse suspicion, he said, 'Ich bin treu,' "I am faithful, I will be a good soldier."

Later he told me that they put him at the train station, to record everyone who was going and who was returning, to write down everything, they were so organized, it was important to them to write everything. He told me that he saw people on the trains of death, and he sometimes managed to give the guards a few marks to save someone each time, because he felt sorry for them. Afterward the war simply ended. All that time that he wasn't there, I couldn't tell you exactly how long it was, I don't really remember, but we remained in the shed, we were quite a lot of people there, and there was just a bit of food that had to last for everyone for all those days.

I don't want to talk about those days really because it was awful. People defecated there in the shed, it smelled terrible, and we would have someone guard the food so no one would take more than what he had received, but I saw with my own eyes how the food guard stole for himself, but those really were terrible times. I think I only managed to live because I would keep food inside my mouth. I wouldn't chew it all at once, so I would still have a little in the evening.

In any case, until he came back, I did not get stronger, I was so afraid, trying but not able to forget. And that was how he found me in the shed, when the war was over, and I was so scared. But then he talked about what would happen, and that seemed incredible. He wanted to move to Israel and I understood that we were free to do as we wished. It's hard to explain to someone who has always been free how amazing it feels, I think that only someone who's been in jail could understand it, and it could have been good if only I didn't still hear that whistling in my ears and if I could forget a little. He brought me to live at his friends' home for a while, and he took any job he could find, which was how he saved money for us for when we took a ship to the land of Israel.

When we arrived, we looked for somewhere to live and he found us a little place in the city of Ashkelon, and even before we married he wanted to learn to be Jewish. He said that it should not be hard for him, after so much time with Jews, it should be easy to learn our customs.

So he went to the Rabbi of the city and he really did learn it all easily, and did everything that the Rabbis told him, even circumcision at the clinic that the Rabbi instructed him to go to, because back then there were no big hospitals like there are today. I was very scared, really, it's not so simple, but he said that when you want something for the right reasons it cannot hurt so bad. That was what he said, my hero…

(When she spoke on this subject, she grew a little embarrassed, and her voice was quiet.)

Later they suggested that he change his name. Herman was not a Jewish name, they told him, and the Rabbi suggested the name Nahum. It suited him so well that name. They also told him to change his family name, but in the end he just shortened it a little and that was it. "Von Bock" is very German, he said, but "Bock" is short, and it's like "book." He loved to read, my Nahum loved books, to this day he loves to read.

Eventually he worked on a kibbutz beside our home in Ashkelon. I wanted to tell everyone what a hero he was. What kind of hero I live with, but he disagreed and told me to forget everything. But I didn't give up and so I'm here.

(At this point she went quiet and I, who was touched by that man's heroism, explained to her that he could easily be considered a Righteous Among the Nations if he would just come here. She went home to try to convince him, and came back the next day to continue the documentation.)

He did not agree, he said that it wasn't important and not necessary, that's what he said, that it's totally unnecessary. I tried to ask again but he said that he was ashamed of his family, and I saw the pain grow in his heart, but I still wanted it, until in the end he got mad and I got worried so I stopped asking.

He always looked after our son, and wanted him to have a strong name, so he looked in the bible and found the name of a great soldier, Avner, so that he would always be victorious and nothing bad would happen to him.

I finished reading Sarah's testimony with tears streaming down my cheeks. Elisheva, who must have been waiting outside the room, came in and sat down beside me.

"This testimony really was related to you," she said gently.

I nodded and she smiled with satisfaction.

"This has been in the archives for years and no one came for it until you showed up and asked about the Berliner family, but also about the von Bocks."

I was unable to speak. Through my tears I looked at this amazing woman, who made sure to check every bit of information in the database that touched upon any aspect of my story, and I was so moved that I did not know what to do with myself.

"I will be direct," she said suddenly. "And ask you something, if you will permit it."

I looked at her quietly.

She looked at me with a sad expression and said, "You are not a young woman, Mrs. Reich. Why did you come here after so many years, why didn't you come sooner?"

I did not have a good enough answer. There was no shortage of excuses: life, its strange pace, the need to survive at first and later to protect my children, and now, in my old age, because maybe there are relatives who survived and maybe I want to know after all. But I didn't make any of these claims because they sounded unconvincing even to me. Instead, I told her about what Maria had said in our last meeting at her house, and of her unwritten will and how I saw in her eyes the wish that I search and not avoid the hard things that she told me.

Elisheva listened with a thoughtful expression. "Herman von Bock," she said, and was quiet. She got up and moved restlessly around the room. "After so many years of documentation and searching that often ends in disappointment, it's sometimes hard for me to believe that…"

It was already clear to me but I hadn't managed to say anything yet.

She said, "Usually there isn't much chance, so I can no longer be certain of anything, but this time I think I succeeded."

~

CHAPTER TWENTY-THREE

At the entrance to the cemetery, under the "petting zoo" graffiti, sits a pleasant man, wearing a worn-out kippah and a kind smile on his face. He offered flowers to cemetery visitors, and a young woman among the recent arrivals takes a bouquet of yellow Gerberas adorned with green leaves.

She bursts into laughter that sounded more like crying and said, "What's wrong with you, what is this, a birthday?"

Everyone looked at her in silence, and Nisim counted the visitors; it's hard to imagine how all of them squeezed into the little Mazda parked outside the gate. He counted four adults and three children. That doesn't make sense, he thinks to himself, and only then does he notice the faded Fiat parked behind the Mazda.

"It's not a birthday at all," one of the men reprimanded the girl, but the woman standing beside him said, "Leave Alma alone, it's good for her to put flowers on her grandmother's grave, what's the matter with that."

Nisim looked at them with great interest, like a theater director whose actors surprised him with text of their own.

The man looked at the woman with an expression that seemed to say. "Who let you interfere with my life?" But doesn't say a word.

The second man said, "Sorry to get involved, of course it's not a birthday party, but flowers are acceptable."

The woman who had been nearly silent a moment before seemed grati-fied. "You see, everyone brings flowers these days, they're pretty."

The first man was quiet, his expression severe. A moment later he said, "Look at this place. Does it even look to you like a cemetery, because to me it looks more like some kind of garden you'd see on a postcard." His voice was loud and shrill, with no question mark at the end of his words, and it seemed that he really was waiting for a response.

The older woman placed a hand on his arm. "Relax, little Yos," she said. "If it looks like a garden from the movies, that's a good thing. Look, it's all clean and orderly, and there in the middle by the bench, what a lovely flower bed."

They entered, almost passing by Nisim without saying a word, when the one that Nisim already thought of as "the quiet one" turned to him and said, "How rude of us, I'm sorry, we are the family of Eva Reich."

Several cars approached the gate, one after another. People emerged from them: a couple, someone on his own, a small group that arrives to-gether in one car.

Someone said loudly, "What is this place? I wouldn't have come if I had known beforehand how long a drive it was."

Another woman whispered loudly, "Stop complaining already. What's the matter with you, we hardly leave the house anyway, just rot in front of the television."

The man seemed unmoved. He then replied in an even louder voice, "Maybe you're rotting, I'm not rotting, I am enjoying my life, unlike you."

But the woman was already moving away from him. She approached the gate and looked at the graffiti with curiosity. Interesting. She said to herself, '*a nar vakhst on regn.*' A moment later she looked at the man with the kippah sitting there and mumbled to herself that even if he heard what she said, he wouldn't understand Yiddish, with dark skin like his. What she meant to say was that whoever wrote that stupid graffiti was an "idiot who would grow without rain,"[8] and she certainly meant no offense to the guard sitting there.

---

8   From the Yiddish expression '*a nar vakhst on regn,*' "an idiot grows
     without rain," implying that idiots are resilient and can be found
     everywhere.

She hurried inside followed by her husband, hunched with the weight of the years.

Nisim saw her from afar, as she approached the family members, imagined her expression mixed with sadness and curiosity. He was familiar with these expressions after so many years here.

He had spoken with Avner about the essence of mourning numerous times, and how many of those who attended funerals are really mourning at all.

Avner had said that he was pretty sure that only the close family felt the pain of the death, but Nisim told him that that was not true, some come out of real grief. Now with this woman, who mumbled in Yiddish, he was no longer certain that Avner had not been correct.

Through the office window, Avner stood watching the guests arrive. He knew that he had to get himself together and go out to greet them, but he remained standing as if nailed to the spot. He watched Eva Reich's family and tried to guess who each of them was. The tall, younger man looked to him like Yossi Reich, and the younger woman who lit a cigarette a moment ago must be his wife. The two boys would be Mrs. Reich's grandsons. The older, full-figured woman must be Hani, and the balding man standing beside her must be her husband. The young woman with the bouquet of flowers would be the granddaughter. He should go out to them. He must. But he could not seem to move.

"Oy," the woman said, "How awful. You must be her children, right? She always spoke so proudly of you. She told us that her son was an artist, a painter or something like that, and the daughter a journalist. Didn't you work at the women's magazine or some other newspaper?"

Avner was concerned that he had been mistaken, he recalled just the opposite, but the two looked at one another with a slight smile and Avner heard them correct her mistake.

"Ahh… oh, well that's what I said," said the woman. "The son is a journalist and the daughter paints, that's what I said!"

The two didn't reply and she continued, "I am so sorry for your loss. I worked with your mother at the university for many years. I'll never forget her. Her memory will always be engraved in my heart, that's for sure."

Avner almost wanted to respond. The expression "engraved in my heart" sounded ridiculous to him. Nobody was engraved on anyone's heart, that was an empty phrase, but he stayed standing in the same place, unable to speak.

He heard Hani asking, "What did you teach, were you in literature as well?"

And the woman replied in a quieter voice, "No, I was a secretary in the department, but we worked together, Eva and I, like this." She held up two fingers.

Another woman slowly approached the gate with a handkerchief in her hand. Nisim offered her a bouquet of Gerberas. The woman took the flowers and smelled them. "They smell amazing," she said. "Mrs. Reich loved flowers."

Nisim looked at her, his expression pleasant, and she felt the need to explain who she was. "Mrs. Reich, you know, she lived in a retirement home in her final years. I managed the place. I knew her well." She turned to go in, then looked back at him. "Thank you for the flowers," she said. "They're wonderful."

Through the window Avner heard the conversation. "Thank you for coming," Hani said to the woman. "And thank you for the flowers."

The woman wiped her tears with a handkerchief. "I really loved your mother," she said.

Hani replied, "We know. We often saw the two of you drinking coffee together when we went to visit. Mom loved you very much, Mrs. Shapira."

The woman replied, "Your mother was a very special woman. You can be proud of her. After what she went through in her youth, to raise herself up like that and build such a rich, cultured life, with warmth and love, that's so rare."

Avner was still standing beside the open window listening to whatever snippets of conversation he was able to hear. A young woman stood with her back to him, and Avner saw that she had a bouquet of Gerberas in her hand. He didn't see her face, nor could he hear what she was saying, but across from her was a young man who looked about the same age as her, and Avner heard as he asked, "Who's going to give Grandma's eulogy?"

The girl said something, and the young man said, "Help me if I can understand what that's about."

Avner grew a little anxious. Did the young man understand that the person who was going to give the eulogy was not among the family that they knew? But a moment later the young man said, "Why is it only after someone dies that we remember to say good things about them? I don't understand that, I don't. Can't we tell them good things to their face while they're still alive?"

Avner saw a boy among the guests; he was not small but still a child. He was standing and crying, and Avner felt his heart breaking. He assumed that the boy was one of the grandchildren and his great sorrow moved Avner to the point of tears.

He heard the younger woman as she said, "Enough, Itamar, sweetie, stop crying." But the boy carried on, his crying growing stronger. "Enough, sweetheart," the woman stated, trying to calm him. "Grandma was very old, and now she is no longer suffering."

The boy did not stop crying.

Through his tears Avner heard the boy say, "But Grandma won't be at my Bar Mitzvah." The young woman stroked his head and was quiet.

He looked at her tearfully. "What kind of Bar Mitzvah will it be now?" he asked.

The woman replied, "It will be fine, Itoosh, it will be fine."

That one sentence took Avner back many years. He was just twelve that terrible morning when he heard his mother's shrieks, but now, seeing the crying child, he remembered exactly what she said, "'*Endet*,'" she cried. "'*Endet!*'" And after that she said a few more words in a language he didn't understand and again and again repeated the word "'*Endet*.'" He recalled the terror that seized him; her shrieks made his blood run cold, but it wasn't just that. He didn't understand most of the words in the other language, but the word '*Endet*' was alarmingly similar to the word "end" which he had learned in English class. Was she saying 'end?' End of what? He was terrified, and tried to understand what she was talking about but couldn't. "Why are you saying 'end?'" he finally asked his mother, worried, but she didn't answer him, just went on in a fading cry, "'*Endet... Endet...*'"

He actually did have a Bar Mitzvah. His mother made a great effort and he was called to the Torah, but he would not read his Bar Mitzvah portion. She pressured him, making him agree to it. He didn't want the whole ceremony, even then he had begun to rebel against religion, but his mother promised that if he agreed, she would throw him a party at home and invite all of his friends. He was terribly afraid that she might have one of her not-so-good days, but now, thinking back to that evening, tears burst from his eyes that he was unable to stop. What a tremendous effort she had made that night. How she tried to stay sane and talk only Hebrew in his friends' presence.

He felt guilty recalling how he warned her ahead of time not to embarrass him, and how it turned out to be a perfect evening. She even bought herself a new dress, something she had refused to do for years. More than once his father had suggested she buy herself a dress, but she didn't want to. But for him, he tormented himself, she had agreed. She even made him a Bar Mitzvah cake, with decorations and the number thirteen in chocolate frosting. His friends had come, and sang, and danced, and the evening looked like something out of someone else's life, not that of a boy whose father had died suddenly only a few months earlier and whose mother…

Avner sighed from deep inside. He must go out. Simply must. He looked out at the graveyard, at the headstones scattered around. Black letters tell of "A generous woman, full of grace," or of "Dad, forever in our hearts," of people who had died at a ripe old age and others who were gone too soon, and a stubborn tear threatened to erupt from the corner of his eye.

A speeding Ford Transit came speeding toward the gate and stopped with a screeching of the brakes. Two men in work clothes get out. One has a note in his hand. "Here," says the second man. "There's nothing else."

They looked around and one pointed at the graffiti and said, "Look at this, that's hilarious!" They smiled for a moment and the other one said to his friend, "Okay, funny or not, we have work to do, let's drop the package off and finish up here."

A moment later they were looking at Nisim and asked almost in unison, "Is this the cemetery?" Nisim nodded and showed them the sign: "Heavenly Rest."

He was used to people noticing the graffiti first, and for the thousandth time thought to himself that without a sense of humor, he could not go on working here.

"Thank you," said one of them and together they opened the back door of the Transit and took out a large cardboard box.

"Heavy." One sighed and the other laughed. "Getting a little carried away are you? This is heavy? It weighs nothing."

Nisim looked at the men inquisitively, and one explained, "This package is from the retirement home in Ramat Gan. Are you Mr.....?"

The man was quiet for a moment and pulled the note out of his pants pocket again. "Ahh... Mr. Avner Bock?"

Nisim said no, he was not Avner Bock, but Avner was here in the little office beside the bench.

From the office window, Avner saw the two men heading toward him. They entered his office without knocking and set the big box down on the floor.

"Sign here," said one of them.

Avner, preoccupied, asked, "Do you have a pen?"

The man wiped sweat from his forehead and laughed. "If I had a pen would I be a porter?"

Avner looked around in a drawer, found a pen, apologized without smiling, and signed.

As they left, he heard one say to the other, "So hot, can you believe it, it isn't even summer."

Avner stared after them and couldn't understand why he was so jealous of simple laborers. He looked at the box but does not hurry to open it. He heard a rhythmic clicking sound from inside. He approached hesitantly, opened the box carefully to find a large grandfather clock, its hands moving agreeably, making a constant ticking.

Avner took the clock out of its box and saw a note attached to it.

With shaking hands he took it out:

"Dear Mr. Avner Bock, if I had known of your existence, I would have made contact years ago. It took me a long time to put the pieces of the puzzle together and find you. It isn't like the photograph that I dug out of the hold because then all of the pieces were there, and this was more complicated. In any case, if you are wondering how I found you in the end, you can ask my grandsons, who must be standing outside already. One amazing thing about children is how they don't ask unnecessary

questions. It took me some time to gather the courage, but as
soon as I asked them, they found you within a few minutes.
Young people today have no trouble finding people online. I hope
that you are living a good and full life. I am giving you this
clock, which has a special power of only showing good hours. Be
well, Eva Reich."

Avner felt exhausted; he had no energy to handle everyone right now. He went back to standing beside the window and saw the big crowd of mourners already gathered. He sat back down at his table, the diary opened to the final page. He placed the note on the diary and held his head between both hands.

The time is five minutes before three in the afternoon, and he can't seem to rise to his feet, let alone speak. He was dizzy, and told Nisim, who entered the office with evident concern on his face.

"You need to go with the family for identification," Nisim stated.

He does not personally do such things.

"You have to go to them, Avner, without full identification we cannot continue. And look, it's already nearly three."

But Avner did not reply. He did not need to identify anything because everything was finally clear to him, apart from the question of how he would get up from the chair and get down to the task for which he was there.

~

ACKNOWLEDGEMENTS

First of all, I owe a huge thank you to my dear mother, from whose chilling life story I have woven pieces into this book. My mother, a Holocaust survivor, to this day visits schools on Holocaust Martyrs' and Heroes' Remembrance Day to tell kids her story in a way that even young children can understand.

A big thank you to my amazing children for their patience and ability to put up with me through the tumultuous days of writing, and their willingness to hear parts of the book and give their opinions.

From the bottom of my heart thank you to my one and only wonderful sister Yehudit Glass who has been my beta reader for every story, poem, or book I have written. She is not biased and always tells me the truth, even if it isn't always pleasant.

A heartfelt thank you to Gali Tzvi Weiss too — author, screenwriter, journalist, and beloved friend — for holding my hand throughout this entire process.

A huge thank you to Avner Pahima and Sherry Ashkenazi and everyone who works at Korim publishing.

A heartfelt thank you to my literary editor Amir Sheinkin. Without your faithful, precise, uncompromising work, I would not be able to put out this book. Dear Amir, the hours of listening and consulting went above and beyond.

And finally, a very special thank you, with all my heart, to Yair, my life partner, who wove the story's narrative with me, listened attentively to every question that arose, supported and encouraged me all along the way, and was a true reflection of the readers' perspective.

And to my dear readers, thank you for holding my book before you. It touches me in a way that I cannot explain!

If you have any response to the book, all will be received warmly. You can contact me at:
tzviag7@gmail.com

Printed in Great Britain
by Amazon

45644909R00131